SEAT

of

TRUTH

———————————

Ezechias
Domexa

SEAT

of

TRUTH

Ezechias Domexa

Zeeks Publishing Inc.
Toronto, Canada

PUBLISHED BY ZEEKS PUBLISHING INC.
Copyright © holder 2019 by Zeeks Publishing, Inc.
All Rights Reserved
© Ezechias Domexa, 2019

All rights reserved. No part of this publication may be reproduced or transmitted in any form, or by any means, or stored in a database or retrieval system, without the prior written permission of the copyright holder.

Published in Canada and the United States by Zeeks Publishing, Inc.
www.zeekspublishinginc.com

This book is a work of fiction. Names, characters, businesses, organizations, places, events, and incidents are either the product of the author's imagination or are plainly fictional. Any resemblance to actual persons, living or dead, is entirely coincidental.

Book Cover Design by Felix Hernandez
https://www.hernandezdreamphography.com
Book Production Design by Book Makers
https://www.thebookmakers.com

Hardcover ISBN 978-1-7752324-0-7
Paperback ISBN 978-1-7752324-2-1
PRINTED IN THE UNITED STATES OF AMERICA 2019

To Grandpa & Grandma: Mr. & Mrs. Eleanor Jeantinor

Are you afraid of the dark?
Then turn on your light.
—Ezechias Domexa

PART I

AN INTRODUCTION

In the world of savvy businessmen, I'm nearly without rival. My business has thrived for centuries and centuries, longer than you care to know. Way back, when dreams — all these modern inventions — were merely concepts, and the folly of human's imagination.

"It's impossible!" you used to bark. Surprisingly, most of you still do. And I've always laughed.

Unlike you, I have always known these things — even greater things — were possible. So I used your ignorance to build an empire. You could say I'm an opportunist. My Competitor, however, vehemently disagrees. He claims that I play and prey on your innocence. That is a lie in itself. For the most part, this is what caused the friction between us before our amicable split. He takes all the credit for Creation, saying that He created the heavens and earth, but fails to mention that it was a collective effort. When I attempted to justify this small misunderstanding, He mounted a coup d'état and surprised me in an ambush. We fought mightily until a cease-fire and agreed to part ways. But He cooked up some story, telling the whole world that it wasn't a split, but a forceful removal.

Regardless, I agreed to supply this introduction, to offer some personal insight into my business strategies and practices in exchange for your opinion on a small, rather personal matter, if you will.

By the time you finish reading this book, of these two things one is certain: either you will become fonder of my perilous assets, or you will begin to see things from a whole new perspective.

I know for some of you no amount of explanation can change your mindset. And because of your ignorance you will always walk in lameness, whine all day, and blame the whole world for your lacks and failures. And for the rest of you, in your dysfunctional, unstable mind, everything is a debate. Trust me, I know debate; I invented it myself. There's nothing pleasant, or fruitful, or noble about it, if you must know. A quick examination of our offices: politics, environment, entertainment, and academia can easily testify to my meaning.

Yet my premonition of which of these categories you will fall into is the least of my concerns. My best guess is that most of you will fall into my laps again. It appears, for some inexplicable reasons and unknown circumstances, that there exists a convulsive torrent, some sort of gravitational force that always puts you in my trajectory. And the answer to our constant crossing-paths lies in the choice of your words – the power of your tongue.

"No I can't." (Lovely!)

"I have no one to help me."

"It's so difficult."

"I'm afraid." (My all-time favorite.)

"I am too white."

"I am too black."

"I am too Muslim."

"I am too Latino."

"I don't have the time." (How adorable, huh?)

"I'm not talented."

"It's impossible." (I mean, really?)

Those are your favorite words. Shall I continue? *Merci beaucoup!*

You see, in your depleted linguistic interpretation of the Old-Fashioned Book, you consider yourself more of a ... uh ... a self-inventor, not as the peculiar people, or royal nation you were designed and destined to be, *Vous savez?* And I'm supposed to be preying on your innocence? Oh, please!

Luckily, everything history taught you about me, you think it is fairy tale – bedtime stories to lull babies to sleep. Over time, the Old-Fashioned Book became a derelict building, crumbling with the passing of the ages. Frankly, I secretly laugh my ass off and begin to wonder what future generations will make of it.

My mission is to make your life miserable and eventually destroy you. And if I can do just that before you reach the end of this great book, I will, gladly. The reasons are not many: humans find me funny. Oh, how I hate that word! I don't see the funny side of what I do. There is nothing, absolutely nothing witty or glorious about dying, or better yet, in his own paranormal vocabulary, "being lost." Such tasteless descriptors disgust me. Even worse is the irony with which the Venom from his mouth insults me, in spite of his general rudimentary insight into his own making and history.

Oh, wait! I often forget my manners. Please excuse my rudeness — I have failed to properly introduce myself. I can cordially assure you, though, that my chivalry is most gracious. My Creators were generous with me. You could say Wisdom is my nickname, for I have wowed many with that virtue.

Anyway, an early introductory isn't important and might well spoil the surprise. After all, we have plenty of time to make each other's acquaintance and will eventually get to know each other quite well, I guarantee.

For now you may call me Counselor — Counselor Tshembow. And I don't take kindly to my name and its spelling being made fun of. Although my true identity is hidden — and you, too, have learned well enough how to stay hidden, but my name? I live up to its expectations.

The name is Tshembow. The *t* is silent, and so is the *w*. I wouldn't have it any other way. And your age doesn't matter to me. From fleshy newborns to old-timers languishing in nursing homes, in all the known worlds, with all my diseases, I see you all the same, and of pity I have none. Assuredly, I'll bet that when you find out who I really am, I will have your undivided attention.

Don't just take my word for what I say, okay? I don't want to scare you away. Sometimes the confusion in my confused state is so confusing that my judgment, counsel, and advice are a guess at best. I just need your personal opinion about something. About a little, a little — uh! — *misunderstanding*. A misunderstanding that I have with a Guy.

We have had countless of great business dealings throughout the ages, and I know Him as a fair and shrewd businessperson. Not that I don't believe in Him, I do. I just need your own, personal opinion in that small matter.

He doesn't withhold what's mine, that much I know for certain. But I find it out of the ordinary that a specific good would be held back for so long. And I now question the how and the why for such unusual delay.

You see, I've been waiting here, at the Gate of Exchange & Forgotten Hope, where our daily business transactions take place, and I've yet to hear from Him. We'll get to His identity a little later. He is not a Guy I truly like to talk much about, really,

4

because the Dude gives me chills each time we meet and I always tremble. But don't be carried away by hearsay, let's just leave it for now. Instead, allow me the pleasure of flaunting my credentials and telling you a bit more about my accomplishments, background and qualifications. Shall we?

I am a Counselor. That means I represent clients and give legal advice. Whether you like it or not, you are most likely among my endless clientele one way or another. My list of faithful clients ranges from the best to the worst, from all walks of life: entertainment and sports, technology and science, business and politics, religion and culture; they are scholars and media figures, celebrities and unknowns, farmers and professionals, soccer moms and coaches, teachers and students, beggars and elites and bourgeois, priests and followers, police and soldiers, bakers and princes, servants and kings.

What's my specialty, you ask? That's a great question.

My specialty is souls.

Human souls.

I guarantee loss and destruction, and all bad things in between.

Well, technically, I don't advertise that with such boldness — an unnecessary arrogance anyway. I operate on a more ... a more — uh — hidden agenda *per se, vous savez* ... hmm ... oh! My agenda is *parallel* in dimensional nature. I know that humanity has a phobia of big words and complicated sentences like "My agenda is parallel in dimensional nature" — honestly, I don't know what the heck that means, and neither do you. Let's just move right along, shall we?

To put it bluntly, I destroy human souls. That's what I do. And I'm good at it.

I take neither breaks nor vacations; I don't take sick days and I don't call in late; I am not afraid of tornadoes, or rain, or

SEAT OF TRUTH

hurricanes, floods or fire, or snow. I just work around the clock while you humans are asleep — not literally, you damned things!

Now I know without a doubt that I have your full attention. I told you, didn't I?

I'm going to introduce you to a guy — not the Big Dude, not yet. Leave Him on the side for now. I'll introduce you to an eyewitness, a nice guy. I'm almost persuaded you've met people like him before, at least once in your miserable, stuck-in-the-middle life. Naturally, there aren't many of his kind around anymore, but I believe you may at least have heard of one or two, maybe three, in the distant past, perhaps from the Old-Fashioned Book, your bedtime storybook. His name is ... uh. Oh! Mitch. Mitch P. Campbell. He will tell you more about the ... *misunderstanding* about which I seek your input.

In the meantime, I urge you to remember my name is Tshembow, with a silent *t* and a silent *w*. I wish all the letters in my name were silent because I thrive in silence.

Mitch, my *frenemy*! Will you please tell these monkeys what led us into this predicament?

6

CHAPTER ONE

"If man learns how to live,
he should necessarily learn how to die."
—Ezechias

My name is Mitch, Mitch P. Campbell, as the Counselor said. My last day on earth was a Thursday. It was the last Thursday of July 2015, my son's sixth birthday.

When I looked back at all the events that led to my demise, with all honesty, I can say that it wasn't the best year to die and neither was it the best day, because no one really wants to die. Do they?

We humans, we love life. However difficult the days ahead may seem we still cling to the dear rope of hope that tomorrow, or next month, or next year it'll be better, and thus, we press on toward our next sunrise. Death wasn't on my schedule. Not so soon.

Anyway, that was the summer of fulfillment. It was, in a way, the beginning of my sanity. It was the time, too, when I had fully reached the pinnacle of personal success and happiness, when I had found out I was more tolerant of things and of people, and

SEAT OF TRUTH

especially of the clashes between cultures. I became more loving and caring than I'd ever been, and my wife became prettier than she had ever been. It was a great year.

Money, of course, I'd never seen it in quantity, although I suspected that my family had plenty. I had stopped dreaming about a family inheritance — had long since stopped counting when my widowed mother would die and pass it all to me, now that I'd become the only heir.

I wanted to live, maybe too much. You know those moments when everything in your life is going so well? Not because you have money in the bank, it's just that zeal, that optimistic perspective about the unknown. There was so much to live for, so much to look forward to. Mostly, I guess, I wanted to witness the growth of my son, Matthew. So I longed to enjoy the age of wisdom and to die an old man as it is wished in all known cultures.

I didn't die old. I felt that so many pages of my life were left empty, so many journeys that I wanted to set out to, but didn't; so many beautiful things that I wanted to pursuit and accomplish but was too afraid of what people would say. My life was just shells of unfulfilled promises, lived in the shadow of others to stay relevant.

Death surprised me that day. It wasn't supposed to be like that. I had thought I'd be the one looking for death, or at the least waiting for it.

I imagined I'd become old, my opal skin still hanging to my bones, only traces of the violet veins, already dying, and simple gestures would make my knees wobble.

I had pictured myself calling on everyone I cherished, dividing my earthly belongings, giving instructions about who would get the paintings, who the old car, who the jewelry, how to divide the land — properly arranging my affairs, making amends with family, high school friends, and neighbors over decades-old grudges, giving proper goodbye hugs. Then death would find me in my sleep, waiting and ready.

If I had to die that young, I'd have hoped for a different day, certainly a different place, perhaps a different time and definitely a different way. Not in that gruesome, uncalled-for, unexpected manner — and in the middle of summer at that, when tourists flocked to West Palm Beach Florida, and my testosterone skyrocketed. It was a close call.

If I were given the choice to pick a day to die — as most of you would — my top pick would be a Sunday morning, when people go to church to confess their sins. I'd want to die there, on the altar, at the rooftop of the Holy Ghost, showered head to toe in the Well of Emmanuel. The magic brew! But it wasn't up to me to decide on the time, or the place, or the manner in which I would go, so I died anyway. I didn't even get to make a last phone call to anyone I knew. Not to friends, colleagues or family, not even my son. What a betrayal! At forty-five years of age, full of power and will and dreams, wealthy and healthy as an Arabian horse, at the peak of my sexual flame, my best years. I didn't want to die.

My mother died within minutes of me.

Oh! FYI: I am speaking to you from Heaven. Lucky me — I made it. Whew! And by the way, there was no blinding light or tunnel if you must know.

**

My mother and I died in a car crash on July 30th, 2015, at 4:36:10 p.m., in rush-hour traffic.

Both of us were pronounced dead at the scene.

You may well ask if I was speeding. I know you *want to* ask. No, I wasn't. Not with my awfully stubborn, impossible mother in the passenger seat telling me when to switch lanes, when to slow down, how fast to go, which lane to keep. She was beginning to get under my skin, and frankly, her bossiness nearly cost me the Heavens. I'm sure you have a passenger like that in *your* family or circle of friends.

There was nothing extraordinary about that dreary Thursday summer afternoon. It was one of many I had seen over many a year — except, one might say, everything seemed to change, but nothing had moved. It was a gut feeling. You must have had one of those, like a premonition, as Counselor Tshembow mentioned, a feeling that something… *something* is incomprehensibly, mistakenly happening beyond your control.

It had started with a simple phone call the night before. Give me a page or two. I'll fill you in.

***

Two months earlier I had lost my only brother, Edmund P. Campbell, to a rogue bullet. The Palm Beach County coroner — under my mother's pressure — ruled his death a homicide. The lead detective, Mr. Laurent Dubois, a man I wholeheartedly despised for reasons I will later disclose, was making some progress, if one can call it that, and wanted to share with us his findings.

The sun was still high in the southern Florida sky when we left West Palm Beach Police Department in South Rosemary. The last heat of the mid summer day scorched everything in its path, from grass to trees. The evergreen foliage went from green to dark gray, except, of course, for the dwellings of the wealthy, where groundskeepers attended to the thriving lawns. Aside from those gated communities, the whole south appeared almost deserted.

From the department to our home in a gated community in the suburbs, the driving distance is a relatively short fifteen minutes. We exited the highway and joined the rush hour traffic, right at S. Australian Ave Bridge. A jazz melody crooned from the car stereo, cutting short further dialogue, including more questions about my son's birthday cake decorations and my late brother Edmund's mystery life: if he planned to get married, if he had a girlfriend, etc. I knew there might be other questions lingering somewhere — after all, she's a mother.

The space between mother and son had gone silent. So I dove into the world I knew best: numbers. I loved the closeness of numbers, their shapes, and the colors my mind associated them with. This was thanks to my illiterate childhood maid, who instilled in me an early dose of arithmetic. "Numbers are beautiful," she used to say. And I, as innocent as I was, repeated after her: "Numbers are beautiful." "Numbers don't lie," she said, and the new student repeated: "Numbers don't lie." "Everything has numbers attached to them," she taught me. "Life has numbers." Although I had no business with any of this, nonetheless, I listened and learned.

Later on in my life numbers took on additional significance in the form of my career as an accountant. Four years in the navy had left me a strict discipline of an introverted man, too busy assessing things. So I took solace in numbers. I became an accountant with an infallible photographic memory and calculation.

As we waited at the traffic jammed, I began to take an inventory of everything around: the cars, the people, even the advertising on the billboard.

In the rear-view mirror I could see the eighteen-wheelers flying northbound on the bridge. I offered a quick prayer of

SEAT OF TRUTH

forgiveness, one that might fit any common criminal, and stretched my body behind the wheel to relax.

My eyes caught a little girl who had both hands covering her mouth; eyes wide open, staring at the highway bridge above us. It was a moment of perfect stillness. For a few seconds everything and everyone ceased to exist. Then I realized that *everyone* saw something, everyone except my mother and me. They had all covered their mouths as though they were watching a horror movie and were about to come face to face with what they dreaded most. Then I sensed a shadow, as if a massive cloud was gradually blocking the sun. It all happened in a split second.

My mother twitched her large body around. She saw it. It was coming from above.

She grabbed my shoulder and I looked at her. Terror registered in her face.

I jerked my head to the side. I saw it, too.

It was too late.

"JESUS!"

CHAPTER TWO

"Are you afraid of darkness?
Then turn on your light."
—*Ezechias*

This is how my last day on earth ended. Just like that, I was gone. Can you believe it?

My last word on earth was a super loud "Jesus!" You couldn't ask for a better farewell.

At the exact moment of the impact, in that nanosecond, my other body — my soul — stood beside me, staring at my physical body as it was tossed like packed meat. Amazingly, I felt no pain.

The speed at which my soul escaped my body could not be measured against the speed of light, or in fact by any scale that human measures speed. The change was so fast and so smooth, I neither felt nor saw how it happened. I was suddenly standing over my own body, mute.

A truck carrying ninety tons of concrete had lost control on the highway and landed on my car, neatly compressing it like a demolition machine. Gone were the bulletproof windows, automated air bags, and other safety features I had paid so much for.

I stood and watched as the world spun in slow motion. I was in shock, and I lost focus. All I heard were screams and yelling voices as people rushed to our rescue.

What happened? I asked myself.

I squatted next to my physical body, still in the driver's seat, and went to touch it; but I couldn't feel it. Hesitantly, I poked my finger at the head and waited. Nothing happened. I slapped it hard in the back of the head, but I didn't feel the touch. Instead, my hand passed right through it. *What...?*

Am I dreaming?

I've had weird dreams before.

My physical body was still alive, but it seemed that somehow my soul had left it in a hurry. I took a good look at the strangeness of my new body, the weirdness of it, and I became angry.

The first thing I saw about it was the reflection on my skin. It seemed to be radiating some sort of electric current, as if it had an invisible force field. When I poked at it, a wave of rings formed and expanded, like shock waves, through the rest of my body and into my immediate surroundings, but I felt no vibration. *What's wrong with me?*

Though the weirdness baffled me, somehow I wasn't worried. Not really. Maybe I needed time to get used to it. *It's just a dream anyway. When I wake up, I'll laugh my butt off and tell Connie all about it. Maybe she had one of those dreams too.* Then I thought, *where's my mom?*

***

I turned my attention to my mother to see if she, too, had turned into a strange creature. I found her body in a much different state than mine: both arms and legs were broken and dangled like loose branches. Her left femur had been twisted so badly that brown fluid was dripping out of the smashed bones. Her left shoulder blade had been torn from its socket and flipped backward in front of her, only the ligaments kept it from falling off completely. She was alive.

She looked at my physical body and called out my name.

"Mitch! Mitch!" she called in a high-pitched voice with a grinding pattern, one she might have acquired after years of smoking.

"Mom!" I quickly answered.

"Mitch! Mitch!" Her voice trailed into dread as she stared at my body.

"Mom! Mom! I'm right here." I knelt in front of her.

"Mitch!" Now her voice came with total despair.

"Mom!" I screamed. "Mom, I hear you! Can you hear me?" I waved my hands in front of her face, but she kept calling out my name. Her voice became more and more somber until she broke into tears.

I touched her, but I couldn't feel her.

I can't feel a thing. Shit!

Stiffly, she moved her fingers. They were held only by thin, torn ligaments and moved as if the commands came from a scattered brain. She murmured my name, nearly inaudible, her voice so tender, so humble and loving.

A flock of motorists scattered around the crash scene. Some were on their phones talking to 911 operators, while others frantically moved chunks of metal to get to us. I approached a man in a medical uniform who seemed to be in charge of the situation. "Excuse me sir," I said. "Are you a doctor?" He didn't answer. He didn't even look at me. "Sir! Can you please help me pull my mom out?" still no response. *How can he be so insensitive in*

SEAT OF TRUTH

a life-threatening crisis? I went to a woman who was crying hysterically. "Ma'am, can you —"

"That one is dead!" she cut in, pointing at my body.

"I'm *not dead,*" I said, waving my arms frantically. "I'm right here!" I turned to the crowd. "Can anyone see me? Hello!" But it seemed they neither heard me nor noticed my gestures. It was as if I was a ghost.

Am I a ghost? Maybe I am *dead for real,* I thought.

But it wouldn't be fair to just die like that. I wasn't sick. Dr. Lenik and I had a lengthy discussion at my last checkup. My health was in perfect order. No, I can't be dead.

My mother withered in her seat. She was trapped by her seatbelt like a wounded animal trying desperately to escape from her imminent death.

"Jesus! Jesus," she said as if she knew what was about to happen. She opened her mouth as if trying to shout, but the sound that came out was more like a muted cough. Finally she composed herself and offered her last prayer, forcing the words out between breaths, sighs, and tears, as if her destiny and mine depended on it.

"Heavenly Father. I confess to you that I am a sinner, wicked in all ways. Your word says that anyone who calls upon your name shall be saved. So I am calling. I am calling upon you, Redeemer, save my son, Mitch! Save me! Have mercy on us, have mercy! Forgive our trespasses as we forgive those who have trespassed against us. I trust the rest of my family into your keeping hands and unto your watchful eyes. Remember me, O Lord! Remember your servant! For I have served you. We receive your forgiveness, and by faith we are saved. In Jesus' name: Amen!"

Then she began to sing her favorite hymn, *When Peace Like a River.*

16

For the record, I must confess that my mother, Mrs. Gandalf Campbell, *née* Marie Grace Miller, was never someone you would want to sing along with. In fact, if singing or dancing ability were a requirement to enter the Heavens, I'm afraid it would be bad news for her. She had always struggled to keep basic music tempo, and as far as dancing goes, let's not even go there. But this time, for the first time in a long time, the song came out perfectly. I was baffled. She sang with boldness and confidence, devoid of emotion and transient enthusiasm, almost too triumphant and sublime. Our survival was at stake. You may sing along, too.

When peace like a river, attendeth my way;
When sorrows like sea billows roll;
Whatever my lot, thou hast taught me to say
It is well; it is well with my soul.

Slowly, as the singing continued, her other body — her soul — began to break free. She started to squeeze out of her physical body as if from a tight rubber shell, and her eyes caught mine. Although I knew my efforts were not needed, I quickly stood up and tried to help pull her out of her body. It was a strange feeling to touch part of her soul.

I held both her hands and pulled hard. She hissed and whined. I pulled harder. I heard her creak and crack between the two worlds as the singing slowly faded away. Suddenly, like a released rubber band, she snapped out of her physical body and landed right next to me, gasping for air.

CHAPTER THREE

"The dead are not dying, the living are"
—Ezechias

The noise around us suddenly fell away. Mrs. Campbell had just turned into the same strange kind of creature I had become. But for some reason, I felt complete peace. "Mom! Mom!" I shouted in the peaceful silence. "We're in Heaven!" I smiled broadly. My mother stood her half squatting position, one hand on my shoulder for support, the other on her knee.

"Boy! Gimme some water," she said, breathing hard. "I'm thirsty."

Instantly, a handsome being in a fine sky-blue garment appeared beside us. His glossy hair was radiant — glowing, even. His beard was young, had never been touched by a razor. A breeze swept past, and an inviting scent wafted through the air. He had not walked toward us. He had magically appeared when my mother said she was thirsty. His eyes held all glory. The smile on His face captured us whole, and we felt safe. We stared at the being in astonishment, unable to move, speak, or breathe, flabbergasted by His unusual manifestation. And suddenly we

18

knew, without knowing how we knew, that it was Jesus, our Savior and Redeemer.

He carried with Him a goblet. Slowly, He placed his hand behind Mrs. Campbell's head, leaned her slightly backward, and brought the cup to her mouth as if He was nursing her. She gulped the drink while looking at Him from the corner of her eyes as if to demand, who are you? But she was too comfortable in His arms to question His provenance. *She knows,* I thought.

After she had drunk enough to quench her thirst, He straightened her and embraced her longingly as if He had been waiting a lifetime for that moment, and said with the most beautiful smile I had ever seen, "Welcome home, beloved sister."

Mrs. Campbell, eyes wide, shouted in a high-pitched voice, "Jesus?" She assessed Him from head to toe, as if He were a kid she had raised herself.

"Yes, beloved sister," He answered with the same hypnotizing smile.

"Where's your Father?" *Oh boy!* I felt the first hint of ungratefulness on my very first day in the Heavens. *Jesus Christ! Mom, say thank you for the drink, at least.*

Jesus lifted His gaze and motioned behind us. When I turned around, I thought I was going to see the car crash and all the lingering bystanders, but what I saw was breathtaking beyond imagination. I fell to my knees.

CHAPTER FOUR

"Forever is too long to gamble
with the little time we have."
—*Someone said that.*

Before I could speak a word, a colorful crystal-like city spread out taking my breath away. On my left was a valley where the moon had apparently fallen and been crushed into broken pieces, and where lush landscapes grew in and around them. On my right a volcanic rock villa bathed in a warm, orange glow and a wide, placid lake surrounding it. A little farther, an aging metropolis where no one aged, or slept, rose under the dormant, settling sun, its lights ablaze with life. Beyond that, another city began, and a mysterious aurora display soared in all directions. Ahead, lay the dusky hills of Golgotha, bordered on both sides by the Fountains of Jacob where strings of illuminating mist erupted from time to time before turning into something I couldn't wait to see. Farther down, at the far edge, immense golden rays of light beamed into forever, and the rest was only OMG! OMG! OMG!

This is the Heavens.

20

I'm in awe.

Without saying anything more to Jesus, Mrs. Gandalf Campbell began to walk toward a hill on which a majestic French-style mansion stood. She turned and said, "Mitch, go look for your brother. Bring him home! You hear me?"

Yes, boss.

"Yes, Mom." I said. She then pushed through the crowds, ignored their warm 'Welcome home' statements, and headed to the hilltops in the far distance where the Lord Himself resided.

Jesus watched her rush off without a fuss, her hands on her waistline as if she had been walking all day long, and said to no one, and with no particular concern, "I think the Old Man is in for something." He turned to look at me, but I was still on my knees.

He took me in with His eyes for a moment, and then pressed my head against His belly in a long embrace. He gently massaged my hair, and I felt what Calvary really meant. I choked in my own tears, tears of peace, tears of relief, beauty and joy. "Ohh, I know," He said with unknown gentleness. "I know. It's okay." He leaned down and kissed my salt-and-pepper hair with such tenderness that I felt down my spine a shiver that renewed my whole body. "Welcome home, brother. The storm is over!" He assured me.

He extended His hands before me and I noticed the scars left by the piercing nails. He smiled at me as I looked up and met His gaze. There was so much depth in those eyes that barely contained His excitement. "I did it for you, Mitch," He continued. "I would do it again and again and again if I had to. I did it to dry tears from these beautiful eyes of yours." His words moved me deeply. He wiped the tears from my eyes with His fingers. His touch felt like alcohol falling against my bare skin in plain winter. And as if a veil had been covering my sight,

SEAT OF TRUTH

suddenly a shadow receded and revealed a world of colors — vibrant colors beyond the simple red and white and blue and green and yellow I had known on earth. For the first time I saw what beauty was really like, and the first person I saw in Heaven was my dad.

CHAPTER FIVE

Home, at last.

Your immediate families are the first people you see in the Heavens, I later learned.

My father looked much, much younger than when he had died. He had been sixty-nine years old when he passed away. The last five years of his life spent in bed, and under the madness of his mysterious malady, his first words in those five years were also the last. He died without speaking his mind. He couldn't. But if sixth sense is real, I believe we had a moment. I believe we had that moment right before his passing, when he reached out, took my hand, stared at me, and smiled the most peaceful smile ever. He died with that smile on his face.

Gandalf P. Campbell and I had not been as close as he had been with my little brother Edmund. In fact, we were not close at all. We could trace the reasons as far back as my brother's birthday and birthplace: the West Palm Beach Medical Center in Florida.

I felt a hint of betrayal the day my brother was born. I was three years old.

SEAT OF TRUTH

The welcoming feasts and acknowledgments he received cheated me, I felt in my three-year-old opinion. Despite my mother's bold assurance and genuine counsel early in her pregnancy that nothing would change between us, that she and my dad still loved me, and that the family was simply growing, now I found the proof of my suspicions in the way they held him and how they spoke of him in front of me. I felt robbed of so much attention that I couldn't recover and found solace around Atelia, the housemaid whose main teachings were in arithmetic and problem solving — how to add numbers, how to subtract numbers, how to decipher numbers. "Numbers are real," she would say. "Numbers are real," I would repeat. Besides her daily dose of problem solving, she taught me how to play soccer and dribble a soccer ball.

As my brother and I grew older and adulthood began to settle in, during college I noticed more of that same betrayal. My career choice, to begin with, didn't impress my parents at all. They didn't tell me so to my face, but the mere mention of it made it seem far from their expectations. You could say they were superficial beings; their beautiful smiles concealed aristocratic seeds that they pursued to keep their good name above everyone else's. I found this to be generally the case among humans' households.

In my basic good nature, I realized a good accounting degree would benefit the thriving family business and I wholeheartedly believed it to be my calling. So I studied numbers. I studied numbers with such passion that many considered me nearly a savant in the field. I admired numbers: they provided safety and comfort that letters lacked. I wanted to ensure, in terms of numbers, all aspects of the family business. I saw it as a necessity, so I did what needed to be done.

24

In my father, however, I sensed that he saw me as a young lad — with good luck and a good name that might amount to something good, something decent, but not fulfilling or exhilarating. I couldn't tell if it was resentment or jealousy I harbored over the years, or perhaps a combination of them at some point during my adolescence; but I made it my responsibility to thrive in the face of his assessment of me and to lead by example for the sake of my little brother. I distanced myself and took to reading math books by the boatload. It was one way to escape his presence and avoid conversation. I couldn't tell if he sensed my reproach through the growing coldness between us. But as if that were the case, he pursued my acceptance by all means, providing everything I dreamed of, as if to make amends for his lack of faith in the abilities of his own offspring. He had put at my disposal all good things to enjoy life to the fullest, for which I was immeasurably grateful and still am, and for which too, especially throughout his bedridden years, I was — along with my brother Edmund, his heroes.

Sometimes when no one was watching, I wanted to hug him, or kiss him, but for some reason I couldn't bring myself to do it. It was only a silver of moment I had with him before death took him away. I reached out and held his hands; he stared at me and smiled. I believed his smile was the equivalent of the most beautiful I love you, or thank you I had ever received. It was the last two years before his passing, for some mysterious destiny — and on my mother's constant requests for father and son bonding — that broke the silence of the long, lost years.

When I first laid eyes on him in the Heavens, there was no distance between us, and there never will be again. That much I know. He immediately reminded me of Edmund, since they were so close, even in their features.

SEAT OF TRUTH

"Dad?" I called out as he rushed toward me with arms wide open and received me in his embrace.

"My son! My son!" he shouted out.

"Dad, dad!" I continued until the whole scene turned into loud sobbing with two grown men locked in an endless embrace, neither willing to let go, and the entire Heavens watching the whole episode. I felt no shame, no pride. We released each other, but still held hands. "Dad," I said, "where's Edmund?"

"Go!" He searched my eyes, now resting a hand on my shoulder. "Look for your brother and bring him home."

"I will, I will!" I assured him.

He had two hologram crowns I observed. One, in the shape of a marquise cut and the other in a pear cut, those are the prizes he received for his race.

***

Hologram crowns are given in the Heavens for earthly fulfillment. They don't in any way turn others into second-class citizens, nor do they place restrictions on access, or on all the features immortality comes with. They are simply emblems, or proof of a person's earthly work.

The second person I met in the Heavens was Atelia, our earthly housemaid. She was stunning, with all the glamor of an elite woman accustomed to giving orders. She wore a turquoise mandarin-collared floor-length dress, with a tinge of green and a seamless accordion-pleated shawl, pinned at the shoulder with a burgundy butterfly pin.

Three hologram crowns hovered over Atelia's head: the Crown of Glory for her teaching, made of a light shade of lapis lazuli stone that glittered with flecks; the Crown of Righteousness, made of ruby in a brilliant full cut; and the

Crown of Life, made of shining diamonds in a *briolette* French cut.

Besides playing numbers with me, Atelia had served as a sanctuary to me when my love had been betrayed. She was like a mother to me, one who seemed to understand me better than I did myself, including when I was curled into a silent ball in a corner. She knew the exact word to make me smile, the food to lighten my mood, and the song to make me dance. Her witty remarks and her mind-blowing, heart-wrenching tales of her own life kept me whole. Her presence had brought me peace and joy in a lifetime of sadness, resentment, and selfishness, none of which I knew how to deal with.

Atelia called everyone in the household "master," except my mother, whom she called by her maiden name, Marie Grace Miller, which was unheard of.

When she saw me she could barely contain her excitement, and neither could I. She dropped the palm branch she had been holding and leapt forward. My father let go of my hand to make room for Atelia. "Master Mitch! Master Mitch!" she yelled. She wrapped her arms about me and rested her head on my shoulder in complete surrender. "Oh, Master Mitch, Master Mitch, He found me," she said. "The Redeemer heard my cries for help."

"He found me too, Atelia, He found us all," I replied as I held her tighter. Then she took my face into her hands, looked me in the eyes, and said: "Go look for your brother. Look for him and bring him home." I nodded as she let me go.

****

However, nothing prepared me for the next resident I encountered in the Heavens: Flannighans L. Molard.

CHAPTER SIX

Surprises, all the way in the Heavens.

When I first saw Flannighans L. Molard in the Heavens,
I was so shocked I thought I had found myself in the wrong
section. Flannighans was not the sort of human you would think
could ever set foot in the Heavens. If he ever saw the inside of a
church, it wasn't to pray. As far as I knew, he had been to
church only twice, for two funerals: my dad's and Atelia's. If
there were any other occasions, it would have been for a
wedding, only to chase the bridesmaids. Because according to
popular belief, if you don't go to church every Sunday, pray as
hard as prophet Elijah, pay one tenth of every hard dollar you've
earned, make pledge to charities, and never kill mosquitos, some
pastors say you're not going to Heaven. So I found this hard to
explain, for Heaven's sake, how in the name of the Holy, did
Flannighans L. Molard manage to make it here?

I pointed him out as he was talking to someone. "Jesus," I
said, "is that Flannighans?"

"Yes, that's him."

"And what's *he* doing here?"

28

"Oh! He's one of us," Jesus replied.

"One of us?" I shouted. "But … he's gay!"

"Was … gay." He raised a finger to correct me.

"But … he was a drug addict, too. He's not supposed to be here. He sold weed back on earth!"

"And you smoked it," Jesus countered. "I remember that."

"Me? Smoking? When?"

"At a sorority house party: Tuesday, October 17th, 1989, at 3:45:23 p.m., on the balcony. Does that ring a bell?" Jesus snapped His fingers, and the event flashed live through my memory.

"It was a one-time thing!" I protested.

"Nevertheless, you smoked it, didn't you?"

"Obviously, you have no idea who this guy was," I went on bitterly. "Flannighans bullied and terrified people for years, in kindergarten, in high school, all the way to college! He dropped out and started selling dope and being weird in all kinds of ways, and now he's in Heaven? Wow!"

Jesus chuckled. "Mitch," He said, His right hand coming to rest on my left shoulder as if He was trying to teach me something I would never understand. "You'd be surprised to find out who my real servants were."

"Yes, but him?" I asked, raising my eyebrows.

"Mankind sees the outside that can be cunning and deceitful. As for us, we look inside the heart where we dwell all along."

"So, for how long is he staying here?" I said.

"Forever and ever. Like you." Jesus said

There had to be something that would get the guy kicked out of this place, I thought. "Did you even know," I pursued, "that he made fun of your name and stole things, back on Earth?"

Jesus laughed. "When the pristine conscience of these so-called Christians is revealed, the true sons and daughters of my

SEAT OF TRUTH

Father, Our Father, will be shown in full plenitude, as it has been today."

With that I had almost run out of leeway to incriminate Flannighans — almost. I looked at Jesus, and in the depths of His compassionate eyes I saw how vain and mundane I was, but, still, I was preparing my next indictment. "Maybe you don't know what he did," I said. "I can tell you, if you want." Evidently some earthly emotions were still attached to my new life form and I couldn't let go. Judgmental people!

"Come, let me introduce you to him," He said, already moving toward Flannighans.

"No!" I crossed my arms. "He's *not* my friend."

"Everyone is your friend in Heaven. Come on!" And He added teasingly, "It'll be fun." With that, He grabbed my hand and pulled a reluctant me behind Him.

"Flannighans Molard!" Jesus called out. Flannighans came running. "I'd like to introduce you to a friend of ours, Mitch P. Campbell," Jesus said cordially.

Flannighans brightened. "Mitch!" he said, and pulled me into his arms as if I was his longtime best friend. I gritted my teeth and coldly accepted his embrace, with a smile — you know, one of those patronizing smiles we humans give sometimes to people we don't like.

"Do you remember him, Flannighans?" Jesus asked.

"Yes, of course! How could I not?" the man answered with a hint of gratefulness, looking at Jesus as if they had planned this encounter. He held my shoulders amicably. "Mitch," he said, "you once told me Jesus loved me. I was coming out of a convenience store in West Palm Beach cursing His name because I'd missed a lottery win by just one number. *One number!*" His voice rose, and he looked at Jesus as if he still regretted the loss. Then he turned back to me. "That sentence

30

began a raging war inside me, one that lasted many years until I gave up my practice and got right with this Man." He looked at Jesus once more and nodded his head in thankfulness.

"It was your seed, Mitch," Jesus added, "that brought him to me, and because of him you have earned your only crown." He put weight on the words *only crown* as if I *should* have earned many more.

Flannighans then raised his hands and out of nowhere a hologram crown somehow appeared. He placed it on my head. It was the one known as the Crown of Rejoicing, for winners of souls, and was made of a variety of precious stones: sapphire, diamond, apatite, pure gold and others. Then he held my face in his hands, offered me two tender kisses, said thank you, tears welling in his vibrant green eyes, and walked away.

I bit my lower lip and held it between my teeth. I stood in silence, shame and guilt splashed on my face, trying to conceal my defeat.

"You see? I told you," Jesus said playfully. "It wasn't sooo bad." Perhaps, he was attempting to save the day, but it was much too late. I was broken.

Flannighans came from a broken family. His stepfather — a man he hated so much that he never said his name — was abusive. By the time Flannighans was ten we had become best friends. He spent most of his time at our house, playing and eating, until one day he stopped coming.

It wasn't until later on that we learned he befriended some poor souls who introduced him into a dubious and unsavory world. And from there we never spoke or saw each other for a long time.

If that frail vessel, Flannighans L. Molard, could turn to pure joy, most of us would be left speechless by who made it to Heaven and who didn't.

SEAT OF TRUTH

Jesus allowed me a few moments — enough time to recover — then He helped me to rise from my knees and said, "It is time to meet your Father." We started a long walk, uphill, to meet my Maker face to face.

How old is He? I couldn't help but wonder.

CHAPTER SEVEN

"Besides me, there's no other Savior"
-God

The sprawling two-story French-style mansion was built on a slope and could be seen from anywhere in the Heavens. It was surrounded by a lush, well-trimmed landscape that looked like living walls composed of flowers and bushes closely grouped together. Concealed lighting added an intimate appeal.

The house stood on a coveted piece of property that He alone could afford: a dead end. Abraham Boulevard held no homes, but the Lord's. Its walls were painted in a rich cream color, and its thick purple curtains showed through the floor-to-ceiling windows matched the roof tiles. On both sides of the giant wooden French doors a series of glass panels rose to the second story and met the roof. A zigzagging walkway and a hedge four to five feet high surrounded the property.

Two giant Angels stood guard at the open gate. With their large folded wings they resembled statues. I wondered, *Should I say hi to them?* I decided to wait and see what my companion did. He said nothing. I tried my best not to look them in the eye.

SEAT OF TRUTH

But the most mysterious thing I saw in the compound was a tree known as the Tree of Life — a tree made of water. Yes, a sparkling water tree that grew in the middle of the front lawn. Believe it or not, it even had underground roots, a stump, and a trunk. About twenty-four feet above the ground its limbs began to spread dividing into big branches, and then into twigs upon which, leaves the shape of apple grows. Occasionally water drops formed on the leaves and fell rhythmically from their tips. As we passed under the tree, I felt every enzyme and every molecule in what made me *me* awaken. The tree had instantly transferred some sort of energy to me. I felt it. I looked up to assess the strange spectacle and saw — like a momentary vision — a portal to another world that I know for certain no one would ever be ready to venture into. I quickly looked back down and redirected an inquisitive glance at my Host. He smiled coyly.

As we approached the house, I heard a distant discussion — rather, a heated argument between two parties — rapid questions with even faster replies, as if they had heard us coming and were in a hurry to wrap things up.

"Then where is my son, I want to know?" Mrs. Campbell demanded in her usual bossy manner.

"We are not to speak of it! I forbid it at once!" a deep baritone voice challenged.

"Not good enough, not good enough!" Mrs. Campbell countered. Jesus looked over at me and smiled. No doubt He had heard it all too.

When we stepped through the French doors, the smell of freshly roasted and ground coffee beans welcomed us.

The interior was nothing fancy or lavish as I had expected, but there was this anointing aroma in every square inch, coziness in every piece of furniture, warmth only found in Him.

The Scandinavian-style family room held an L-shaped sectional across from an off-white fireplace against a gray wall. The color scheme of light blue, orange, yellow, green, red, and white brought a cheery vibe to the room's Nordic theme. Two accent chairs made of bamboo and lambskin sat next to a recliner across from the comfy sectional. Expansive windows backed the sofa, and the flooring was grey hardwood. A mix of artworks, musical instruments, and books were creatively placed on the walls. Jasper stone vases held cedars of Lebanon leaves. Wooden bowls were filled with small stones and incense, vases of flowers, others with plants and a bamboo ceiling light fixture that cast a three-dimensional picture of a lion, ready to roar, onto the Persian rug.

Every element was both historical and timeless. There was nothing over the top. The organic touch, with bits of nature, made the place unique.

There was, however, no mirror in the home. Everyone and everything was what it must be. No reflections were needed. Enough.

In the kitchen Mrs. Campbell had already assumed her new responsibilities and made herself at home. She stood at the counter drying dishes with a towel. The Lord was taking a cake pan out of a wood-fired oven. Neither displayed their emotions. Neither showed the least sign of being disturbed, despite the argument we had heard.

"It is well, it is well!" Jesus announced joyfully as we stepped in.

"Yes, it is. Everything is fine," God quickly replied. "Please come in!" Mrs. Campbell shot Him an accusing look as if to say, *No, everything is* not *okay — Lordy!* "The lasagna," God continued, "is outstanding today. It's the best lasagna I've ever produced in

SEAT OF TRUTH

all my Heavens." He laughed loudly. "Ms. Dylan ate *twice* already."

Well, I thought, *this is going to be interesting. His Heavens?*

"We will enjoy it too, as always," Jesus said as we made our way to the dining table, where the Scandinavian theme gave way to a touch of the Hamptons.

Mrs. Campbell brought two hot dinner plates and served us as the Lord busied himself putting a few utensils in order. *I thought God was supposed to look like some sort of power source, so bright that mankind cannot look at Him. How come He,* I wondered, *is doing human chores?* Nonetheless, although surrounded by immortality, I felt at home. This was where, in my being, I knew I belonged.

During my sojourn on earth I had quite a few good lasagnas, but this one — holy!

The gourmet kitchen was designed for connoisseurs. It featured opal blue appliances, off-white granite countertops, and deep blue matte cabinets.

The kitchen housed a long, rustic dining table with enough chairs to sit twelve. There was also a dinette in a corner of the kitchen, with four antique chairs made of Chinese bamboo and lambskin.

Most things in the Heavens were made of cherry, oak, walnut trees, gemstones and bamboo. The furnishings here were ancient, but retained a fresh and a modern feel — deep blue cabinets, stainless steel appliances, and lots of shelves and drawers to store God knows what.

The Lord had a blue apron wrapped around His waist over a white T-shirt with a bold slogan: "I am God alone; besides me there's no other Savior." *Is He showing off?* I thought. He turned to continue his business and the back of His t-shirt read, "... and I'm *not* showing off." I looked over at Jesus, who was choking back laughter. *They know my thoughts?*

36

The Lord wore khaki army pants. They showed obvious signs of age and were covered in patches. He was barefoot.

"Mrs. Campbell and I were about to go out for a stroll, weren't we, my child?" God said, and looked at her for approval with scornful eyes. My mother stared at Him accusingly and between gritted teeth said dryly, "Yeah, it looks like it Lord."

God undid the apron from His waist as did Mrs. Campbell, and they headed for the door.

On the way out, God stopped beside me and casually rested a friendly hand on my shoulder. "You did great, Mitch. You did great." He said. I pulled my chair aside and stood to look at Him, but I couldn't return the love, for those piercing eyes beheld something unknown to a mere mortal. I bowed down.

"Thank you," I replied, biting my lip, "Sir ... Your Majesty ... I mean Your ... Your Highness." Jesus let out a quick laugh and muzzled his mouth with his hand to stop that laugh from turning into something spectacular. I didn't know what to call Him. Almighty? Holy Ghost? You know, the usual titles by which we referred to Him back on earth. I didn't know the protocol in heavenly parlance, so I'd butchered it.

"Is he what you were expecting?" my mother asked with a hint of curiosity.

"Mitch is everything my Son stood for," the Lord said to no one in particular.

"I am very pleased in him, Father," Jesus concluded.

"Why don't you boys join us?" God said. "Take some cake with you!" It was more of an order than an invitation. With that, the Lord knotted His hands behind His back. So did my mother. She walked side by side with the Almighty as Jesus and I tagged along behind carefully, getting to know each other.

SEAT OF TRUTH

I grew closer and closer to Him with each passing minute, as if an essential part of me had been missing and was now finding completeness in His nearness. He is so easily entertaining.

"Where are we going?" I asked Him, almost whispering.

"Sightseeing. I don't know," He answered as if something else was on His mind. I noticed recent wounds on His forearms and was tempted to ask about them, but didn't.

"You don't know?" I said, clearly surprised. "I thought you guys were supposed to be ... I mean ... one ... with ... with Him?" I pointed at the Lord, still ahead of us. Jesus let out a laugh. "Well, my Sunday School teacher put it as if you guys were like ... like a triplet or something," I said. "So I was half expecting to see three-in-one kind of ... you know. I mean, you know, the Trinity. We were taught about that back on earth, right?" Jesus chuckled again. "And what exactly are we going to see?" I asked Him, sensing perhaps, my explanation was a bit off.

"Stuff," He casually answered.

"And where's the Holy Spirit?"

"Sleeping," He answered.

"Sleeping?" I stopped in my tracks. "You guys are *sleeping* now? And what about the people back home?"

"You're home, Mitch."

"I mean on earth?"

"They're fine," He said, His loving eyes searching mine. "I'm just kidding. You'll meet Her in due time."

Ahead, the Lord was pointing out a large, distant fireball to Mrs. Campbell.

"This is Nebula," the Lord declared loudly with a big laugh. "I created it myself," He added, as if we didn't know. He opened his hand and pulled the whole fiery ball closer and suddenly we were merged inside a maze of colors and diagrams, chambers,

38

pictograms, passages, corridors, shapes, exits, and lights. The complexity of the mechanism was mind-blowing. "Though I created it all, things still amaze me, you know," God said.

Mrs. Campbell, meanwhile, was in the same bad mood as earlier. Nothing seemed to impress her. "Where is my son?" she said to Him. "I'm not interested in sightseeing right now. I need to see Edmund."

They walked on silently, side by side, but more was said in the silence than necessary. Passing across the infinite, He gazed at every sight as if He was seeing it for the first time. My mother, on the other hand, showed no interest in heavenly sightseeing. All she cared about was her son's whereabouts.

"You know," God eventually said, "there are so many wonders in this place, don't you want to enjoy them? I can never get used to them." God pointed at another large solid body and pulled it in front of us. "This is Nanova. You guys call these 'comets' back on earth." He let out a small chuckle and said, "It's a carrier. It carries the provisions it was designed to carry and spreads them where it was destined to spread them." He pulled it closer and we found ourselves in a current of particles of sand, dust, threads, light, wind, and other forces moving in a precise harmony that I thought was musical.

But my mother clearly did not. "I've seen enough," she said, "and I have plenty of time to tour the Heavens. Am I not here forever, as you promised? Eternal life, John 3:16, hello?" She displayed a pinky finger and raised her eyebrows. God offered a weak chuckle. "I want to see my son," she added boldly. "I'm going to follow you everywhere until you take me to see my baby."

"Your baby left you a long time ago, Mrs. Campbell," God replied, not looking at her.

SEAT OF TRUTH

We came to a stop as a blue silicon horse swept toward us. He bowed down on his front legs and said: "Your Majesty!"

"Old Pale, how's it going?" The Lord replied, sweeping the animal's back. *How in Heaven,* I thought, *are these two speaking as if they're normal human beings?* The animal had a long mane that glowed with tendons of blue, red, and yellow fire. He moved off at a trot.

My mother then broke down, falling to her knees at His feet. "Then where, in your name's sake, is he? For Your love's sake, take me to him, Lord. Please, please!" Her voice was nearly gone. All that was left from the car crash and the crying was a low grind that broke between phrases.

The Lord sat down next to her and wrapped His arms comfortingly around her. Jesus and I left them in this position and headed for the Square.

***

On our way to the Square or Stone of Creation, where trials took place — also called the Mercy Seat was, Jesus had to take leave of me to welcome a new baby. But before He left, He told me that Flannighans could be a good guy to hang out with, especially for the next six days. And just like that, with a smile, He was gone. I was suddenly left to wander alone.

Six days, I thought. *Why six days?*

CHAPTER EIGHT

The things we carry

I found Flannighans Molard in the Square watching a couple of kids playing soccer. Because of the earlier episode, I felt uncomfortable addressing him. So I stood by a tall lamppost made of pearls and sodalite gemstones. Inside the post, lava was moving inward, forming curls and twirls of different shapes and colors and brightness. It was a spectacular sight. From there, I observed the game.

"It's beautiful, isn't it," Flannighans said from across the street.

"Unbelievably beautiful!" I answered, still looking between the gorgeous posts and the children's activities. He stared at me as if he already knew what was on my mind and was waiting.

"You only have six days to find him, you know," Flannighans said as he crossed the street toward me.

"Yeah! I've been told," I said to him. Waiting to see if he would offer to help me. He said nothing.

"Look, Flannighans. Have you seen him around here?"

"No, I haven't," he said.

41

SEAT OF TRUTH

"You remember Ed, don't you?"

"Of course I remember little Ed."

"Don't call him 'little Ed,' you *know* he doesn't like that," I said. "And I'm sure name calling is forbidden in Heaven, isn't it?"

"You don't know anything." Flannighans said, and laughed.

"Do you have an idea where I might find him?" I asked, observing him closely. "After all, you seem very familiar with the place better than anyone—"

"Flattery doesn't work here," he responded flat out, and then added, "Dylan might. Dylan knows everything!"

"Who is Dylan?"

***

My first job in Heaven was to find my little brother and bring him home. You heard how boldly Mrs. Campbell told me so. But Heaven — as I'm sure you can imagine — is not exactly a football field's length, or a city block. Although everyone knew each other, rules governed the place like any other. I didn't know them yet, but the rules were there, and they applied to even newcomers.

For instance, you should not ask anyone if they've seen someone. You will get not an answer, but a laugh. You cannot go to the Gate of Exchange & Forgotten Hope. It is forbidden. I later learned it is also called the Gate of Hades & Forgotten Hope.

However, Flannighans secretly told me I shouldn't even be asking questions, and that I must wait until I was told things in due time. When I returned to the subject of how I was the one who brought him into the Heavens, he made sure to remind me of the compensation — by which he meant the hologram crown over my head. When I pressed him for information, he said,

42

"That's where He brings them at dawn — lots of them." He almost whispered, while looking around as if the words were some sort of contraband goods.

"Who brought who?" I said, half angry with him now. I held back from grabbing him by his lapel.

"Man! You really don't know anything, do you?"

"Obviously! I just got here two days ago."

"You're not supposed to count days or keep track of time here, Mitch," he snapped at me, as if I had just broken a sacred law.

"Can someone bring me up to speed here?" I said. "I'm lost. Why all these secrets?"

"'Lost' is a forbidden word here, too." Flannighans arched his thick eyebrows. "Only the found are here, Mitch," he said boldly. "The lost people — He brings them to the Gate of Exchange & Forgotten Hope and hands them over to Tshembow, without a word."

"Hands them over to Tshembow?"

"He just hands them over." Then I had the fearful realization that, perhaps, it *would* be better to leave things alone and wait until I was told.

CHAPTER NINE

The amazing, complex,
Mindboggling, supernatural
Human beings

The next morning, I found Flannighans Molard waiting for me at the Square. This time he had a companion. A boy.

I took the opportunity to examine Flannighans in his entirety. Back on earth his aging features had always been a mystery. He was one year younger than Edmund, but could easily pass for our father. It was said — and it could have been only rumor as far as I'm concerned — that addiction to weed, and later to hardcore substances and other experimental mischief, had taken hold of his reason, and he had begun to age at a rapid rate. Atelia attested that he came from a family that was supposed to leave earth a long time ago, but for some reason he got left behind and his existence became a burden to society. We heard his origin story when Edmund got badly cut climbing a tree by the shore. I thought that in Heaven the effects of physical degeneration could be reversed. However, in the case of Flannighans L. Molard, either it was irreversible, or he just didn't care.

44

Flannighans was tall and lean, virtually free of fat. He had cropped short brown hair, a long forehead, and an even longer, pointed nose. Thick eyebrows and high cheekbones accented his deep eye sockets, and his large ears had earned him the nickname "Jedi" back on earth.

Flannighans always looked like he was smiling. This was partly because he barely blinked, so it seemed as if he was in a perpetual state of shock, and because his two front teeth, divided by a large gap, protruded over his lower lip so that when he wasn't smiling, he still appeared to be, even with his mouth closed.

His long arms hung beside his tall, slim frame, which was supported by even longer legs and big feet. He had grown a goatee that he considered aristocratic, just a few long strings of hair that looked like a worn-out, out-of-place ribbon. He wore his brown pants pulled up to his torso, with a light-yellow T-shirt properly tucked in and a pajama top that he claimed to be a suit jacket. On his head was a gray beret; on his feet, light brown moccasins with four eyelets that made him look like a seasoned pirate. In all, his features belonged to someone who'd popped out of a time machine. I found myself asking which part of his attire was most offensive. He was neither old nor young, neither healthy nor sick. Flannighans was simply Flannighans. To anyone who knew him before, he was a monument.

Flannighans and his companion sat chatting on a bench that glittered with gemstones. "Mitch, this is Dylan. Dylan, Mitch," Flannighans said, and displayed all his bony teeth in this one short sentence.

"Dylan?" I repeated and extended my right hand. He let out a giggle, and then I realized that Dylan wasn't a boy, but a girl.

"Welcome home!" she said with a lame, failed high-five.

SEAT OF TRUTH

"Thanks!" And, in that instant, I sensed a transfer of energy between us. I felt closer to her than I had ever been to anyone else. *God, I love that kid!* I thought, taking her in. The tomboy had an urban look. Her hair was short, in a pixie cut, curly, and the color of corn stalks. Her complexion, I supposed, belonged to a child born from a white and a black parent, from whom she had inherited the good genes of both so that she fell into a new category of human being.

She wore indoor soccer shoes, ankle socks, and short shorts, and an oversized soccer jersey covered much of her shorts, which could have fooled anyone.

She roamed the streets of the Heavens either on her skateboard or on a bike that her Grandpa, as she called God, had made especially for her. The bike came equipped with a basket in which she carried her soccer ball.

Flannighans filled three cones with pistachio almond ice cream from a bucket next to the bench and gave one to each of us. This, I thought after my first bite, could be a distraction from finding my brother.

"Let's go!" Dylan said to no one in particular. She set her skateboard down on the pavement and jumped onto it. The former drug addict stood up and started walking in the general direction of Adam & Eve Boulevard, and I followed.

"Isn't she cool for a seven-year-old?" he exclaimed as Dylan rode the skateboard free-style across the rugged gold ground.

"She is," I admitted with a smile. "Did you tell her what we're up to, Flannighans?"

"I guess she already knew."

"You guess? Aren't you supposed to tell her?"

"Yeah. But she knew."

We walked along Isaac Boulevard, where the street lamps were made of colorful rings of crystal and varieties of colored

46

gemstones unknown on earth. Everything in Heaven is alive in its own right, the streets are as sleek in design as they are beautifully stunning.

The tomboy entrusted me with her God-made skateboard and started dribbling her soccer ball between my legs and Flannighans'.

From Apostle Luke Crescent we turned onto Moses Lane, where lush hills of trees thrived, and a jaw-dropping variety of aquatic life was on display in a nearby stream.

Flannighans had said, according to Dylan, that the place we were about to see was known as Checkpoint, and that this was where people were held until further decisions were made about their final destination, whether they'd be admitted into the Heavens, or handed over to Tshembow at the Gate of Exchange & Forgotten Hope. These people believed that they had been good enough back on earth. They also believed in the good deeds they had performed, their philanthropy and charitable contributions, their fundraising, and the countless little things they spent time, energy, and resources on in the name of love. They felt entitled to an audience. They wanted explanations.

"There are a few more places I know of," Dylan volunteered.

"How do you know these people are waiting?" I inquired. Dylan looked over at Flannighans as if seeking permission to answer the question, and I quickly concluded that these two, although not remotely resembling one another, complimented each other in so many ways. Now I couldn't help but wonder.

"Well," Flannighans said to Dylan, eyes slightly narrowed, "they're in transit. Remember?"

"Yeah! They're in transit." She agreed.

Between rows and rows of Germany's cherry trees we walked in silence.

SEAT OF TRUTH

The cherry of Germany is a soft-pink flower. The flower blossomed, fell on the ground like cotton balls and formed a soft, uneven mattress. Flannighans and Dylan fell freely unto the cushion. They bounced back a little. I, too, let go. A little. I was more concerned about finding my little brother. But I played along. The odor was light and addictive. We could hear the rose petals breathing under our bodies. They made vibrating musical notes that were in tune with the rest of us.

After a couple of awkward backflips on the soft bed, I started walking as if I knew where I was going. It worked.

They followed.

Dylan had taken her skateboard from me and was now busy, flipping and sliding it on anything nearby in a series of 360s, as if her body were nothing but smoke. She did a 540 against a wall that looked like a frozen cake and bounced back into another 360 before I caught her in the air. She then grabbed the soccer ball from Flannighans, who was lagging behind.

"Who gave you your name, Dylan?" I said to her.

"I chose it," she said, now passing me the ball as if to introduce me to soccer. To my own surprise, I responded with impressive skills. "Grandpa told me I could choose my own name since I didn't have any," she continued, "so I chose Dylan."

"Why Dylan?" I asked her, passing the ball to Flannighans, who immediately lost it.

"Dylan is unique, stylish, and mysterious," she said, "especially for a girl."

"Mysterious?" I caught myself repeating, a little too loud.

"Grandpa told me so."

Flannighans had finally caught up with the ball and was coming back. "You always lose the ball," Dylan called out to him. "Did you play any sports at all back on earth?"

48

"Sports were never really my thing," he quipped as he again struggled to control a simple pass.

Coke and weed didn't leave you enough time for them, I wanted to say, but I let it pass.

"So, Dylan," I pursued, "where are your parents?" She took the skateboard from me, placed it on the glittering road, leaped on, and flipped it 180 to face me as she rode it backward.

"They didn't want to have anything to do with me," she said, "so they killed me in my mom's tummy the day they found out she was expecting. She learned that from a stupid little tube she bought at a pharmacy. She drank some bad pills a so-called doctor prescribed her on purpose to kill me as Grandpa was weaving me in her matrix." She spat the last sentence with hatred. "No one has claimed my existence yet except Big Brother, Big Sister, and Grandpa. So I'm kind of waiting, you know, to see if someday they'll come and search for me like you're searching for your brother, Edmund."

"I'm sorry, kid," I said, "that your parents didn't want you. Frankly, only a coward would butcher a baby."

"Yeah, I know," she said dryly, not taking part in my sentimentality.

"But if you were killed before you were ever even born," I asked, searching her face, "how come you're alive, and seven years old?"

"Every baby that was never born will grow to seven years of age," Flannighans offered as if he had made that special rule himself. "Not a single day more." He was carefully holding the ball in his large hands.

"Why seven?" I said.

"Seven is perfection," Dylan said, "and it took Grandpa seven years to teach me all things. So you're staring at the Old Man's masterpiece, my friend," she teased and giggled.

49

SEAT OF TRUTH

Dylan's comical way of laughing grew on me more with each passing minute. The dryness in her raspy voice and her giggling were so contagious that I began to long, and anticipate for her to speak. The suddenness of her laughter excited me and reminded me of the joys of being a child.

There was nothing not to love about Dylan. You couldn't help but be fond of her big, soft, grey eyes, always searching. Her cute little round face and her large front teeth exuded royalty and ordinariness at once. I observed a few freckles on her face; they looked like an artist's rendering, but they were real. Her mannerisms were nothing short of a typical girl — like, crossing one leg behind the other when she stood, twisting her shoes, sitting on both her legs, brushing her short hair to the side with her fingers, and fidgeting with hands so delicate I feared touching them might hurt her.

"So, Mitch?" Dylan began, and did a back kick before reaching a yellow lamppost with grey, ink-like threads; visibly live stitching inside it. "How many people did you lead to the Light?"

"To the what? The — the Light?" I fumbled. The difficult question had altogether surprised me. She stopped and looked at me as if to say, "Of course! How many people did you lead to Grandpa?"

"Oh! I brought ..." — I paused, and made it look like I was counting — "Flannighans. Over there," I added, pointing at him next to her. She lifted her chin to look at Flannighans, who nodded.

"Just one soul, out of billions?" she shot back at me. "What were you doing down there?"

"Kid, you have no idea how hard it is to be human—"

"Oh, Flannighans!" Dylan called out. "We're here."

***

50

Our arrival was a relief for me, providing a perfect alibi to avoid digging into humanity's twisted, complicated society. The search for my brother seemed promising now.

The entrance to the Checkpoint was through a tunnel formed by date palm trees, except instead of dates they grew honey. The bees formed ball-shaped honeycombs like grapefruits welded into a branches. Way at the end of the tunnel we came face to face with what had to be an abandoned soccer stadium. Its dome was covered with a white tarpaulin fabric. We noticed a few entrances. But the main gate was secured with sharp barbed wire. Access was strictly prohibited with no security guards at either entrance, and all of which were locked anyway.

This location, according to Dylan, was one of several Checkpoints. People who came here went through rigorous questioning about their earthly life. If their answers proved satisfactory, they then moved ahead to the next Checkpoint, somewhere else, where a lighter version of their life's account was further reviewed. This information had come to Dylan through the privilege of having never been born. Not only could such people choose their own name, they were also gifted with special skills. Grandpa methodically instilled in them certain abilities, which served as compensation for the loss of the right to be born — they've been robbed of their calling.

Dylan indeed possessed amazing abilities. She's able to explain in lay terms the theory of black holes if need be. She dazzled us with the correlation between dark matter and space and the dimensions of the human soul. As we toured what we could of the Checkpoint, she explained to us that when her Grandpa said that the Light is able to pierce as far as the division of the soul and the spirit, as both joints and marrow, these were simple formulas of quantum physics and biology. The human soul is like tiny little drawers made of fibers, little motors, and

SEAT OF TRUTH

apps, as well as chains of neurons of different colors and shapes that illuminate the body. Imagine a knitting factory with different stitches, patterns, and weaving threads, Dylan said. If we could reach the dimension of Oneness, we would be able to see with naked eyes the true anatomy of our own soul as if through the lens of a microscope. Therefore, at that nano level, we would be able to heal the physical body from any disease, or release it from any form of bondage because the soul is an exact replica of the physical body. "Gentlemen," she searched our eyes, "we are but self-aware machines. Our soul is like the inside of a computer board, a mingling of chips and wires and processors and sensors with different colors and shapes and vibrations and sounds. And inside these tiny little references Grandpa stored love, kindness, gentleness, compassion, long sufferance, dreams — provisions ready-made for us to solve any problem and discover the mysteries in all He created." She brightened with a smile at the end of her grand exposition, as if she too was amazed at the depth of her knowledge in quantum mechanical theory about the anatomy of the soul. My lips had become so dry that I found it difficult to breathe or swallow, and Flannighans' already wide eyes had become even wider.

We came across a small contingent of beehives filled with honey and buzzing insects. Flannighans reached out his large hands and plucked off a honeycomb. He divided it in three pieces and shared with us. There wasn't any wax left after I put the magical sweet in my mouth. It tasted so good that it felt unreal.

We sat outside the dome sucking honey and peering in from time to time through a tiny hole we had found, but we couldn't see much. There wasn't anyone there except us and only solitude. Dylan leaned over and peeked through the hole while licking at the honey on her fingers. "Edmund P. Campbell was here," she said. I leapt to my feet and asked her how she could tell. She grabbed my ankle. And then I saw it. I stumbled backward.

"Whoa!" I pulled back and yelled, "Edmund? Edmund?" I looked frantically around for a way in. "Is he still in there?" I asked Dylan. "Edmund? Edmund?" I called out until Flannighans shouted something along the lines of "He can't hear you!"

Gripped with anticipation, I crouched back down touching Dylan's feet, as if she were some kind of antenna, and the reception needed adjustment.

"That's as much as you can see," she said. "Only once."

"I told you!" Flannighans took a deep breath. "I told you Dylan knows everything. What did you see, Mitch?"

The encounter had been so clear and so fast that I now feared that it had been not a reality, but a flash of memory, like a quick vision. "I saw him, Flannighans! He wore yellow overalls, with straps over his chest, he was barefoot, he …he sat on a chair and nodded at someone in a blue medical gown."

"Is he okay?" Flannighans asked.

"He's fine. I don't know. Now what?" I turned to Dylan.

"We'll find out," she said. "But we should probably get back."

***

Half the day was already gone by the time we left that place. It had, in a way, been a small relief. At least my brother wasn't where I'd feared he might be.

On our way back to the Square, Flannighans showed me the road to the Gate of Exchange & Forgotten Hope and told me that it was forbidden to go there. From the look of it, it was too terrifying to even remotely consider venturing there. But Dylan offered to help with her special gift. She would go there with us the next day. "We might find out more about Edmund," Flannighans said.

CHAPTER TEN

*"Someday, we will know
the price for everything."*
—*Ezechias*

The next day, coming back from the Gate of Exchange & Forgotten Hope, I suspected that Edmund's whereabouts were shrouded in even more mystery than I had anticipated. That place had temporarily traumatized me and made me wish it were all a nightmare.

The street the Gate was on, Lucifer End, was the shortest in the Heavens, only about a block long. On one side, long, curved branches of oak trees fell to the ground and looked like moldy dew. Long mosses dangled from them like ripped linens. The beech trees on the other side of the road were also draped in moss and dreadful looking. At the end stood the Gate of Exchange & Forgotten Hope.

The entrance — the only way in — was a sight of sheer horror. It was a dark arched metal gate made of something that will forever remain rusty. In hot red ink, the following statement was written at the top: *Abandon All Hope, You Who Enter Here.*

SEAT OF TRUTH

We peered through the iron bars and could easily see bizarre street names that were even more dreadful than the entrance: Murder Trail, Confusion Way, Hypocrite Crescent, Adulterer Street, Resentment Avenue, Hatred Lane, Unforgiving Boulevard, Liars Court, Gossip Lane, Pride Road …

But the most terrifying part was the unending cacophony, a musical mess that was hurled from inside when we came into contact with the iron bars: the squeaking of handsaws on metal, the suddenness of drums that jolted the heart through the roof of the mouth; the screeching, eerie, dreadful resonance of cymbals; the brassiness of trombones that came from nowhere and everywhere as if the whole world were playing at once but in different keys and in no particular tempo: the sound stung and peeled at the skin, cutting and piercing every square inch, it scorched and bled the eardrums, it made the senses twitch and cringe, it caused the body to ache from the head all the way to the soles of the feet and it burned the eyes and the nostrils until it engulfed and enveloped mind, body, soul, and spirit. It was Hell.

The experience was unlike any other. *Abandon all hope, you who enter here,* I thought. What a hopeless, daring statement!

Dylan, as always, was riding her skateboard on everything while Flannighans was trying to figure out with which leg exactly to kick a soccer ball. Then, "Guys! I have an idea," Flannighans blurted, his face beaming with excitement.

"What is it?" I said, coming back to the present from the musical madness of the Gate of Exchange & Forgotten Hope.

"Let's find out what your widowed wife is up to on earth!"

"Yes, let's go!" Dylan shouted enthusiastically. Without waiting for my reply, they grabbed me by the lapel of my coat and in the twinkling of an eye we were all standing in the master bedroom of my earthly house in West Palm Beach, Florida.

Ezechias Domexa

***

It was evening; Connie was in the room and had just finished dressing. *Thank God!*

I noticed the bedroom had been repainted with a different color, and the bed had been moved from facing east to north. I had stepped outside the bedroom door and realized that not just the master bedroom but also the entire house had been repainted.

"She changed the whole place! Why?" I asked the others.

"Maybe she never liked the way things were," Flannighans responded, and left the room quickly. None of my clothes were in the closet. As I was about to tell them that, Flannighans called from the kitchen downstairs. "Guys! She's cooking." Dylan and I raced to the kitchen. "She's expecting company," he declared.

"How'd you know that?" I said to him bitterly.

"Your four-year-old son is sleeping, she just put on a new outfit, and there are no dirty dishes in the sink," Dylan observed. "*You* do the math, genius! Something is definitely going down," she high-fived Flannighans. I stared at them ruefully, as if they were a poorly matched couple, and seriously questioned which part of my existence these two really belonged to, the past or the future.

"Something *bad* is going down tonight," Flannighans said. "I can smell it. How long has it been since you died?"

"About four weeks, maybe more," I said, as I checked the calendar on the wall.

"And she's already dating?" Flannighans snapped as he opened and closed every drawer in the kitchen.

"Maybe she missed me?"

"Does it look like it, Mitch? Think about it. You just passed away and she's already changed the color of your home, probably gotten rid of your old clothes as well. She just moved on. In a way, she might even be *happy* that you're dead. She probably wanted all these changes all along."

"It must be the detective," I decided.

"What detective?" Flannighans said.

"The one investigating my brother's death, Laurent Dubois."

"You know you mispronounced his name," Dylan scolded. "This is a French name, proper pronunciation is required."

Flannighans stood in front of me and said, *"Monsieur le detective, Lorahhn Doobwah,"* in a funny French accent with his big mouth so puckered that Dylan went crazy with laughter. *God, I hate him!*

***

Laurent Dubois was a man I wholeheartedly despised. He had come to my family in the late spring of 2015 to investigate the death of Edmund, my little brother. When he saw Connie, he immediately had the hots for her. I explained this to my companions as we watched Connie arrange plates and tall wine glasses on the dining table. My wife then had expressed a fraction of interest in the detective's French background and accent and was always available to answer questions during the investigation. But at this time of the night I found investigating a bit bizarre, and equally suspicious. After all, the case had supposedly gone cold after my passing. The agents on the case must have sighed in relief without Mrs. Campbell's constant harassment for updates.

"Talking about French people, there's someone at the gate, guys," Dylan warned us from Matthew's bedroom.

We climbed upstairs to take a peek out the window and confirmed. The car headlights were coming from the gated entrance toward the house. Then we hurried down the stairs and crammed together at the living room's floor-to-ceiling window glass panel that overlooked the parking area, and waited for Mr. French's arrival.

He parked the black sedan and killed the engine. *Surely government property,* I thought.

He took a bouquet of fresh flowers from the passenger seat and exited the vehicle and walking away from it. He then stopped, and looked back at the car as if he was parking in the wrong spot before deciding to make his way to the front door. "Oh! He's a gentleman," Flannighans remarked gaily. "The guy brought flowers."

"Flannighans, what do we do?" I said to him.

"We do nothing," he said. "We're just going to sit down and watch them fornicate until sunrise." Dylan giggled. "There's nothing to do but watch and listen."

The detective knocked at the door timidly and waited. We stared at him from the window.

"Go away!" I shouted.

"He can't hear you, Mitch," Dylan managed to say through laughter. A moment later the man knocked again, this time a bit harder. Then he scanned the perimeter as if he was trespassing. *You sure are,* I thought.

Connie wore a black cotton skirt that stopped just above the knee with front and back pockets; a gray V-neck sweater only partially covered her belly button. She wore her champagne hair in a ballerina bun that transformed her long neck into an accessory for temptation. Her shoes were open-toed and low heeled. The dimmed light in the foyer and the sixteen-year-old's smile on her face worried me a little. What husband wouldn't be worried? She seemed to have just found her youth.

At five foot eleven, with plump, glowing skin and perfect teeth, even though she had a four-year-old son, forty-four-year-old Connie Crichton Campbell still stopped traffic around West Palm Beach. She had missed her chance at professional modeling — that had been her first choice when it came to careers. Nevertheless, she had managed to keep her body fit and enviable, and vultures around the county would kill for a piece of it.

She finally heard the knock at the door. *Make him wait, honey. Make him wait!*

He had his head down when she opened it. He turned and feigned surprise, like he was at a loss for words, and said, *"Vous êtes très belle, madame!"* Connie appeared overwhelmed by his compliment *en Français* and was clearly blushed.

"Ah oui? Merci beaucoup, Laurent," she joyfully responded in near perfectly accented French as the detective kissed her on both cheeks. She inspected him almost unnoticeably — a move that made me jealous. I didn't like the way she looked at him.

"Eh, eh!" Dylan teased. "This dude's got swagger!"

"Dylan, what do you know about this stuff?" I snapped at her.

"I'm just saying," she said.

"Please come in!" Connie said to the detective. He stepped into the foyer and gave her the roses, and she thanked him.

"I trust that wild orchids and lilies *sauvage* will brighten your heart tonight, Mrs. Connie Campbell," he said. *How I hate the way he pronounced the word "sauvage"!* I thought to myself. *I hate French people! I hate everything French.*

"Please, call me Connie," she insisted.

"Oops!" Dylan cried, rolling her eyes. "Kicked to the curb!"

"Good Lord!" Flannighans discharged loudly.

"I love wild orchids!" Connie exclaimed, smelling the bouquet. "How did you know?" She searched his face.

"It was a wild guess." He smiled with obvious satisfaction, as if her liking the flowers might mean something more.

Back in my schooldays, I told the others as we took our positions across from them in the living room; I never understood why people were so obsessed with French customs. My parents visited Paris frequently when I was young. I went back with Connie once, maybe twice. She wanted me to speak, or even try to say a few words. I didn't. I suspected she would kill to speak the language of *des amoureux*. Did she resent me for it? I seriously questioned.

Connie's face showed excitement, a sense of hope that made her alive with almost too much enthusiasm in welcoming a total stranger. Even more shocking, she already allowed him to use her given name, like she had no recollection of her so recently defunct husband. As if she found a silver lining in my passing. What had happened to our twenty years, our child?

Matthew was already asleep, and the nanny gone. Last time I checked the time, it was nearly 9:30 p.m., the weather was pleasant, and the French songs on the stereo — *my* stereo — weren't helping the situation. The mood had changed, and every God-given defense mechanism against fallen man seemed to have vanished from Connie's mind.

The detective sat down on the sofa with his legs crossed as if he paid the bills. We sat across and staring at him while my widowed wife poured drinks at the bar. She came back with two half-full glasses. "I brought you some red wine," she announced, with a full smile and a nod.

"Wine is a tradition in France," the detective declared. "We drink it every day, with every meal." He thanked her for the drink, and they toasted.

We watched them like owls, listening to their conversations until their glasses were empty. Connie excused herself to check

SEAT OF TRUTH

on things in the kitchen. We sat across from Laurent Dubois, judging his shoes, his shoelaces, his pants and socks. His body was as trim as if it were made of cables. I wasn't jealous — I thought I could take him down. He seemed to be one of those rare folks who spent most of their work time in outdoor activities, and over time, the sun damaged people like him in a way that made them immune to its dangers.

After a second round of red French wine, Connie announced that dinner was ready and invited him to join her in the dining room. We followed them hurriedly.

They sat down across from each other, but in my eyes they were too close. We sat on the remaining chairs, close enough to monitor their every word and movement.

The three-course dinner I had seen waiting in the kitchen consisted of a Burgundy salad with poached eggplant, roasted lamb chops with mushrooms, a variety of sautéed vegetables, and crème brulée for dessert — my favorite dishes. I hoped this time they were too salty, or too bitter, or the worst, too spicy.

Connie served a healthy plate of salad to the detective and then to herself. I despised his nearness to her. He thanked her with a smile as she tucked a wisp of hair behind her ear, and they began to eat. The detective was grinning.

"They didn't even say Grace to Grandpa," Dylan said in disgust.

"Something bad is happening tonight!" Flannighans said again.

"Can you stop saying that?" I said sternly.

Just one month after my death my wife was already fornicating — well, at least, emotionally. This was nothing short of an amorous affair. The most frustrating part about my new life was that I couldn't speak to living people. They could neither hear me, nor see me. Yet I could see and hear *them*.

62

After dessert Connie and the detective moved back into the living room and settled down on the large sofa, still savoring their drinks. She sipped from her glass, treasuring her wine as she tried to impress Mr. Laurent whatever-his-stupid-name-was with her taste for French customs, French traditions, French décor, French culture — in fact everything from France. I was suddenly glad we hadn't gone to Paris for our honeymoon.

The detective, too, nursed his drink. He spoke with enthusiasm about Connie's elegant taste in décor — compliments that made her blush. She took the opportunity to give the detective an account of her experience in the field of interior design. He, in return, told her new things about the paintings on the walls, most of them European: the Thomas Couture, the Charles-François Daubigny and the Eugène Boudin. There's always a story behind a painting, and he knew them.

My parents had been great fans of European art, I told my companions.

The detective seemed to have a perfect story for every single one of the pieces and told them in a romantic way, a talent I lacked. For Connie it all seemed an adventure, perhaps one she had been missing for decades. What had I done wrong all those years? I was getting the impression that I had never known her when I thought I knew her well. "Who knows the heart of man?" I asked no one in particular.

"My Grandpa does," Dylan assured me.

"What about *that* painting?" Connie asked, pointing at the wall across from them.

"Ah, *oui!* Alphonse de Lamartine." The detective's face brightened. "Lamartine was in love with a beautiful young woman named Julie Charles," he began. "After her sudden passing from tuberculosis in 1817, Lamartine mourned his loss in solitary confinement, in a state of near suicidal delirium. He gave up his previous life, purged himself of the things of this world, and embraced the sanctuary of loneliness. He composed one of the most epic, heart-wrenching poems ever written. And Henry de Valcourt was inspired by that poem to paint this: *L'isolement,* which mean *Loneliness.*"

"Wow!" Connie sighed longingly. "Tell me about the poem, Laurent," she pressed, almost pleading now. *Ooh crap, Connie!*

Dylan had been jumping her skateboard from rail to rail, but now she stopped. She sat down with her legs crossed, curled herself into a ball and listened attentively.

"The poem itself is a grim representation of abandonment," the detective was saying. "It begins with a picture that immediately draws us in." The detective stood up and walked to the wall, near the painting, to show Connie the old oak tree where the author had sat to write his first verse. Connie came closer too, as if she couldn't see from where she had been sitting. "From there," the detective pointed under the tree in the painting, "the poet was able to view humanity through a much different lens. He went on to paint in words, a charming layout of the landscape he was observing below: the rivers, the sunrise, the sunset — everything a man could wish and dream for — only to conclude, *One being is missing, and everything is depopulated,* which many believed to be the poem's focal point, referring to Julie's death." A look of wonder filled Connie's blue eyes and the detective seized the moment to recite the opening lines of the poem in a much lower, seductive tone, while taking dramatic steps around Connie.

Loneliness
Often, on the mountain, under the shade of the old oak,
At sunset, sadly I sit; and walked my eyes on the plain.

From hill to hill in vain bearing my view,
From south to north wind, from dawn to sunset,
I travel all the points of the immense extent,
What do I make of these valleys, these palaces, these cottages,
These Rivers, rocks, forests, deserts so dear,
My soul remains indifferent to such wonders;
does not experience before them neither charm nor transport.
I contemplate the earth like a wandering shadow
Vain objects, which for me the charm has long gone,
And I said, "Nowhere happiness awaits me, because
One being is missing, and everything is depleted."

Dylan's expression shook me. It was indescribable on her cute little round face. I caught a glimpse of something very familiar, but I couldn't quite place it in my recollection. Her mouth was wide open in awe, as if she too had been much in love and mourned a lost lover. "Wow!" she said with tears and a broken voice. "That's so sweet."

"Ooh! Enough, Dylan!" I said, raising my voice in consternation. "They're just words. That's just how French folks talk."

"No, they are *not* just words, Mitch. This is the language of love and of the soul, the language of Oneness. That's how Grandpa speaks to us all. That's how one's heart truly speaks." Her voice cracked with emotion. "Once we purge ourselves of all things mundane, that's how we find Him, that's where Grandpa is waiting, Mitch — in a dimension of wholeness and serendipity. All Grandpa ever wanted is for mankind to see himself as a mere speck of dust in His universe." She sniffled.

"Oh, Dylan!" I waved my hand in the air in frustration. "You and your Grandpa's stuff."

"I wish I'd known these lines back on earth," Flannighans said, succumbing to the poet's charm.

SEAT OF TRUTH

"You too? Really?" I looked at them with pity and couldn't decide if they were my guides, or criminal accomplices.

By the end of the poem, Connie was drooling. She swallowed hard and managed to speak: "Laurent," she paused to swallow again, "do you really think a man can be so madly in love with a woman that existence itself bears no charm?"

"Absolutely!" he said with a trace of romance in his eyes.

"That was so sweet! So moving! So touching!" Connie said, her skin glowing. The detective moved closer to her. Slowly he reached out and took her hands in his. He stared into her defeated eyes. Her breathing became labored. She looked like a deer caught in headlights. The government official brought himself even closer. He held her right hand in his left and with his right, searched her waistline. Julio Iglesias's *"J'ai besoin de faire l'amour"* grooved in low volume from my stereo. *My stereo!*

"Guys!" Dylan cried out; her voice suddenly filled with dread. "It's happening!"

"Oh *non!*" Flannighans lamented, covering his large mouth with his large hands.

They stood so close by the painting; they almost became one.

"We need a distraction." I said to Flannighans, panicked. "Dylan, go to the other room!" I said to her.

"No! I want to see what's happening." The detective took the last step as Connie lifted her chin to meet his gaze. The old house phone suddenly rattled, and they jolted apart.

"Hallelujah!" I shouted, pumping a victory fist in the air.

"Oh, man!" Dylan complained.

Connie excused herself to answer the phone; I followed her. It was her mother checking on her. Connie quickly got rid of her with an "I'll call you later." Meanwhile, the detective had reclaimed his seat on the sofa. Connie joined him as if it were nothing. And then there was a slight awkwardness between them, which pleased me.

The night began to fade. The conversation wound down to casual inquiries. The detective shriveled in his seat, then moved a little closer to Connie and gently touched her hand. We jolted to our feet.

He held her hand and examined her fingers one by one, as if he were a doctor, except there was burning desire in his eyes. Connie closed hers passionately as she received his touches.

"Good Lord!" exclaimed Flannighans, crossing his hands on top of his head.

"He's a bad boy," Dylan said. Connie didn't even attempt to remove her hand from his. She just sat there like a statue.

"You ... uh ...you have an incredibly beautiful smile," he said and held her eyes in his. She wasn't even smiling; it was a trick, and she was falling for this crap. She smiled. *Oh boy!*

"You sure ... you're not exaggerating?" She timidly searched his face. Dylan took my hand. Flannighans was now practically between them on the sofa, looking from left to right to see who would make the first move.

After a good minute of silence, the detective drew a deep breath that conveyed something along the lines of fatigue. *I hope he's dying.* It was already past eleven-thirty. Connie must have felt the urgency of the time, given the way she turned away on the sofa while cracking her knuckles.

"Well," the detective finally said, "I have a ton of work tomorrow. I think I must go."

"Don't think — just leave," I said as if he could hear me, and of course Dylan couldn't help but laugh.

"I bet you do," Connie replied as she stood and picked up the glasses. She rushed them off to the kitchen and hurried back to Mr. French.

SEAT OF TRUTH

Detective Laurent Dubois walked to the door at a bride's pace, obviously not really wanting to leave. Connie followed. He stopped and inspected the corner by the door as if he had just forgotten something. "Well," he said to Connie, "I've had a great time with you tonight. I'd love to see you again."

"I'd like that too," she cheerfully offered.

"Very well then," he said, as they finally made it to the doorstep. He went to hug her, but instead said something in French that made Connie blush. It was a simple *"Au revoir et bonsoir, Madame"* — our good old, "Goodbye and goodnight, ma'am." *French people!* I thought to myself.

"I'm looking forward to ... to actually seeing you again," she said, as if she meant something else.

"How about Friday — Friday next week?"

"Sure! Sounds good. I'm available."

"I'll pick you up at, say, seven?" He waited for her to reply.

"Oui, monsieur." She nodded. After many unfinished sentences and an even longer goodbye, he finally turned to go. Thank God, the worst had been aborted.

He closed the door behind him, allowed some air to pump into his lungs — *I hope they're not working,* I thought — and walked toward his ugly sedan as my heart regained its rhythm.

68

CHAPTER ELEVEN

Who knows the heart of man?

On our way back to the Heavens, I felt disappointed, defeated. I had known Connie my whole adult life, I told my companions. We had met at a south Florida International University soccer game in Miami. She was a sophomore — hot, just like the rest, looking for fun where it could be found. And in college there's always fun to be found. In fact, it was at a sorority party that we met.

I was a member of a fraternity, she of the sorority in question.

The latter decided to invite us to one hell of a party, one with "all things permitted." *All things?* we'd wondered. For one, to have a sorority secretly invite a fraternity into their own living quarters for fun was unheard of. Second, this was something we boys dreamt of, once in a blue moon, in our deepest sleep. In fact, no one from the group believed it, especially the last part — "*all things permitted.*" To entice them into keeping their promise, we offered to provide the supplies: food, weed, and booze. And we boys prayed dearly for the day to come quickly.

69

SEAT OF TRUTH

Beforehand, we gathered together and dispatched a few spies to check the surroundings, to make sure this wasn't a prank or a setup with law enforcement as payback for some emotional harm one of us may have innocently caused a sorority sister. Our scouts came back grinning, and that was all we needed.

When we quietly stepped into the sorority sisters' living quarters, we found an exact replica of the Garden of Good and Evil: an exotic oasis of youth, ecstasy, lust, beauty, and abandon, where everyone craved nothing but pleasures and fun. The party began with a few sentences prepared by the sorority sisters, and ended on a good note: "Ladies and gentlemen, condoms save lives!" They distributed the goods liberally.

We boys smiled dreamily.

The immediate details of Connie's person hounded my instincts. I found her long legs, casually graced with black tennis shoes near a stack of beer cases. She wore a short black skirt and a taupe tank top. As I made my way farther up, I found the weight of her eyes on me, and a torrent of unspoken words passed between us. We began to seek each other throughout the night. She was different from the other girls. Surprisingly, I became accustomed to her smell, her stare and her voice. All of her was a magnet, pulling me in. And from that first night on, the anticipation of her coming and going, doing, and being, was inescapable.

I was falling in love.

In the wee hours of the morning, the dancing and the music were dying down, and so were the drinking and the weed. Everyone longed for closeness and comfort. Everyone wanted to tell his or her story to someone — anyone willing to listen. But Connie and I had an immediate understanding, some sort of silent agreement made through smiles and nods. After that night, we turned it into a regular *va-et-vient*, my-place-or-hers. As love is nothing but habit, over time it became easier to propose than to leave her. From that moment we ate the same food, drank from the same well, and eventually, after we got married, shared the same roof. We slept on the same bed and above all worshipped the same God. Yet twenty years later, I knew nothing about her. I was crushed.

If I were to look closely at it, I must admit, in a way we had ceased to love each other, more so before the birth of our son Matthew. Her fascination — even obsession with fashion — had taken a sudden turn when she and a few anorexic housewives from around the neighborhood decided to enroll in a summer class on French Renaissance. *How sad,* I had thought. This interest, with no immediate source, had brought out her worst, bordering on pretentiousness. Her time was now divided between women-only tea parties, with large straw hats, and *belle robes d'été,* reflective *tête-à-têtes* about paintings and art exhibitions, *salons de café* to discuss general interests, and vintage wine tastings with the county's toxic, high-society wives. Meanwhile, all I expected after a full day's work was a decent meal.

She regarded my lack of interest in fashion as odd, old-fashioned, and sometimes even retarded, which I found annoying. She became so engrossed in consumption that in her own eyes other people lacked sophistication — hadn't evolved enough. She developed a chronic longing and predisposition for French customs as if she was a mad scientist. In the end, she considered most people savage, prehistoric-minded, with no sense of culture or *savoir-faire.* Eventually I found it difficult, often confrontational, to communicate with my own wife. She existed now only in the clouds, above the world, riding on her high horse, far from the mortal realm. And quite frankly, I'd had enough of that nonsense.

SEAT OF TRUTH

Over time, she came to suspect that her new devotion was not well regarded. Not that I wasn't a supportive enough husband, but it wasn't a mutual adaptation. After all, I was the one who had to become accustomed to the new her, the one I never knew; the one I hated the most.

She became reckless with her religious devotion, putting more effort into her physical appearance, and now during our occasional bedroom closeness my wife looked and felt like a small pack of bones that I might break at any moment. In several genuine attempts I gently inquired about her health regime, but my innocent remarks were met with stern reproaches that I was suspicious. It wasn't until one of the women — their leader, Melody — collapsed on a sidewalk and died from her vain pursuit of appearance that the rest of the pack considered the seriousness of their eating disorder. It was a few months later that I found Connie attractive again, just before the birth of Matthew, right after she began to eat like the rest of us mortals, put on a few rolls, and her derrière benefited with an obvious bump. She began to wear those tight miniskirts around the house, and something woke in me again.

"Well, the worst is over," Flannighans said now.

"At least for tonight," added Dylan. "Matthew has a soccer ball too, almost like mine. Did you know that?" She searched my face for an answer.

"He loves to play soccer. Edmund was his soccer buddy," I said distantly.

"What's the matter with Edmund anyway?" Dylan asked.

"He's in transit, remember?" Flannighans warned Dylan quickly. I caught a glimpse of Dylan staring at Flannighans. Instantly I had the feeling that they had held out on me over my brother's whereabouts. They knew more.

CHAPTER TWELVE

Falling in love, head over heels with the Comforter

By the end of my third day, I had become closer to others, surprisingly, including Flannighans. I spent that whole day patrolling around the Heavens looking for Edmund, alone.

I went to the metropolitan city where no one either aged or slept, which reminded me of my college days. From there I crossed the lush valley where the moon had crashed. People had built houses among the scattered fragments, but few people were around when I walked by, there was no sign of my brother. So I headed for the lake. Or maybe I didn't know where to look for him. I asked a few elders if they'd seen Edmund. They stared at me as if I was out of my mind, but they said no, nonetheless. I knocked on a few doors, but the reception was nowhere near encouraging. So I stopped altogether. Eventually, Jesus found me sitting near the Well of Jacob.

I was in my own twilight about the search for my brother when He took a seat next to me. I noticed wounds again around His arms and neck, even blood spots. They looked recent, as though the bandages had just been removed. When our eyes met

SEAT OF TRUTH

He gave me a weak smile and kissed my forehead. There was something about Him, some sort of current that I was falling into. Now, according to the Old-Fashioned Book, the Guy died a long time ago. What was going on in that place that no one was willing to tell me? Why did I feel on the verge of something bad was about to happen? A feeling of mistrust was taking hold of me and it made me anxious. According to Flannighans, humans had caused those wounds because they came to judge Him. He had not dwelt much on the subject and offered no additional insight into his claim.

He sat quietly next to me.

Kids were chasing the water jets around the fountain. We sat in silence watching the kids play and laugh. They all had hologram crowns, the most coveted one: the Crown of Life. We didn't talk. *Maybe He knows where I came from,* I thought. *Maybe He knows why I'm here.* But neither of us spoke his mind.

The kids decided to take their appetite for play into the middle of King David Boulevard. We tagged along behind them. They played like they had no destination, as if they didn't have to go home for dinner, as if no one expected them. The silence grew even longer between Jesus and me, but I longed for His companionship. Eventually He spoke.

"The world is on the brink of moral decay, Mitch," He declared distantly. "Meekness, wisdom, patience, love, and God giving virtues are no longer revered. The contrary alone thrives." He looked at me for support.

"You mean your own people, who are supposed to be the light in the world?" I asked without searching His face.

"I fear that the faith of my house is faltering."

"It *is* pretty bad," I said, remembering my own treacherous sins.

"They approach failure not from a place of grace, but from inability; they consult one another not from a place of brokenness but from pride; they reason to one another not from a place of compassion but from contempt and under threat. From these vantage points spiritual decisions are made in a business-like transaction — no place for the human being, no genuine caring. What hurts the most is that they do it in the name of Love. My name! I never taught that. I don't view them in the past, but in the now. Because the now and forward is the moment of grace and abundance."

The tone with which He spoke reached an intimate part of my soul that I had just discovered. His eyes filled with sorrow and pain as if He was under an unbearable, crushing weight from which He couldn't escape. I felt an avalanche of guilt as if I was part of His constant sufferings. His voice pleaded, almost begged for help — *any* help.

I cleared my throat. It had become tight and dry.

"Is this why there are so many kids in the Heavens compared to adults?" I said to Him. There were scores more children in the Heavens than adults, men and women combined. *Where are the men and the women?* I had once asked Dylan and Flannighans. According to Flannighans' statistics, there were fewer of them in the Heavens because of their stubbornness and generally unforgiving nature. They were grudge holders and always angry over trivial matters.

"For one, yes," Jesus answered, looking at me. "Our kingdom belongs to whosoever has a childlike heart." Then we fell into a longer silence. "Dylan is a fun kid, you know," He said with a smile. I caught His serene eyes. He measured and weighted the words as if they were challenges.

"She knows so much," I added with my own smile.

"She's very fond of you. You know that?"

SEAT OF TRUTH

"She talks non-stop about Grandpa," I said with a grin, and He too smiled even broader.

"Aha! Those two are inseparable!" He finally let out a laugh. "Look!" He said to me, pointing at the far horizon where a large, white winged horse was flying toward us.

Within moments the mammoth beast landed in the middle of the street in full gallop and stopped short in front of us. It bowed down in worship and said, "Your Majesty!" The sheer size of the animal left me flabbergasted. Its mane was like an incendiary bush; its enormous thighs looked so strong; its hoofs were like iron claws except they were made of something precious. Its large wings were blue-grey, but their contour feathers were metallic blue, yellow, and red. Its tail matched the mane on its gigantic neck. I had never seen an animal of that size before.

Jesus petted its back affectionately, jumped on, looked at me, and said, "You know, my sister is waiting for you."

"Your sis— Who? Your sister?" I stuttered.

"Yes, my sister. She's waiting at the end of that road." He pointed behind me. When I turned back to speak to Him, He was gone. Then I heard a sound.

* * *

I started walking down a boulevard, the name of which I didn't know. It was by far the largest boulevard I had seen in all the Heavens.

The rhododendron shrubs were closely cropped, but much taller than I'd known them on earth, especially in Canada. Their purple-rose petals looked unreal. If there was a sound it must have come from somewhere there, I thought. So I resumed walking toward the far end of the road where my companion had pointed.

76

My sister is waiting for you, I repeated to myself.

How long had She been waiting for me, and more important, why?

I followed the boulevard as it gradually turned into a country road. Not too far ahead a tall structure rose out of the landscape. Its massive stonewalls rose upward and overwhelmed everything nearby. As I got closer I could see it's an old cathedral in the middle of a farmland. White smoke rose from the top of the bell tower. I heard the sound again, but still could not find its source. I stopped to look around to locate where the sound was coming from. There was a familiarity in it here. It felt so close to home. It gripped me as if it had been part of me all along. Then I recognized the soothing, comforting sound of a cello.

Besides the tall structure, there was no other. So if there was a sound, it must have come from there.

I followed my instincts.

The building resembled a ruined fortress where apparently treasures had been hidden from prying eyes. Its portal structure, although large, had only one big door in the middle. It was open.

I knew it was She.

Flannighans had suggested the idea of visiting the farmhouse during one of our conversations. I just couldn't bring myself to admit and believe at the possibility. Of all things, a farm seemed inconceivable all the way in the Heavens.

I entered the structure and took a seat in the nearest pew at the back. Immediately, I began to count everything. There were three rows of pillars, and each row had seven massive columns that were joined by carved arcades high above to form a triangular vault. Some of the columns were made of onyx, diamond and ruby, others of pearls, gold and sapphire; the rest were a combination of other gemstones and they all stretched high.

SEAT OF TRUTH

All the seats were empty. A few kids were playing hide and seek among the pews, but mostly it was quiet. The pews were warm and soft. Far ahead, at the other end, the triangular vault reflected seven dazzling lights in a rotunda. I noticed now that someone was sitting behind the last column, before the apse.

She sat with Her back against a beautiful onyx pillar. I watched how Her right hand swayed with a bow as a gentle breeze blew the baby blue dress She was wearing. I took in all of that from the back pew. But I couldn't quite make out Her face. Not yet.

When I first saw the Holy Spirit playing the cello, like most of you would be — and believe me, you would be — I was broken. She was singing a melody well known to me, *As the Deer Panteth for the Water*, accompanied by a host of other instruments. But I couldn't see those musicians, only Her.

Beside Her a grand piano made of rare and rich black wood stood in the open. And from time to time She'd switch from the cello to the piano.

The Holy Spirit plays the cello and piano? I thought.

Her voice rose in sadness as trombones reached for the chorus and then rose in agony and comfort together: *I alone am your strength, your shield ...*

Her voice seared in my soul and searched every joint down into my marrow, and it was then that I understood the impact and weight of the lyrics. The words stung me like bees. They hit me like hail from the skies. Her voice roared again, rising through the building in a crescendo. The acoustic was a pure joy. My body braced itself, heightened with the music and the sound, ready for whatever came next.

She repeated the chorus once more and I caught a glimpse of Her face as She moved to the grand piano. She had freckles — between the left side of her nose and her cheek, just a few nearly imperceptible red dots, like Dylan's, and I began to wonder, could the little girl be Her daughter? The Old-Fashioned Book never mentioned that the Holy Spirit had a child. I frowned at the possibility. Somehow the technicalities baffled me.

The song faded away until there was only the piano echoing everywhere, from the pews to the columns, from the walls and especially inside of me.

"Come on in, Mitch!" She said without looking. *So friendly, so loving.* I was sure She said that with a smile, too. Again, the voice came to me, except I couldn't see Her face. The ease and sweetness with which Her voice called out my name was so familiar that I couldn't deny that I must have known it for a lifetime. An adjacent marble wall brought me Her reflection. She looked at me with a grin from the piano bench. Finally, like a baby, I took my first magical, unbalanced step forward. I moved ahead three rows and quickly sat back down, not really wanting to get too involved with the Holy Spirit — for the most part, because I didn't speak in tongues back on earth, and also because I knew I had knowingly caused Her untold grief back in my heyday and I was ashamed.

"Come closer, Mitch," She pleaded. "I don't bite. I'm the Healer, the Comforter, the Keeper, remember?" I moved into the next pew, still distant from where She sat. My legs could no longer bear me. "It is I who always come to mankind no matter how hard I tried. Oh boy!" She said. With that, She stood up, and took her first step toward me. I froze.

I heard Her footsteps echoing in the sprawling compound as if the steps came from an abyss. Some echoed like snowflakes, inaudible; others like thunder in my soul. Her cadence and demeanor spoke of timeless perfection, and Her smile struck every nucleus in my being.

SEAT OF TRUTH

She wasn't in a hurry. Each step was measured with absolute perfection. She advanced slowly, her hands balancing her bold, confident structure. Her body moved as if eternity could wait, and it certainly did wait. *Holy!*

I thought of running away, but there was nowhere to go. And where can I go that Her hands wouldn't reach me? And besides, my legs felt like in a vise-like grip.

The Holy Spirit, or simply Holy as Dylan referred to Her, wasn't beautiful or pretty as one might expect. She was simply an ethereal expression of love and kindness and grace and compassion and mercy and joy and peace. So the nearness of Her exuded absolute comfort and felicity that cannot be expressed in words. As simple as that! She was *it*.

With Her pixie haircut and Her large front teeth (I had caught a glimpse of them when She was singing), She was almost a carbon copy of Dylan. *Maybe She's the one who inspired the little girl's fashion sense, to wear her hair short like the Holy Spirit*, I thought. *Maybe She's Dylan's role model.*

"I'm glad you accepted my invitation right before your dying moments," She said as She took a seat next to me. I bowed my head and kept it down. *Is She waiting for me to say something?* I thought, *because She isn't getting anything.*

The scent of burning myrrh oil and fresh-cut cedar wafted in our proximity. Between us was nothing but silence, the kind we all long for, and the kind that morphs into hope. And then I experienced weightlessness, as though Her presence had slowly dissipated an invisible burden I carried.

There was nothing but us.

She moved closer to me now, so close that our knees rubbed.

My blood turned to syrup.

She took my frozen left hand onto her lap and began to massage it with both of Hers. I felt Her touch in my every

80

heartbeat, in every breath I drew in, in every involuntary pulse I contracted in my wholeness. I felt Her gaze on me. I raised my chin and turned my face away, unable to look into those forgiving eyes. They were probably grey, maybe blue, or hazel, or green, or black. They could be anything. I wasn't sure.

The silence.

I can't breathe.

How can one looks into those comforting eyes?

The eyes that provide strengths?

The eyes of atonement?

Those compassionate eyes?

She held my wrist with one hand and with the other She slowly made circular movements as if to cause the blood to circulate in my body. *She knows. I'm trapped.*

Atelia had taught me well. She had taught me the necessity and the importance of assessment, especially when overwhelmed. I put my childhood lesson to the test. I made a quick retrospective assessment of what had transpired over the last few days so that I could have a better grasp at what was going on.

Three days ago, I had been driving northbound on the I-95 in Fort Lauderdale Florida, in the United States of America, on the North American continent, on a planet called Earth. A place where mankind mastered the art of speech with nothing to show for it; where there is enough, but where more have none; where there is division, but one needs another; where access is protected by firewalls and guards; where diseases share beds with lesser ailments; where joy and peace became ghost stories. And now, here I was, seven existences away, sitting mere inches from the eyes that behold all glory beyond the grasp of knowledge. How surprising was that! Finally, I said — or rather, the words escaped my mouth, "I'm sorry ... for everything I did."

SEAT OF TRUTH

My eyes blurred with tears. I used the back of my right hand to clear my vision, still looking away.

Her hands slid up my forearm and elbow, and She rested her chin on my left shoulder. She was so close to my ear that Her breath raised goose bumps on the side of my neck, and She said coyly, "Sooo…" as if we were longtime lovers, as if She longed for me, as if She was about to propose to me. "I'm not going to see those beautiful eyes of yours that I spent an eternity designing?" She giggled, almost like Dylan, and I chuckled a little too. *Is Holy flirting with me?* I thought. With that, She slowly pressed her lips onto my left cheek and planted a kiss there and said, "Come more often. We have lots to talk about, don't we?" She waited for my answer and I nodded yes, still looking away. And like that, She was gone.

They all do that.

***

I left the farmland still feeling the soothing press of Her lips on my skin. Her touch was divine.

Unreal.

Magical.

Miraculous.

Mysterious.

I felt a pang in my heart every now and then as I walked back in the general direction of the main road. The scent of fresh-cut cedar, of jasmine and burning myrrh oil, wrapped around me like layers, and I found myself longing for Her.

CHAPTER THIRTEEN

The particles of life

Mercifully, I escaped the farmhouse without having my ability to speak in tongues tested. Dylan was waiting outside the main road. This time she was alone. She was riding her skateboard around a curved wall made of amethyst and emeralds, while holding her soccer ball in one hand. "How did you know where to find me?" I said to her.

"Oh, I know. You saw Her, didn't you?" she asked curiously, now holding her toys.

"Saw who?" I played along.

"She's so pretty, isn't She?" she said with a wide smile.

"What are you talking about?"

"Aaaah! You like Her, don't yah!" she gushed.

"Stop it!" I blushed but smiled.

"I knew it," she declared.

"Dylan! I can't believe you said that!"

"Have you seen those eyes?"

"Nope."

SEAT OF TRUTH

"They're violet — I mean real violet. And if you look a little longer, you'll see something else in them."

"Like what?"

"Next time, look a little longer!"

"Can I ask you a question?" I said.

"Yeah." She slid her skateboard and did front and back 360s as if it were a bike.

"Why doesn't She live with your Grandpa?" We started to walk and turn left on King David Boulevard heading toward the Square, called Stone of Creation where all the roads lead to.

"Well," she began — and I braced myself for another wave of quantum mechanics equations and dark matter challenges — "the mystery and the dynamic between the three of them is really simple, you see. The three of them are a ring through which mankind must pass to attend eternal felicity and join the circle of Oneness, once and for all.

"Grandpa called mankind — every person. Those who answered the call He then qualified and handed over to my Brother. Then my Brother accepted them with their baggage, took on His own back everything they carried — I mean everything emotional and physical — set them free and handed them over to my Sister." She counted them off on her fingers as if she planned on reaching one hundred. "Her job is to teach them how to stay free and lead them into all truths and mysteries, eventually to Oneness — in other words, back to Grandpa. But mankind seldom lets Her lead. So Her job is the hardest." She said that last sentence as if I should have known that basic answer. "Did I lose you?"

"How old are you again?" I asked as I sat down on a bench. She giggled like any happy child and then some more.

"I am seven years old," she managed to say. "Why, because I'm so smart? Grandpa taught me a lot of things. He's a mean

84

Old Man, but wise beyond your wildest imagination. He explained to me the mysteries of all the creation and the theories of life —".

"The theories of life?" I asked her, anxious to hear about that.

"Of course." She looked at me, as if to say, *duh*. "They're simple algorithms that regulate the flow and transport of all energy in all things and beings, and between all things and beings, in all states, and between all states. In all that was and is, in all that can be, and in all that will ever be.

"For instance, between any given point and another exists an invisible mass, transporting information and obeying laws of the universe — the Ether theories. Mankind has gone to extreme lengths trying to figure out these mysteries but never will because, not only they have approached it from the wrong vantage point, they also have hidden agendas.

"Ether theories, or the invisible mass, is the foundation, or better yet, the hub that rotates, shifts, transmits, connects all things and beings visible and invisible into a singularity: the Oneness. These computing rules are a combination of science and spiritual law, which in the customary physical dimensional mind is inconceivably inconceivable. On your seventh day, you will see it in all its infinite splendor: all the logic, the mechanics, the distances, the chemistry, the configurations, and all that it illuminates, the apps, the bonds, the transmission, and all," she concluded, as if she too couldn't wait to see it again and again.

"You really are a wonder, Dylan," I conceded.

"Grandpa *partly* agreed with Stephen Hawking when he said that 'the universe is governed by the laws of science. The laws may have been decreed by Grandpa, but He does not intervene to break the laws.' Grandpa breaks and defies them all the time,

SEAT OF TRUTH

for anyone who truly seeks, knocks, and asks. But sadly, Grandpa says, the physicist declared himself an atheist."

We stopped again and sat on a bench next to which stood an upright barrel. She then raised herself on her toes to reach inside. "Can I ask you something?" she said while filling two ice cream cones from inside the barrel.

"Sure, go ahead."

"If it's okay with you, can I call you Dad until my real one comes?" She handed me an ice cream cone of pineapple almond and immediately licked her fingers.

"Well, kid —"

"I asked Grandpa about my dad once. He told me" — she now mimicked her Grandpa's deep baritone voice — "'*Ms. Dylan, it is forbidden. We are not to speak of it.*' That's His favorite sentence. I'm sure you'll figure it out on your own with Him there is no negotiation. So, can I call you Dad, please?"

"Sure, why not? You can call me Dad all you want, until yours comes," I answered between bites of ice cream. The fruity, delicious savor of the ice cream was so good that I didn't see Flannighans coming.

He showed up from nowhere in his boney smile-structured face and grinned at us as he took a seat next to me. "You guys want to come with me to see something cool?" he announced immediately as if he had just found something new. Dylan stood up and shouted, "Let's go, Dad!" She was obviously eager to test the new title. Flannighans filled an ice cream cone for himself. I demanded a refill, and he took the lead.

86

CHAPTER FOURTEEN

The frequencies of the Heavens
The path to Oneness

We strolled along the dreamy Adam & Eve Boulevard, also known as Eden Boulevard where rare flowers bloomed: the Netherland tulips whose petals grew in the shape of a round vase, the intoxicatingly fragrant of Syrian jasmine, the *fleur-de-lis* of France, the tall sunflowers of Ukraine, orchids of Hong Kong, and an equally rare assortment of trees. Among them were Japanese wisterias — a beautiful, light purple flower often used at fairs and as wedding decorations.

"These species are so unique they can only grow in certain parts on earth," Dylan explained. "But people know so little about the amazing effects and purposes of trees. Trees sacrifice themselves by breathing the carbon dioxide that could kill us and turning it into pure oxygen. Yes, trees produce the oxygen you're breathing right now! They provide shade, fruit, and wood; they are used for fire, houses, paper, tools, and transportation and much more on earth." Dylan said they could be used to do all things. You only have to know the proper use for them.

SEAT OF TRUTH

In a science assignment back in high school we were told to write a short paper about why we must not cut down trees. I wished I had known these things then. I would have had an "A+".

We took a sharp right toward Joseph Court, where more flowers and other rare plants grew than I care to name. We kept going until we reached the city limits. The road forked into two gravel roads. One gave way to a narrow passage leading to a plantation field, another to a small descent but much narrower.

We stopped.

We'd been walking for almost two hours. Dylan and Flannighans looked right and left as if they were lost. But after a few minutes of standing, Flannighans found his way. We took the plantation field road. Both side of the entire field stretched with rainbow eucalyptus and mango trees. The mango trees branches joined together, threaded into arcs, and the gravel road looked like an illuminating tunnel with band of lights of gradient colors.

The unmistakable multi-hued bark of the rainbow eucalyptus trees was unique. During the day, the reflective, bright-colored barks resembled oil paintings. It was said that the trees were created when Grandpa first demonstrated His genius to Noah by displaying a rainbow in the clouds.

At night the tree glowed with the seventeen heavenly colors, and whoever touched it would turn into a rainbow until sunrise. Only the Tree of Life could undo the effect.

Flannighans' daily lessons were filled with surprises, sometimes passing as strange. One never knew what to expect when he opened his big mouth. And lately it had gotten worse. It appeared, too, that the little girl was falling for his moribund theories.

88

"It's this way," said Flannighans, pointing at the tunnel-like path beneath mango trees whose mouth-watering fruit hung so low. Scores of birds perched on the branches. Dylan had handed me her skateboard, and Flannighans, her soccer ball. We plucked off mangoes and ate them as we continued in single file and eventually found a larger road of dirt and rocks where we exited from the tunnel. I was last, making sure that no one touched the rainbow tree.

We found two benches and quickly took seat to continue to enjoy our mangoes. Evidently no one spoke for a while. Then I slowly raised my hands over my head and took hold of my crown and began to look at it for the first time. It had all sort of cuts, gleaming and glowing in wonders. The Crown of Rejoicing is exquisitely breathtaking. Flannighans looked at it longingly as Dylan went on to explain the geometry and the science behind each facet.

"Would you like to hold it Flannighans?" I said to him.

"Yes, Mitch. Let me hold it a little." He held it with a grinned face and fondness.

I had to admit there was something different about Flannighans — this ability to define things with such simplicity, this bold acknowledgment of the nature of his existence, this freedom, and this assurance that his demands and requests were attainable. He displayed attentive awareness of my lacking in spiritual respects, and the immediate exercise of humility and compassion to help. Was this really possible from a former drug dealer/addict?

We hadn't spoken since our delicious mango treats and crown inspection. We resumed our walk but my mind was somewhere else. I was thinking about Edmund. Maybe this time they were taking me to see him. Were they trying to surprise me?

SEAT OF TRUTH

I knew Dylan had abilities. She was gifted. Maybe she could perform a miracle for her new "dad."

"How did you die, Flannighans?" I asked in the oppressive silence, trying not to think of Edmund.

"Oh! From a drug overdose," he said bluntly, clearly surprised by his own bold admission, which stopped me in my tracks.

"A drug overdose?" I barked. "What exactly *is* this place, anyway? Who's allowed in here?" I asked angrily. "I thought you gave up all those habits to make things right with Him!"

"Yes, but it didn't mean I became a saint instantly Mitch," he said in his own defense.

"So you died from a drug overdose, *and* you made it to Heaven?" I found myself saying. "How convenient, isn't it! And there are folks — *good* folks, I might add — who probably made one little mistake, did one little bad thing, and are ... and are ... nowhere near here." I feared using the fitting word — the one that I'd been thinking the whole time. I was making a point about Edmund. I felt a knot in my throat.

"It happens, Dad," Dylan interjected, as if to calm me down. "Grandpa says it's all or nothing, that ninety-nine percent is exactly the same as one percent. In other words, there's no continuum between these numbers. People are like software in His eyes, they're either a *one* or a *zero*.

"I told Grandpa, 'Mathematically, it doesn't make any sense.' He explained that if He'd allowed categorization of sins, mankind would have been right to judge each other. Comparing one's level of wickedness to others would have been fair game, and complacency would have been justified. And as a consequence, my Brother's sublime atonement of all wrongful proclivities wouldn't mean much." She looked up at me. "Did I lose you?"

90

"I'm following you, baby girl," I said, and she took my left hand in hers. "Continue," I added softly.

"Mankind," she said, "already spent the majority of their precious time judging each other — especially churchgoers, from the crown of your head to the soles of your feet. They place so much emphasis on sex, murder, and homosexuality as if these were the ultimate sins for which redemption seems almost inapplicable, while little lies, resentment, manipulation, selfishness, trifling, and hypocrisy thrive among them. They categorize sins into big and small, bad and not so bad, heinous, and social or casual. In doing so, they have opened a gateway that Tshembow has used to his own advantage. Tshembow doesn't appreciate a sinner walking around like clashing cymbals — too much wickedness is problematic, Dad. Counselor Tshembow estimates that in the natural, and in the supernatural law of things and of mankind's own making — I mean his subconscious — lies a reset button that can retaliate against insanity even for the sake of civility or moral compass. With such a potent principal spiritual order, mankind might find his way to Oneness. In wartime flocks of people find the path to Oneness, albeit at the cost of many. So Tshembow prefers them to thrive in the luxury of complacency and focusing more on façades and *good person* title. The Counselor bets and relies heavily on trivial sins, those that yield no earthly appearances, such as hypocrisy, resentment, lust, jealousy, pride, gossip, and plain selfishness.

"In Grandpa's big fiery eyes, a former drug addict, like our good old friend Flannighans over here, is as holy as the Lamb Himself so long as he leads a new life. A preacher is as filthy as Tshembow himself as soon he tells a white lie or is biased in his executions.

SEAT OF TRUTH

"Grandpa also says that mankind focused too much on religion in the last few remaining days than pursuing a relationship with Him." She sounded as if she too had had enough of mankind's routine religious activity. "I must warn you too, Dad, that religion and spirituality are nearly equally needed," Dylan continued. "But the latter is most important, since it is the portal through which one can attain the circle of Oneness. Humanity and the infinite cosmos is a combined web of frequencies filled with energies that Grandpa Himself carefully designed for us. We can tap into that energy and extract the very essence or reason for life, which is: joy, fun, peace, love, fulfillment, patience, forgiveness, compassion, accomplishment, longsuffering, meekness, and much more, Dad."

I could only look at Dylan, at how she held up her palms, counting with her little fingers, as she wowed me with her simple explanation of life, death, love and above all, mankind.

In the silence that followed, she walked very close to me, holding my hand from time to time as if seeking protection. I took advantage of the long silence to process it all and tried to see where Edmund's longtime church attendance and performance fit into all that.

Back on earth my little brother Edmund had been a role model in the eyes of many. What exactly had gone wrong? Where had it gone sour? Or was this a bad joke? Was I hallucinating? As far I knew, I was dead. What I had thought was a dream wasn't a dream after all. It had turned out that I really was dead. There was no going back. So where was Edmund? Who knew? There were so many questions to answer that I forgot my original train of thought until Flannighans spoke again.

92

"What about you Mitch? How did *you* die?" he said. I looked at him, trying to figure out what he was really looking for, and how to best deliver the news.

"I died in a car crash last Thursday," I gave him enough information so he wouldn't ask more questions.

"Ouch!" exclaimed Flannighans, as if someone had just pinched his skin. "Did it hurt?"

"You think it's funny," I said. They both laughed.

"You know, Mitch," Flannighans said, "He really loves you. I mean *really.*"

"Who?" I said distantly, still trying to make sense of Dylan's notions on spirituality and sin.

"Jesus," Flannighans said.

"Why do you say that?" I asked, again processing things.

"He's so happy around you. You make Him laugh. Mostly He's sad," he continued with a trace of his own sadness.

"How can He be sad?" I said, slowing down, as we were about to cross a small wooden bridge.

"Well, the way you guys treat each other down there, how could He not be—"

"Were you not down there too, Flannighans?" I snapped at him again. "If anyone made Him sad, it would have been you. From what I know, you broke *all* the rules. You broke *all* of —"

"Me?" Flannighans defended himself, now becoming angry too. "Are you comparing my sins to yours?"

"I didn't do those heinous things you did." I waved him off and crossed the bridge.

"You did far worse than you think."

"Oh really? Really?"

"Oh, yes."

SEAT OF TRUTH

"From being a bully all your academic life," I hurled back at him, "to being a drug addict, stealing, to selling bad stuff, and to ... to ... God knows what else!"

"Yes, I know you humans! All you do is judging, judging people. You so-called religious, zealous people! Always judging!"

"Yeah! Shall we talk about sins now?" I challenged him. He looked at me, his face contained, and I saw the beginning of tears shaping in his deep gray eyes, which made me happy.

I won. I thought.

"I didn't know, Mitch." His voice was now broken. I felt a small rush of victory inside of me.

"You didn't know what?" I asked. I wanted him to confess.

"I didn't know the truth. I didn't know the truth, okay?" He mopped his eyes with the back of a hand. "I didn't know the truth Mitch, but you did." He paused and waited for it to register, and it certainly did. "Worst of all," he added, "you came all the way into the backyard of the Heavens to judge me."

The guy had a great and powerful point, I had to admit, but still I was thinking about my next strategy: *pride.*

"As if you could do any better," I offered, concealing my defeat.

"I would try. I would try, Mitch." He sniffled. As my own eyes were blanketed with tears, a giant drop escaped and Flannighans noticed it. I looked away. He saw my defeat.

The night Edmund had got himself badly injured at the lighthouse had not been Flannighans' fault but my own. He had taken the fall for me.

After that episode, my family — especially my mother — always turned him away whenever he came over to play. He was deemed a bad influence on us. The door was always shut to him. Now I seriously questioned whether we were not somehow responsible for much of what had happened to him.

Dylan stepped between us as if ready to break up a fight. She watched and listened to how two human beings replayed their old burdens of daily living. She seemed unsure whom to believe.

"Religion," she began, "compares people. It sees them according to how one defines good and evil. Spirituality is a progressive achievement made through seeking, knocking, asking and a combination of the practice of good virtues that leads to the circle of Oneness. Flannighans' escaping punishment is not a miracle unheard of in the Heavens, on the contrary. In fact, my Brother — hypothetically speaking — warned your species during His sojourn on earth in a series of parables: about the rich man and the poor man, about how the first will be the last and the last will be the first, about how not everyone that comes in His name is from Him. In conclusion, Dad, a person's spiritual journey is a secret known only to Grandpa, no one else."

Dylan's explanation crushed me. But it also left a smile on my face that I still carry.

Indeed, human beings classify and codify everything to assess one another. With that scale, the infinite manifestation of possibilities becomes what they can justify, explain, and comprehend in their narrow mental framework. They become judgmental in the process. Once we've made our psychological profile of someone, there's no escaping it. And in spite of these unruly emotions, humans blossom in blindness.

As much as we don't like to admit it, there are only two choices. Sometimes we wish there was a gray area where we could safely harbor our inadequacy, our self-doubt — some sort of mechanical back door through which to manage life.

What a bunch of fools, mankind!

SEAT OF TRUTH

The road now entered a small rural town where people stood on their front porches and watched us passing by as if we were extraterrestrial invaders.

We spotted tall Madagascar baobabs behind the small homes. The trees were a sight to behold. They looked like giant upright wine barrels. Each tree had three branches at the top. They grew large, odorless white flowers that never died.

There is no dead tree, or branch, or leaf in the Heavens. Nothing suffers decay.

These giant barrels stored enough water to have lasted for generations back on earth. Flannighans and Dylan declared that the baobab has a direct energy exchange with the Holy Spirit and is also a replica of a human being. They brought me closer to one and had me touch its glassy trunk. It was super cold, then warm, then super hot. All in an instant! That is why they said the tree is a replica of a human being, because of its quick, changing nature.

"Its very nature is unstable," Flannighans said.

I've never seen a tree so mysterious. Some of the inhabitants laughed at my initial reaction. They probably think I'm an alien.

"What is this place?" I said to Flannighans.

"These are people who choose to live the life they dreamed of living back on earth," he answered.

"Are you kidding me? In a slum?"

"Ah, Mitch!" Flannighans warned. "You'd be surprised to find out what makes some people happy."

"They don't look too happy to me," I countered.

"Some people want the whole world to be happy, while a few require nothing but the breath of life." Flannighans laughed, as if it made him sound more knowledgeable about heavenly stuff. But what he said made sense. Back on earth I had known people who would happily have traded their life in a heartbeat if they

96

could live for one more week. I knew people who would have handed over all their gold for good health, or to live for one more day.

Flannighans said the majority of these onlookers had been rich back on earth — in fact, very wealthy people or superficially wealthy — but unhappy. These folks understood that wealth is a tool to better understand themselves and others. They knew well all along that money couldn't bring them *la joie de vivre* found in the simplicity of life, and that only total abandon of self and things could. Now, they had the opportunity to live like that without having to prove anything to anyone so they chose this lifestyle. "They're happy, Mitch."

We arrived at an area fenced with barbed wire so sharp that even looking at it felt harmful, almost the same security-like features we had seen at the Checkpoint. We managed to ascend an embankment built alongside the fence. Then it was a few steps up until we landed on a flat surface facing a small hill partially fogged. Before he took another step, Flannighans looked at me with defiance in his eyes and said, "We never came here, okay?" threatening me, as if that he would vehemently deny his involvement.

"Won't they know?" I asked, but no one answered.

We crawled up the hill on our bellies. Flannighans went first, then Dylan. I wanted to ask them why we had to crawl. Couldn't we simply walk? Again, with these two, there was no way I could win an argument. So I crawled.

Closer to the summit we felt a pulling, as if gravity trying to pull us into another world. We reached the tipping point of the hill and could barely see each other as the fog had become heavier. Then Flannighans said, "Wait for it, wait for it! Voila!" and suddenly the fog lifted off, and there we were staring at a

SEAT OF TRUTH

mechanical device below. "Look!" A delighted Flannighans pointed below the cliff.

"Wow!" Dylan whispered in awe.

We stared down at a spinning device resting on a thick blanket of white fog. It looked like a complex gear assembly that rolled, rotated, and spun around aimlessly. From time to time, things fell off the device and were lost forever in the thick cloud below.

"Where do they fall to?" I asked, in wonder.

"Earth," answered Flannighans.

"What exactly *is* this place?" I finally demanded.

"Oh! This is Heaven's warehouse my friend," Flannighans said. "This is where all blessings are flowing from. All these things you're looking at are blessings — things people are asking for, or hope to achieve in their lifetimes. Mankind calls them dreams."

The vastness of the treasures my eyes could see was immeasurable and indescribable. I saw all good things hoped for and dreamt of by mankind: mansions, cars, jets, clothes, yachts, trucks, bikes, high-rise condos, hotels, diplomas, motorcycles, helmets, designer bags, shoes, soccer balls, birds, wedding dresses, land, silver, gold, diamonds, cows, rings, mules, chickens, children, donkeys, lions, tigers, elephants, plates, knives, watches, bracelets, televisions, cellphones, chairs, virtues, toys, husbands, wives, kids, twins, body parts like: arms, legs, hearts, kidneys, eyes, bones, ears, fingers, blood, toes, and much more. Everything was neatly packed into transparent boxes ready to ship to earth. I could barely contain the smile on my face as I witnessed an old lawn mower just fall off the cloud. I laughed.

"Is that a donkey?" I asked. "Somebody is asking God for a donkey?"

98

"Yes," Dylan said. "You'd be surprised the things some people lack in some parts of the world."

"That's a loaf of bread, isn't it?" I laughed out loud again.

"Yes. Some people can't afford them," said Flannighans.

"Why are some of those houses look like mansions and others are so small, almost like huts?" I remarked.

"The size of any mansion is the same," Flannighans said. "This is called the 'natural affinity law of faith.' The wish is granted according to the petitioner's work. If you dream big, you'll work harder and smarter to achieve that dream. And likewise, if you dream small you will achieve small things. It's just a natural attraction."

I looked at him. "Then why are these things still here?"

"There could be many reasons," Dylan jumped in. I turned to face her. She had both her elbows planted on the ground and rested her face between her palms. "When someone is asking God for something, or dreaming of accomplishing something, Grandpa immediately releases it, then the universe catalogues it in Heaven's warehouse and assigns it to the proper frequency of Oneness. Anyway, the reason these things are still here can vary. Some petitioners give up on themselves; others are too lazy to truly seek the proper frequency. And some of these things, as you can see, are days away from falling into the Great Mist. Others are mere hours, or even minutes away from the dreamer. The dreamer just happened to use the wrong language. The thing is, whenever, or wherever you speak a word, a transaction takes place somewhere, good or bad. It is a supernatural law that no word comes back void. It is called the fruit of one's lips. And it must find the related frequency — in those cases, Tshembow. Then those people lose their passion and focus. Discouragement settles in, and worse, they quit, often under the pressure of

SEAT OF TRUTH

society, family and friends. They become the victims of trends and waste precious time."

"Then why did they give up, when what they were seeking was within reach? I don't understand," I said. I was a little angry now at humans.

Flannighans answered: "They failed to practice the virtues that build the relationship to Oneness: patience, justice, mercy, forgiveness, altruism, love, longsuffering, compassion, and meekness. These would have eventually led them to where they needed to be. One of these might have been the last step between the dreamer and the frequency to Oneness where the dream itself awaits. But they just threw it all away because they wouldn't wait a few more seconds to help someone. They wouldn't show mercy to one who needed it most. They wouldn't forgive someone who sought their pardon. They wouldn't share the pain of others who were heavily laden. They refused to extend a helping hand to a beggar, or lead a stranger, or guide the blind across the street. You never know what can stand between you and your dream."

"Some people think," Dylan interjected, "that by the mere thought of dreaming they are entitled to the desires of their heart. As you can see, everything here has an expiry date. That is the day the requestor passed away, or will pass away. And almost everything here is way past its expiration date. Mankind has made a lot of requests, but claimed so little.

"Dad, human beings misunderstood the concept of faith and success, especially religious people. Some think only faith, which is the evidence of things we cannot see — in other words, the conceptualized or the imaginary — is enough to get what they so fervently desire. So far they have gotten half of it right. What they don't realize is that faith must come to a point where it's no

100

longer an idea, but an experiment, the manifestation of the substance itself.

"To put it on a human scale for your understanding," Dylan continued, "consider the first day you attended pre-school as an act of faith. It was by your own admission that you didn't know how to read and write and do basic arithmetic. Teachers welcomed you, held your hand, and showed you how to draw letters and numbers: A, B, C, D, 1, 2, 3, and so on. On your first day it appeared hopeless, you must admit. Later on, teachers connected those letters to form words, numbers to amounts. As time went on, it seemed somewhat easier. The more you practiced, the better you became. Then you started jumping from first grade to second grade, and before you knew it, you were in high school and no longer needed guidance to read and write and do basic arithmetic. Now, your reading, writing, and arithmetic abilities were no longer a belief but a fact: faith became palpable.

"In reality," she said, "everything exists. We invent nothing. The very tools of our lips and the practice of the imaginary, by means of virtues, bring everything into existence. Grandpa created all things before any of us were. That's why mankind is able to call those things that are not – the imagined – as though they were – the manifested. The truth is, whatever mankind can think of, or imagine, is already somewhere waiting for us to find through the game of seeking, asking, knocking, and the practice of good virtues.

"Grandpa said He was done with mankind's nonsense. He placed the cookie jar just a little above the shelf. All mankind has to do is rise onto their tiptoes and shake it. It will pour over them. But they looked for the mechanics of the shelf and got confused about the whole thing."

"Are you sure you're seven years old?" I asked her.

SEAT OF TRUTH

"Yes, I am seven years old, Dad."

"You know too much, and too far ahead of your time."

"There's no space and time in the Heavens. Eternity is a timeless dimension."

"That's my girl!" I said, tickling her ribs as she screamed with glee.

Flannighans stared intently into the distance as if something had caught his attention. I followed his gaze.

"Are you thinking about that Lamborghini?" I asked him.

"No," he said, still gazing into the distance. "My life could have stood for something. I saved no one, Mitch."

"That's why you don't have a crown?" I said, laughing at him. "You're crownless."

"There are so many people who would do anything for the right to live. I saved no one. I helped no one! My life was a total waste," he said with remorse.

Dylan looked at him as if he had just thrown something good out of the window. She seized the moment to breathlessly express her discontent. "I'd love to know what it is to be human, to grow up in a family, have a birthday party with my friends, play an instrument, hold my dad's hand, go to college, and be a good servant. I've been robbed of my right to humanity and my calling. I might have cured cancer," she said.

"You didn't miss out on anything, kiddo," I said.

"I missed out on everything, Dad. You don't understand," she said, her voice cracking with emotion. "It's not about you. Being alive is a mission in a big world, Grandpa told me. You have no idea the amount of planning that goes into bringing forth a life and sustaining it. The sheer amount of mathematics, the energy rules, the chemistry, physics, biology, sociology, bonding, apps, and much more, all of which work in perfect

102

harmony, not near perfect." She raised a pinky finger in defiance and arched her eyebrows. "In perfect harmony."

"The whole universe," she continued, "is inside of you, Dad. Life is a gift to be given. It's not for you to waste, abuse, or neglect. You are the carrier of what is most precious in all the Heavens and in all the Creations. Life is precious, but humans do not regard it as such. I can't understand how in a lifespan of ten to one hundred years humans could achieve next to nothing. Nothing!" Flannighans looked guiltier.

"Human beings are the worst mistake your Grandpa ever made," I said with confidence.

"Grandpa doesn't make mistakes! He fixes broken things." She searched my face for something.

"You think it's that easy, kid? It's not that simple," I lamented. "Baby, you have no idea how hard it is to be human, let alone to live among them. I was human all my life, and trust me honey, most of the time I thought I was from somewhere else because the things I thought, the deeds I did, and the things I wished for were so outrageously malice—"

"Exactly! Of course you're from someplace else ... on a mission," countered Dylan, now with both arms open, as if I had finally caught a revelation of what she had been saying all along. "You're an alien. We're the aliens, Dad. The problem with humans is that they fall in love with what's going on in the mission field and they give up their heavenly citizenship. Grandpa became the tiniest in His own creation, to show you the way, so you might experience Oneness with Him. And you gave up all your fame and glory and glamor and honors and royalty because you were too lazy to seek and knock, too impatient to wait, too selfish to share, too proud to ask. And at the same time you forgot you were simply on a mission. There are protocols to follow, and you died idling in complacency

103

because of fear of changing and moving on." I looked at Dylan and wondered how, for Heaven's sake, she knew so much.

We fell into a long silence, each of us contemplating below.

Finally, I asked Flannighans, "Why is your name still on that Lamborghini?"

"Those are things I prayed for in my youth and adulthood, but did nothing to achieve them, so I never had them," he said with a trace of regret. "Things that I asked for with the wrong intentions."

"Wow," I interjected, with half a smile.

"And you know one thing? I was struggling to make ends meet, dude, when I had it all at my disposal." He said the last word as if he might vomit.

"Well!" I said with a chuckle. I don't know if planet Earth would've been able to handle Flannighans terrorizing the neighborhood with that red Lamborghini throughout high school and college. Heaven forbid!

"You see that house on the cliff, Mitch?" Flannighans said.

"Which one?"

"The one next to the yacht ... you see it?"

"Yes, beside the high-rise hotel. Yes, I can see it." I pointed to show him. "Just a little nudge," I said, almost to myself.

"The requester grew weary, which He forbids us," Flannighans said.

"Wow! Three bikes just fell off the cliff! Did you see that? Did you see that?" I yelled at them, grabbing Flannighans by the shoulder.

"The bikes, helmets, toys fly off the shelves by the truckload," Dylan said. "Those are kids' prayer requests."

"Yeah," Flannighans confirmed. "Those are kids' prayers. All kids' prayers are answered within one day if not mere hours, because kids ask with great and divine intention."

104

"Ok, let's go!" Dylan said, as if she had seen enough.

CHAPTER FIFTEEN

A heavenly date

The Montezuma cypress tree at the base of Mount Sinai has the stoutest trunk in all the Heavens. Even when Flannighans, Dylan and I stretched our arms, we still couldn't make out its circumference. On earth, cypresses grow in southern Mexico. The tree's lustrous, silky bark made one think it was worth dying to touch it. It grows one branch at a time. Holy said that its existence dated way back to antiquity.

We sat down with our backs against the trunk, staring at the immense beauty below and talking. The entire time Holy did all the talking, and boy, Holy could talk!

I wanted to simply ask Her about Edmund, but my words were lacking. I didn't know how to begin this sensitive conversation.

This was my fourth visit to the farm. I still couldn't tell if Her eyes were blue, hazel, green, or something else. The comfort I found near Her made it difficult to dwell on the subject of my brother. She knew I had something on my mind. She had made that clear the first time I'd come and had insisted that I come

106

often and soon, for we had much to talk about. So She knew. Today was no different from yesterday, or the day before yesterday. It seemed to me that whenever we met, nothing and no one else mattered anymore. She was *that* companion.

The last time we had held hands was when we came all the way from Mount Moab. She had said She was preparing me for my big day, whatever that meant. I didn't know. The whole time, too, my head was either down, or straight ahead.

We talked about time.

"Time is the only true measure of your existence," She said. "Without time, you don't exist."

"Then why does our existence have time limits?" I asked Her. What I really meant to say was: *How much time do I have to find my brother? Is he in some kind of trouble?*

"Your existence is a trial to temporarily experience what it is to be without us. We don't want to hold your hands here. We want you to know what we know and to discover your true nature. Pride, or other elements that brought you to sin, will never go away. You will always have to make choices, as do we. And that is why we've given you joy, so you can fear pain. We've given you mercy, so you can avoid affliction. To understand judgment, we've given you grace. To value strengths, we created you with weaknesses. We allowed you to experience lack so that success would humble you. This is the balance we're bringing back, the beginning of all beginnings. We're embedding the truth in you so that you can know the how and why of Creation and discover the mysteries in all."

The more She talked the less virtuous society became with all its smugness. You woke up one day, and a dude from some obscure field of science had declared that black holes might not be so dangerous after all. Next day, another one in the West made a new discovery about a new planet from the comfort of his office. Three weeks later the planet was not a planet after all but a star. Then again someone from another continent came forward with new supposed proof alleging that there may, or may not be traces of water on Mars. These are people who never see a real tree in their city life.

How presumptuous these silly human beings were, making claims with nothing to back them up but speculation!

But Holy's words wrapped around me like silk. They melted like cheese and bonded with my being. Each added more excitement, reached new heights, until attainment became oblivion itself, until the words became timeless. More powerful than wind, gentle and light as an autumn breeze, more silent than the night. The words were older and faster than time. I breathed them in the air; they made their way into my nostrils until they reached that special place.

"Who writes the law upon your heart? Brings you joy in the morning?" She gushed and opened her arms wide. "Mitch, I am the rhythm of life, the One moving in every sphere of influence. One who walks with me shall experience gravity and feel the rotation of the earth beneath. He must feel every vibration of living things and witness the amazing way the trees absorb nutrients. He must understand the infinite capacity of Creation, from the smallest atoms — the quantum Realms — to the largest things they are composed of," She said with a joyful fist pump. "The purpose of science is to better understand Grandpa. All He ever wanted for you is to know Him through the means of His Creation," She concluded excitedly.

That day was the nearest I came to looking into Her eyes. The descent of Mount Moab was a great stretch. At the bottom of the mountain, before we reached the valley where the moon had crashed, we came across a quiet waterfall where giant charcoal rocks looked like prehistoric eggs, ornate with green

108

parasites. Among the rocks were small basins here and there. The stones at the bottom of them were white and shades of gray. The water was limpid and serene. Nearby a small tree cast it branches over the waterfall. She must have caught me staring at its beautiful flowers that changed color by the second. "This is the Silk Floss tree, found mostly in the tropical forests of Paraguay. However, despite its beauty, the Silk Floss has painful thorns. The crown that rested upon Your Savior's head was made from it." She said.

She stepped into a small pool between the rocks, right under a branch of the Silk Floss. The water reached above Her ankles. She held up her hands like a vessel, collected a handful of water from the waterfall, and drank it. "Are you thirsty?" She said.

"Yes," I heard a voice saying, but it wasn't me who spoke. It was my mouth that spoke the word, an answer I had no part in. She reached out again and collected another handful of water and extended her hands before me. As I looked down, I caught a reflection of Her eyes that will forever be seared in my inner being. I wasn't ready to get caught up in the rapture of her eyes. It was like momentarily entering a forbidden dimension. I quickly closed my eyes. I leaned forward into Her hands and began to drink. Now I know what Dylan meant by *Look you'll see something.* The more I drank, the more Her hands were filled until I was satisfied from that inexhaustible source.

✳ ✳ ✳

Today, She had given me a talk about compassion, love, gratitude and forgiveness; the wonderful gifts of virtues that we're born with. "Compassion is a progressively learned virtue that yields to the ability to love others regardless of their education, pain, ignorance, inadequacy, incapacity, color, gender, possession, and social rank. And it is also the only virtue" — She

SEAT OF TRUTH

raised a finger like Dylan would — "with which one can flow from grace to mercy, and that makes forgiveness easy. Lack of forgiveness is the hardest wall between mankind and me. And you know what?" She giggled. "The funny thing is, the offenders often moved right along once they have repented and made amend. The victims on the other hand, are still terrorizing their own souls with decades-long grudges.

The truth is, mankind talks about lack of empathy, but in reality you all have limits because your emotions exist solely on a continuum basis."

"What do you mean? Aren't our emotions always subject to the singularity of Oneness?" I said to Her.

"Yes and no. Human emotions can be broken down into small parts. It is the sum of them all that makes you unique. And that is why you change. Consider the following: your concept of love at the tender age of seven isn't the same as that during your teenage years and is definitely different in your young adulthood. Old age will surprise you even more when you find out what it really was all along. That is different from me. I am what I was, and will forever be what I am. I change not." She paused and waited for my input.

"I know what it feels like, rejection," I said, attempting to look in her direction as we slowed our pace and entered a tunnel of flamboyant trees. Their vibrant orange-red petals blossomed on a bed of green leaves, resembling bouquets. This was called the "autumn tree" on the tropical island of Haiti. Here, it grew to be the same length and height, but the colors are mesmerizing.

"What you held against your parents was a natural survival instinct mechanism," Holy explained to me with enthusiasm. "During inception we imbued all mankind with this set of DNA that develops into attachment, attachment then becomes love,

110

and love, dependency. That's why babies cry for their mommy and daddy the second they leave them to get a baby bottle from the fridge. It is an inherent threat that they don't know how to respond well to yet, and that's how we'd love humankind to rely on us.

"Humankind, however, drifted and wandered alone, far away from the glitz and glamor of the life that we imbued them with. They codified everything and fell into day-to-day routines. They gave a one-way definition to all things that exist. And if you're not on that bandwagon, you become abnormal, outcast. Slowly, your potentials: ambitions, drive, and abilities — your best weapons for achievement — lose meaning. And now you can't tell the difference between humility and curiosity. Where humans should have been more curious, they became passive, and they became silent disciples when they should have spoken. Where they should have been more prudent, they became more generous for fear of retaliation.

"Most living people are waiting to die because they are not living. They simply exist conditionally to wake up and go and come back. They exist without even a streak of curiosity to venture one day a little farther and ask what's on the other side. Concurrently, life slowly becomes only that established institution they revere: family. Comprised of mom and dad, son and daughter, maybe a dog or a cat, the SUV, a mortgage, a career, and the basic civic duty of all citizens. At this stage, they focus more on *having* than on *being*. Therefore knowledge becomes personal, and everything personal needs safety. Safety causes fear, which creates politics. Politics creates enemies, and with enemies, war becomes inevitable.

"In their fear to leave the past behind, their present becomes tormented with regrets, and the future is automatically on hold. They become slaves of their own minds, obsessed with what their lives could have been, had they made different choices. Like a piece of them gets stuck into something, maybe a place, or a person. But they fail to realize that one can always start over with me, which is my only purpose, Mitch.

"This fastidious mold of unforgiveness erects the impenetrable wall between mankind and me, stopping all blessings from flowing, all dreams from coming to pass, all creativity from being released, all desires from being fulfilled." The smile on my face was unmistakable as we arrived at the farmhouse.

We stopped in front of the humongous structure. The silence between us made it even bigger. We were still few inches apart. She took my hands in hers. I was now looking down at her toenails, in a shade of taupe, as if they were CGI. I knew Her eyes were on me. What I heard next drained every ounce of blood from my body.

CHAPTER SIXTEEN

"Time kills everything."
— Someone said that.

I left the farmhouse and headed to the Square, or Stone of Creation, intending to reflect on what had transpired over the past few days, to examine and explore my options, to get a better perspective on things, only to find Flannighans and Dylan suspiciously debating whether or not to tell me about something. They went quiet when they saw me coming.

"Tell him!" Dylan ordered Flannighans.

"No, *you* tell him!" Flannighans countered.

"No, *you* tell him!" Dylan stood up.

"Tell me what?" I asked, searching their eyes.

"Go ahead, Dylan!" Flannighans said. "Tell him!"

"There's another way...," Dylan began, looking at Flannighans.

"Go on, girl!" Flannighans encouraged.

"There's another way to know for sure what happened to your brother." She was now staring at me.

113

SEAT OF TRUTH

"But we must go *now*," declared Flannighans and stood up at once. "This is your last chance, because tomorrow is your seventh day — your *last* day."

***

It was already Friday night, past eight o'clock, when we invaded Detective Laurent Dubois's office at the Police Field Office in West Palm Beach. According to my handlers, having a peek at the ongoing investigation might give us a clue of what Edmund had been up to before his passing. Flannighans had also reminded me that we could kill two birds with one stone, meaning spying on my widowed wife's love life as well.

Dylan went straight to kneel on the chair at Detective Dubois's computer desk. She stared at the computer screen as if it might tell her something. Flannighans and I shuffled through a load of folders from on top of a cabinet looking for the murder case.

"Dylan, can you find out what's on that computer?" I asked her.

"I can't read," she said bluntly.

"You can't…wait a minute…you don't know how to read?" I asked her. Flannighans, who had abruptly stopped reading began to derail from the top of the cabinet and landed hard on the concrete. I laughed.

"You don't know how to … what?" Flannighans stuttered.

"Nope." She blinked her big, bold eyes as if it were normal.

"What's up with all those impossible equations, quantum physics, theories, and formulas your Grandpa taught you? He never taught you how to read?" Flannighans pursued.

"Grandpa says there's nothing to read about in the Heavens, nothing to write about and nothing to build. But to see, hear, feel, discover, enjoy and experience," she said softly, holding her

114

fingertips together. And it was then that I realized I'd never read anything since my arrival. I knew God lived on Abraham Boulevard, and I'd been to many other streets, but there were no street names. I just knew. Sometimes Dylan's claims came across as unreal, but somehow this settled in as the impossible truth.

"Can you spell your name, at least?" Flannighans continued.

"No. I don't know how to do that either."

"I got my high school diploma," Flannighans boasted.

"It was a GED, Flannighans," I reminded him.

Flannighans easily bypassed the system and logged onto the computer and began to read.

The more he read the web of lies and deceit, the more I shook my head. Unbelievably unbelievable! The whole time I was thinking how for Heaven's sake was I supposed to sit my parents down and tell them what I knew so far? Would they ever believe me?

The gossip about my widowed wife's love life became less and less interesting by the minute. But to satisfy my companions' curiosity, I went along with them to the house.

***

My son Matthew had given up waiting for the soccer game I had promised him for his birthday. Connie must have taken on the painful and difficult task of explaining what death is. Sadly, he had accepted that I was no more and consoled himself by saying that I was in heaven with Grandma, grandma, Atelia and uncle Edmund.

Each night, Connie and I used to take turns reading bedtime stories for Mathew from the Big Old-Fashioned Book, as the Counselor called it. And thankfully, he had grasped the basic concept of prayers before my passing. Lately however, his bedtime reading routine had drastically changed, especially since

SEAT OF TRUTH

this …French guy had begun to conduct late-night interrogations with Connie. So the boy had taken matters into his own hands and prayed alone.

He knelt beside his bed, joined the palms of his hands, and bowed his head. Dylan knelt beside him, adopting the same humble posture. Flannighans and I took a seat on the bed and watched them.

The kid began his prayer by thanking Grandpa for His blessings. He thanked Him for giving him eyes to see and read His Word, ears to hear His words, hands to write his homework, legs to walk to church, to school, and to the candy store (at which Dylan giggled), and a mouth to speak and eat with—not to curse. Then he made a sudden switch in his prayer. He insisted that God do something about recess time allowed in kindergarten. He also complained about one of his teachers, Ms. Chelsea, and said that she should be lenient on his best friend Jessica. And in closing he emphasized the odd school hours and suggested, if possible, that it starts a little later, after enough sleep and video game time. It would be awesome! And if Jesus could call school off once and for all too, that would be genius. That way he would be home-schooled like Jess and Meghan, his neighbors. "And baby Jesus — say hi to Grandma, my dad and Uncle Ed and Atelia and Grandpa for me.

"I miss them.

"And Dear God, please send the angels to protect the house from bad people and thieves and evils, in Jesus' name. Amen!"

He switched off the lamp. Not even one second later he was snoring, and squads of armed angels descended upon the property and formed a ring around its perimeter. The army of angels stared and smiled at us, then they bowed as we got ready to leave. If only I knew the power of prayer back then, I thought.

"You see? That's how Grandpa responds when you seek Him with your whole heart," Dylan said.

She stood up, leaned forward, and kissed Matthew.

"Let's go to the library," I said.

"You're sure you want to do that?" Flannighans asked.

"I've never been so sure before."

CHAPTER SEVENTEEN

The library.
Nothing is lost,
The truth is out there.
—Ezechias

Who would have thought, or remotely believed, that there is a library in Heaven? Yes, there is one: the library of the universe, which records the history of mankind: wars, elections, trials, fights, earthquakes, tsunamis, rains, floods, fires, all the songs, all the poems, all the bands, all the jokes, all the essays, all the concerts, all the movies, all the games, the funerals, the deaths, the deals, the reunions, the wakes, the accidents, every spoken and unspoken word — all properly arranged into subject categories. Everyone has full access.

When I say *library*, I know what's going through your tiny brain: a nice old lady sitting at a fine mahogany desk, staring at a computer screen with a phone nearby, juggling teenagers', parents', and stranger's requests. Right?

Every life from the beginning of creation, from the first man and woman — Adam and Eve — to the very last one, all properly and chronologically archived. Every life arranged in perfect lines of multicolored crystals shaped like candles, stretching in endless rows and columns in divine perfection, linked with endless multicolored threads, like a giant factory.

Like one big story, everything joins together at some point.

Everything leads to Oneness.

You think of something or someone, and there it appears, effortlessly. You can sit down and watch an entire lifespan from the first second at birth until the very last second after death. We call it *earthly life reviewing*. You watch the whole thing on a big screen without interruption. Every little and big secrets are exposed.

Many natural disasters — or so we thought them — such as forest fires, were begun by human malfeasance, others by plain carelessness. Homicides passed for deaths by natural causes, and murders saw the wrong person convicted. Young kids who went missing, but who actually lived next door in plain sight. Big secrets that family members hid from each other, husbands from wives were exposed. Earthquakes, some of which were caused by mankind's search for superpower. Rings once lost ended up found in some small hole in the house. Goods were stolen and the wrong person blamed.

The actual arrangement of these things is mind-boggling, the simplicity and ease of finding them all the more challenging to comprehend. *How long,* I wondered, *did He spend to come up with such a complex and yet so simple a cataloging method? Maybe God is more than just God, as we vaguely imagine Him. Maybe He is God but our fundamental view and definition of Him is mundane enough that the depth, the width, the height, and weight of His infinite knowledge are so immeasurable to us that we see Him as another guy down the street.*

All led to the singularity of Oneness.

We were connected in more ways than we could imagine. Maybe that's why we were not to hurt each other, because in the end it would all come full circle. Society in its own myths may have connected a few dots, or we may have been taught by nature, or may have come to an awakening of His Omniscience by the whispers of our own hearts.

After our last episode on earth at the detective's house, Dylan had said that the library contained all the records of mankind, and that there, I could see everything Edmund had ever done in his life, even secret things, from the day he was born until the day of his passing.

"Why did you guys keep this information from me the whole time?" I said with tight lip.

"I wanted to hang out on earth," Dylan admitted.

"You wanted to hang out on earth?" I repeated after her, angry that they had wasted valuable time. She looked over at Flannighans for some sort of backup, but he said nothing.

"I ...didn't want to ...It was Flannighans' idea," Dylan claimed.

"You guys could have gone whenever you wanted to," I said with a flash of anger.

"Not exactly," Flannighans said, raising a finger as if he wasn't done talking yet. "We can't go alone. We need a conduit — someone who is still in the transition phase," he said. "You're the only link between us and Earth."

"You guys were using me the whole time?"

"I'd never been on earth," Dylan said. "I wanted to know what it looked like. How humans live."

I mimicked her: "*You wanted to know how humans live.* You don't know how to read, you don't know how to write, you can never experience what it is to be human, and yet you —" I stopped, the words stuck in my throat. I swallowed them back. They tasted bitter, and sad, and sour.

We looked at the names and found Edmund's. Then we began to watch his life.

CHAPTER EIGHTEEN

What's your story?
What will you tell Him,
When you see Him?

Today is my sixth day in the Heavens, the last day before my complete transition. Whatever that means.
Not only had I come back from Earth with some familiar and unwanted feelings, but also the trip to the library had added to my burden.

We were headed toward the Square. I had my hands tucked into my coat pockets and my head down, lost in my thoughts trying to process what I just saw. Dylan and Flannighans walked not too far behind me discussing the World Cup Soccer championship. He found it hard to understand which countries made it and which didn't, and Dylan never found it tiresome to explain the technicalities and mechanics of the game. Flannighans keenly asked all manner of questions until at one point the kid asked him if he was from Earth for real, and had he ever seen a soccer match before.

"How do *you* know so much about soccer?" I heard Flannighans say to her.

"I watch every World Cup game with Grandpa."

"Oh! Your Grandpa is in the business of watching soccer games now?" Flannighans said.

"He watches all sports." Soon their discussion about Grandpa's sports fandom seemed of no interest to me, and my thoughts turned back to what I had just seen at the library.

As we arrived at the Square I heard a distant "Good night, Dad!" from Dylan as she took off down Abraham Boulevard and headed home to Grandpa. I waved at her and Flannighans and continued my walk to a lonely bench near the lake by the Canaan border.

What will change tomorrow, and how will it affect me? I wondered.

I lay down on my back, helpless, thinking in the silence of the night about what had happened to Edmund.

According to the report from the detective, Edmund may have been indirectly involved in some overseas plot against a CEO who owned a giant medical supplier in Asia. The medical examiner's report said that the cause of death was poison. *Impossible,* I thought.

They had found the presence of deadly foreign agents in the wound that killed him. The concussion Edmund had during the stampede at the restaurant, continued the report, may have been a diversion to disguise the murder as an isolated accident.

Independent chemical experts traced the deadly agents found in his body to some very nasty people whose names were forbidden to even mention in the report. What could my brother possibly have done to people who would warrant his death? But the reason Edmund had been killed ultimately had nothing to do with these people in China. It had been twenty years in the making in the most secret chambers: in the heart of one man.

SEAT OF TRUTH

Revenge.

Where is Edmund? The thoughts about his whereabouts gnawed at my existence. It was too much to bear, so I left the lake in the general direction of the Square to clear my head.

***

My first fight in kindergarten — if one can even call it a fight — had been because of Edmund. Although his birth had been a buzz kill, over time I had grown to love him, and he grew up to be very protective of me. He was always eager to defend me, regardless of right or wrong. He simply couldn't stand the idea of anyone hurting me. I remembered his first day at school when he held my hand and never let me go, to the point that Mrs. Smith let him sit with me in my first grade classroom. He was adamant that someone might take me away from him. Edmund was everything I had. We always got the same clothes, the same shoes. Though we had our own bedrooms, we would sneak into each other's room to share stolen cookies and candies and tell each other stories in the middle of the night. We often slept in the same bed when our mother allowed it. But over time, it appeared we lost touch, focusing on our personal desires to succeed in life. College choices, studies, and time away from each other weakened our bond, and somehow we became like most distant relatives. I placed this squarely on the collective conscience of society's thirst for wealth and glory.

I claimed a bench in the Square to assess the situation for the tenth time, but my head wasn't any clearer than it had been. As reality settled in, I felt a bead of sweat on my lower back and a few more along my ribcage. My grip on the bench began to tremble and I came to the only logical conclusion: He knew where Edmund was.

***

Being a seasoned accountant suited me well because I dealt with numbers. Numbers are facts. *Numbers are beautiful,* I whispered; and the silent night sang the words back to me. "Numbers give the assurance that letters lack," I recalled Atelia saying.

My logic was perfect because it was fact-based. Sit back! I'll lay it down for you. Perhaps I might earn a small measure of your sympathy.

Fact #1: Everyone in the Heavens refused to talk about my brother's whereabouts for it was forbidden because of some rules. Who wrote those damn rules? He obviously did.

Fact #2: According to Flannighans' account, as he couldn't keep his yap shut, there were transactions taking place at the Gate of Exchange & Forgotten Hope every day. Had He given my little brother away? Only He could answer that question.

Fact #3: Fact number three needs further details before you can grasp it. Just hear me out.

My fondness for Jesus had become fragile at this point. I didn't want to risk it with overburdening inquisitions. Moreover, He had enough on his plate, and was still going through so much due to the human race and their poor choices. Twice during the past six days He had staggered into the house as if He had been beaten to a pulp. When He stumbled in, God and I rushed to grab Him before He collapsed to the floor. He gave into the waiting arms of His Father, who I thought was about to annihilate the human race with just one breath from His nostrils. He looked so furious at the sight of His Son's bloody face.

We took Him to a table that Mrs. Campbell had quickly cleared off. She ran cold water over a towel and started cleaning the blood from His temple and all over his body. His breathing was painful and slow at times. I trembled in fright. I had never seen someone beaten so badly.

Mrs. Gandalf Campbell began to sing *Jesus, Blessed be Your Name.* The Holy's cello was on fire.

Mrs. Campbell bandaged the wounds and took some new clothes and neatly dressed Jesus.

God stood up and went to the large window overlooking Earth as if He might just evaporate the monkeys at once. But when I looked into His eyes, there was as much love for mankind as He had shown to His own Son. *How could you let them beat Him like that and do nothing?* I wanted to ask. I let it pass.

Later on, when I asked Flannighans what had happened, he said he didn't know. Nonetheless, he said there was a place not too far from here, and every time He went to that place, the humans judged Him, put Him back on the cross, and beat Him up.

"Can't He stop going there?" I said to Flannighans.

"I guess ... He loves them so much."

"How could they do that?" I said with bitterness and contempt for my own race.

"You're just like them, Mitch. You'd do the same to Him."

"Shut up, Flannighans!" I ordered. "This is not the time for your insensitive remarks, okay?"

"You just don't know yourself." And that was the last conversation I had with Flannighans on that subject. I didn't want to put Him back on the cross or involve Him at all.

Fact #4: Mrs. Campbell spent most of her time following the Lord seeking answers, and He, as stubborn and unchanging by nature as He is, refused to communicate or reveal her son's whereabouts.

Fact #5: Well, this one you probably already know. I had been tempted to ask Holy many times, but I couldn't. My list of transgressions and assaults on Her and untold grievances made it impossible for me to even look into Her eyes, and all I could do was secretly admire Her. The last time I was with Her, we had just arrived in the farmhouse from the wilderness. She held my hands and asked me to dance with Her. I knew I said something, but I can't remember. She had wrapped her arms around my neck and timidly I held Her at the waistline. Luckily for me, I was probably two, or maybe three inches taller than She was, so I was staring at her husky short hair. We danced at the rhythms of a piano until I was standing alone. She was gone.

Was I falling for Her? Flannighans and Dylan had teased me about that. Maybe I *did* have the hots for Her. Maybe *all* humans do, after all.

My conclusion was this: If He made the rules and forbade talk about Edmund then, He alone knew where my little brother was.

Time was running out.

I had to find him before it was too late.

It was now or never.

I bolted up like a rocket and headed toward His palace.

CHAPTER NINETEEN

A piece of flesh,
a piece of human.

First came the jogging. Then came the slow running. Finally the sprinting, which gradually crescendo to a reckless, unstoppable speed I had never before experienced. I was fully awake and aware of what was happening. An invincible zeal — it seemed a foolish emotion — took hold of my body, and distance and time became one.

Flannighans had warned me about the excitement of immortality and constantly reminded me that I had only six days before completing transition to experience it. He had taken the time to explain to me that all newcomers — who are extremely rare, apart from babies — have six days to transit. He said that human beings were shielded by earthly emotions all the way to the backyard of Heaven, that the first six days were crucial, and that on the seventh day I would be like Him, Jesus, and I would understand everything. "Why seven days?" I had asked him. That is another heavenly lecture I certainly can't afford to give you under the present circumstances.

As I zapped through everything that came into contact with me, I realized that I was furious, and furious at none other than God. I ran faster and faster until my body was no longer physical but a light smoke with a human form, like a ghost. *Is the transition already happening?*

I broke into Mount David, flew over the lush valley of Canaan, and aimed for the Hill where He resided. When I looked behind me, all I could see was a storm of fury, whipping the foliage, but none had been destroyed. Still, the violent speed at which I zapped through it had bent branches and trees nearly to ground level.

With a fist pump I made a dramatic landing outside the Palace, much like General Zod seeking Superman for a vicious fight. The Tree of Life gleamed metallic red in the night — not good. The gates were always open, although it baffled me. What was the point of having gates that were never closed?

I kept a safe distance from the two robust Archangels sentineled at the main entrance. Neither showed the least sign of excitement, nor awareness of my triumphant landing. Neither asked me why I was here, or how they might be of any assistance. I looked at them with a streak of curiosity waiting for a reaction.

They did nothing.

Behind them the French mansion was deserted. The street lamps around the Palace were low, almost like an amber glow among the lush flowers and plants of the garden. The bottom rings of the lampposts were of strange metallic blue and Swarovski crystal, and even in my madness I had to admit they were stunning. I shook a post, hoping to cause some sort of blackout. It didn't work.

Although there was a main gate to the house, the place wasn't walled. Flowers and shrubs, meticulously cut to half a human's

SEAT OF TRUTH

height, surrounded it. I stationed myself outside the compound on the walkway and surveyed the neighborhood. He had no neighbors. If a fight broke out — which I suspected would happen — there wouldn't be anyone to break us up. It would be a fight to the death. *I'm ready for it.*

The lights in the second story were off. That must be where He slept, if He ever did.

Tonight, I'm going to give Him a piece of a human's mind, I thought. *I'll show Him what it is to be truly human – to be flesh.*

I must admit, there was a streak of fear in me of waking Him in the middle of the night. I didn't know what to expect, or what He might do to me. But then again, what did I have to lose? The Guy wasn't helping, or cooperating in any way. Even when His own Son came home badly injured, He did nothing to those who hurt Him. I will stand for my little brother, even if it means breaking the rules in the Heavens.

So I took cover behind a small, but puffy Christmas tree. Under it an amazing assortment of decorative stones of all sizes and shapes had been carefully placed. The tree wasn't tall enough to hide my tall frame completely. Occasionally I had to duck for cover. I stuffed four stones in each front pocket, three in each back pocket, and secured a handful, maybe six or seven.

I took one of fair size and looked momentarily at the Archangels, who were now staring at me with no particular concern. I casually threw the stone at the window on the second floor testing the Archangels' reaction.

No reaction. No answer.

Nothing happened.

The lights remained off.

I waited a few moments to see how fast those two-winged beasts would shred me.

130

They did nothing, so I threw another stone on the roof and ducked back behind the tree.

Still no answer.

Is He dead or something? I thought.

With a little bit of muscle, I threw another stone at the window, hoping to break it.

No one woke up, and the window didn't even budge.

The Archangels now looked away. I took a much heavier rock, with sharp edges. *This one certainly should break a window, or at least crack one, and hopefully wake Him up.*

I served a powerful throw. The stone hit the window frame with a muffled thud and deflected onto the ground.

No damage.

Still no, "How may I help you?"

The windows are bulletproof. They must be. I might need to fire a gun or something. I thought.

I threw all the stones at the doors, the windows, and the skylights like a madman, with intent to break them. *God cannot be such a dead sleeper. He has to wake up and respond to me about my little brother.*

A long moment passed. I had no more stones left. I sat idle behind the tree in the somber night, not really knowing what to do next. I then came out from behind the tree into the open. "I know you're in there!" I shouted in the oppressive silence and waited. "You're not asleep. Oh! Aren't you the Alpha anymore? … The … the … the Omega, huh?" I yelled with sarcasm. "I want my brother! And I'm not leaving here until you take me to him."

Silence.

I sat down facing the windows, waiting and thinking.

Edmund, from my opinion, wasn't a bad person. He certainly may have had one or two bad friends in his lifetime, but who

SEAT OF TRUTH

hasn't? Edmund would do anything for me, or anyone, without question. No bad judgment ever passed his lips as far as I knew. During the years of my depression, especially following my discharge from the Navy when I felt utterly useless in the aftermath of the war, he had sung me songs and kept me sane. I remembered that morning when the whole world became obscure and all I could think of was the obvious. The years in deployment for war had left me with some damages. He and Flannighans had cheered me up and taken turns telling tales of how they had stolen candy from the department store back when they were six or ten years old. Edmund had reminded me of the major event that had happened when I was fifteen, he twelve, and Flannighans eleven — when I had accidentally fallen into a murky swamp in the Everglades. That was one reason I had enlisted in Navy, to learn how to swim. Without thinking, Edmund had jumped after me, and had cut his left leg severely. We had lied to our mother because we had been told never to go there, but somehow she knew.

The last time I climbed a tree I was ten years old and Edmund had just turned seven. Now I felt like climbing the Tree of Life and ripping it to pieces. It might be trespassing, though, if such a law applied here. The only problem was those giant creatures standing there.

I stared at the Tree of Life, now crimson red, almost like velvet. Then I had the sudden realization that these bad boys weren't watching the house — they were watching the *Tree*.

Two angels armed with glaring swords guarded the Tree of Life after Adam and his girlfriend were removed. I wonder what would happen if I were to taste it. So what? I thought.

The image of the Gate of Exchange & Forgotten Hope flashed through my mind and I stood up straight. Edmund is my family, my friend, and my brother. God must wake up.

I found four more stones that had bounced near to where I had been sitting, and I threw them at the windows with every ounce of strength left in me.

Nothing.

"Try these ones," one of the Archangels said to me with a smirk on his glorious face. I glanced to where he pointed, and found a pile of solid uncut rubies, and immediately launched the biggest one at a skylight. The stone slid down the crystal roof tiles all the way to the edge and stuck there, making an annoying reverberating sound, like an ancient Chinese drum.

I waited.

A light in the upper level came on. I looked at the Archangel and he winked at me.

Did this thing just wink at me?

A shadowy figure moved behind the curtains. "I want my brother!" I shouted. "You heartless Old Man, come out!" I ordered Him. I emerged from behind the puffy little tree and began pacing around.

He opened the window and pushed aside the curtain to look at me pacing along the walkway with a handful of ammunition. He leaned on the window frame. A feeble breeze blew His short-cropped hair.

I waited for Him to say something.

He said nothing.

Then I stopped moving.

Fear came over me, and this time for real. For the first time since my ranting, I felt His powerful presence. Silence is a powerful weapon in the right hands, and He knew that. I kept my silence too, and began to consider an escape route, in case it came to that. We stared at each other for a long time, blinking now and then. He stared at me with so much kindness and

133

compassion and love, and I, with so much disdain, hatred, anger, and bitterness.

"All you do is sit — sit on your Throne judging people all day," I began as I looked for more rocks to throw at Him.

Edmund and I used to go to the beach to skip rocks. *I might as well skip a flat one at the window to provoke Him,* I thought. "What did you do with my brother?" I asked Him. "Why did you create us if you knew you wouldn't care?" I paused and sniffed at the quiet night air. "I want my brother," I yelled at Him. He leaned forward, rested His sorrowful face on one hand, and uttered not a word.

The shadow of sadness came over me and enveloped me whole, and out of nowhere Her voice came.

Holy began singing *Tis So Sweet To Trust In Jesus,* accompanied by Her cello, but I couldn't see Her. The soothing sound of Her voice haunted me like a childhood dream.

This hymn had been Edmund's favorite. It was the song that gave him strength when our mother denied him candy before dinner. It was also the song that consoled him when our father gave him a whooping for breaking the windshield of our neighbor's brand-new Chevrolet Cabriolet. When Edmund had bad flux, I still remember, it was that same song that I sang for him until he fell asleep. From what I knew, that song was his anchor, his healing power, and his escape when the world was too much to bear.

It was his sanctuary.

So I sang alone.

I sang until there was no music left but the whispering of the words echoing in the night. Then I started talking again, loud enough so He could hear.

"Do you have no shame? You created us, and you let Tshembow take most of us? You just sit there while my brother is rotting in Hell. Don't you have a conscience? All you care for is your law. Why you made it in the first place, nobody knows. Why couldn't you place that stupid fruit where no one could reach it, so even if Adam and Eve wanted to, they couldn't? A caring, responsible father would have known better, except you. Except you." I paused to sniffle and clear my runny nose. "I know I can't fight you, but I know people back on Earth who really know how to hurt people. They would hurt you so bad you would fly right back into your hidden place." I sniffled again except this time my nose was almost dry. "The thing is, you aren't real. How can people trust in you when all you do is hide? We don't believe in what we can't see, what we can't touch. How am I supposed to enjoy your Heavens while my little brother is rotting in Hell?" I hurled the words at Him. "How?"

"The same way you did back on Earth," He said, "when you had a mansion, cars, clothes, and money while others all over the world were dying for a piece of bread, for a bottle of water, naked, homeless, in Sudan, Syria, Haiti, India. Were you not sleeping; were you not laughing; were you not dancing; were you not having sex and cheating on your wife?" I looked around to see if anybody else had heard that last part and considered my next line of defense.

"You don't know anything about me!" I insisted in a not-so-convincing tone, sniffling more air into my lungs.

Defeated.

God chuckled and shook His head.

"Oh!" I continued. "For the record, I read the Book of Instruction Before Leaving Earth, and it's filled with misleading information and confusions. First, you promised Moses Canaan — the poor guy gave up his personal ambitions to follow you. He made just one little mistake — just one little mistake! And

SEAT OF TRUTH

you banned him from seeing the very place you promised him. And you said you don't change your mind. Hilarious!

"Furthermore, you led the poor Israelites through the hot desert for forty years — *forty years* — and you claimed they were confused. How could they be confused when *you* were the one leading them? Huh?" I asked, trying to make fun of Him. "Remember a pillar of fire by night, and a pillar of cloud by day?" I spoke that last sentence as if it was an operatic demonstration and did little walks around, showing Him how He was leading them around in a circle. "That's funny!"

How come God is so slow to anger? What else can I say or do to provoke Him? I thought.

He stood there, unshakable.

For the first time, I took a really good look at God, without the fear that He might just delete me from existence. He wasn't that old, as I had imagined Him when I was a small child. He was neither young nor old. He had the vibrant, playful demeanor of a healthy adult in his early sixties, a short-grizzled beard, and lustrous salt-and-pepper hair that most would envy.

When I had first come to the Heavens, I had thought I was going to meet the oldest of the oldest of all. I really was hoping to meet a frail, ancient-looking Guy, limping around with a cane. That wasn't the case.

"Who put you in charge anyway? You're a terrorist," I said distantly. I laughed dryly at Him as he stared at me. "You think you're all that perfect. You need to be one of us." I paused. "Oh! FYI! I went to the Gate of Exchange & Forgotten Hope. Yeah! Your secret place where you handled the humans' transactions, gave out their souls like pieces of crap. Newsflash! I went there. So what? Are you not going to punish me for disobeying your rules, your Law? I thought you said your breath is like a consuming fire. Why don't you breathe fire on me and consume

136

me?" I yelled at the top of my lungs. "Oh! FYI again, the stupid circle of Oneness you taught that little robot girl is nonsense, and she's not real anyway. It's just software, some sort of Star Trek trick to impress people. Show-off! Come on out and face me if you dare!" I snapped and looked around for more stones.

Suddenly He stepped away from the window, and in a twinkling of an eye the main door of the Palace opened. He came out.

When the main gate slowly began to open wider, the only thing that I could remember was an earthly saying: *Be careful what you wish for.*

He usually walked with both hands behind His back, but this time He was coming at me with determination. I took a quick look around for more stones. I found and took a handful, ready to defend myself.

It was human instinct.

He sprinted toward me. The Archangels joined Him on both sides. Each carried a long scimitar. *Think! Think fast!*

Three against one?

They were getting closer and closer. Their footsteps shook the gold pavement. Fifty yards now. *Think! Think! Shit!*

I took two, three, maybe four unsteady steps back surveying my surroundings and considering other options.

Escape?

Too late!

They were coming faster now, almost like determined rescuers. I took more steps back until a sweet, thunderous voice startled me from behind.

"Come, my dear son!" the voice echoed in the farthest reach of my soul. I turned quickly, fumbling.

"*What the* ..." Before I could speak more, He swept me from my feet into His arms. "It's okay, son. It's okay," He repeated, swinging me as a human would a baby. His arms were strong and comforting. He smelled like my father, like a gardener. He spoke in his most soothing voice. He swung me and danced with me in His arms to comfort me. "My child, my son, I know what it is to be flesh. I know!" His eyes filled with compassion and pain and hurt and grace. And they were moist. What had I done?

"I'm sorry, Grandpa, I'm so sorry!"

"I know, I know," He assured me.

He began to hum the tune, *Tis So Sweet To Trust In Jesus*, as a gust of wind gently lifted me up and lulled me into a deep coma.

CHAPTER TWENTY

"Immortality is a gift to all man.
But eternal life is a choice.
In the end, we're all going somewhere."
—Somebody said that.

I woke up the next morning — my seventh day — in a strange room and a strange bed. Strange, that is, but also somehow familiar in a way that I couldn't quite place in memory. I knew for sure that I'd not slept here before, but the familiarity was indisputable. *Am I in His house, in His bedroom?*

To the sound of utensils and plates, to the aroma of fresh-brewed coffee and cinnamon, I woke up. I had adjusted my eyes and was looking around to gain a sense of direction and recognition when a friendly voice startled me.

"Wake up!" the voice said. It was Jesus who spoke. He was sitting in an accent chair across from the bed I had been sleeping in. The chair was covered in black and white striped lambskin. He stared at me while holding two big plates of egg whites with spinach, cheese, avocado and French toast. I noticed a fair-sized red duffel bag on the floor next to Him.

SEAT OF TRUTH

When I opened my eyes again, He smiled at me with his mouth full and said, "Good morning?" as He handed me a plate.

"Good morning," I answered, stretching to accept the plate. The morning sun had already risen, and its feeble rays pierced through a joint in the doorframe. "Where am I?" I asked, assessing my lodgings again.

"Home," came the reply. "Where else could you be?" He mused, and then stuffed a forkful of spinach leaves into his mouth with a laugh.

The bedroom was practically empty, I observed, except for my photographs. Every single photo I had ever taken, even my selfies, was glued up in chronological order. They covered the walls. But a strange-looking man held my hand in them, even sometimes carried me. I cocked my head a little and looked at Jesus for answers.

"Who's that holding my hand?"

"Grandpa," He said without looking at me. Another bite.

"Grandpa?"

"Yep! He does that. He loves holding hands."

"Why is He so frail? He needs a burger," I said, staring at the picture of Him looking like skin and bone and a hundred years old.

"Because that's how you conjured Him in your imagination as a child."

I shut up. It was true.

As a child, I used to think of Him as very old. For someone who had been around for eternity, He must have aged, I had figured. So I was expecting someone of about fifty pounds or less. Someone who needed his angels to carry Him around the Heavens while he held in a tight grip the Scepter where He hid all the mysteries of Creation. In fact, I thought He was so old

140

that he became paranoid that someone might steal His Scepter, which He never let out of His sight.

Another time, I imagined Him so old that He became blind, and I imagined that the angels carried Him to bed each night and brought Him out in the morning to bathe in the sunlight. But, somehow, He managed to keep bad angels from the Scepter where all knowledge was stored.

It was Mrs. Jamerson who told us during Sunday school class that God is Spirit and that He doesn't age. It didn't sit well with any of us, who looked at Mrs. Jamerson as if a crucial wire in her brain had been fried. Everything and everyone aged. Although she somehow convinced us that a spirit can't age, even then it didn't stop me from conjuring Him in my mind as old and frail and paranoid with a magical Scepter.

"Nice haircut dude," Jesus said as I stared at the pictures.

"Nice ... What?" I ran a quick hand over my scalp. My hair was gone.

"What's in that bag?" I asked, trying to change the subject. Did He know about last night? *Maybe.*

"Something for Grandpa." He said vaguely.

There was, however, one more detail about God's suspicious bedroom, one that jolted my curiosity more than anything else: a jar. Sitting in the corner, tall enough that it wouldn't be missed. Presumably this was where He kept all souls, the good ones and the bad ones, according to Flannighans and Dylan. I had been wrong. I'd thought He kept them, or hid them, in His Scepter.

The jar startled me when I laid my eyes upon it. *How can that small jar hold souls? For China alone, He certainly would need not jars but containers upon containers,* I thought.

"What about that jar?" I asked Him, keeping my eyes in the corner.

"That's life. That's where life comes from."

141

SEAT OF TRUTH

I almost dropped my breakfast plate as I stared at the strange little container in complete disbelief.

"Life?" I shot back. "You guys found it?" To which Jesus laughed uncontrollably. Suddenly the door pushed open, and without warning the Lord made His majestic entrance.

"Morning, Dad," Jesus offered, trying to contain His laughter. I immediately looked down at my feet. I had suddenly lost all appetite in heavenly breakfast.

He gave each of us a sliced orange, then took the bag from the floor and said, "Why don't you boys join us in the kitchen?" And He left.

We took our plates and headed for the kitchen.

Mrs. Campbell was staring out the window, sipping cinnamon coffee from a Chinese porcelain cup adorned with a gold rim. She seemed to be in a good mood this morning, more than any other day since our general admission into the Heavens. *Did she see Edmund last night?* I wondered. God was busy by the counter, pouring wine into a few glasses.

Jesus immediately took a seat across from my mother, leaving the remaining seat across from me for the Big Guy. He came back with three glasses of wine and placed them in front of us. I said thank you with my head down.

He sat down across from me.

Silence again.

His best weapon fully brandished.

My mother got back to her food. Jesus was halfway through, God was sipping wine and shelling green peas for dinner later, and I was fidgeting. I tried some water to calm my nerves, but my drinking sounded like gulping from a giant goblet. *What's wrong with me?*

"Why don't you have some wine, son," He said, more like an order than a suggestion. I had noticed that about Him. He didn't

142

suggest things, or seek one's approval, He just ordered: *Why don't you boys come along!" "Why don't you join us!" "Why don't you boys have some cake! Bossy!* I thought.

I took a sip of wine and awkwardly placed the glass down. The grape was soothing and very rich, but did little for my fidgeting. I scratched the side of my head, looking for something to distract me.

Mrs. Gandalf Campbell stood and began to clear the table. Jesus eagerly aided her, leaving the Almighty and me sitting. It felt as if I was in a desert with Him. I swallowed hard and my eyes darted here and there, looking around for nothing in particular, avoiding eye contact. *Where's Holy or Flannighans, or Dylan? Where are people when you need them most?* I would have had a great conversation with any of them, even Flannighans. I would be happy to talk about anything on Earth.

Small talk ignited laughter between Mrs. Campbell and Jesus as they cleaned the dishes. She said something to which Jesus answered a little louder, "I know — it's so obvious, isn't it?" *I hope these two aren't talking about me,* I thought, *'cause I'm right here.* "Oh boy!" my mother said. *I can hear you, guys. Hello?*

She looked satisfied for some reason. She smiled and looked toward the table where God and I had been idling, like two lovers in the verge of breaking up.

I held my hands under the table and gripped the edge, desperately looking in their direction, hoping they would ask me to join them. Suddenly the Lord stood up and said, without looking at anyone, "Mitch, why don't you walk with me!" Immediately, I observed a hint of pain in Jesus' face.

With that, the Alpha and Omega threw onto His back the red duffel bag that Jesus had brought with Him earlier and started walking toward the front door.

I followed.

CHAPTER TWENTY-ONE

Atonement

Mrs. Campbell and Jesus crammed in front of the floor-to-ceiling windows as if witnessing a farewell procession. After maybe thirty steps, just as I was about to reach the main gate, right under the Tree of Life, Jesus called out my name. He ran toward me with His arms wide open and hugged me. The hug was so tight I felt the throbbing of His heart in mine. Then He let go of me and ran back inside.

Twice the Tree of Life had sparkled with the glitz of gold, metallic green, and blue. It always took the color of the heart of the observer. Last night it had been sparkling red. Now it was almost colorless, with lavender-hued and rose petals. For some reason, last night when I had stared at it there hadn't been that enigmatic vision of the portal I had experienced the first time I had passed under it. Flannighans had told me that this was the same tree that was in the Garden of Eden, and that they'd had to remove it for fear that Adam and his girlfriend Eve might be tempted to override their misdeed. He also said that it was the only landmark that could be seen from anywhere, because it is in everything and every being. *It is a compass to Oneness,* he mused. I remembered staring at Flannighans and wondered if he was really worthy of the afterlife. He even said that many inhabitants believed that the tree's water drops drift into a parallel stream and arouse other souls, giving them strength and comfort. In fact, he went as far as to say that the Tree of Life is an extension of Holy. But this was Flannighans L. Molar. Because his academic achievements were marred by mischief, I found it difficult to accept some of his claims.

God and I left the Palace and headed down the hill. The Lord's strides were brisk and steady; mine, sluggish and defeated. We passed many streets of stunning design, streets I had not yet ventured into, notably Hope Street, also known as Blue Street. That street is made only of blue gemstones, such as sodalite, topaz, lapis lazuli, blue chalcedony, larimar, and benitoite — stones mostly found in California. Blue was my favorite color. When I was feeling off balance, there was something soothing about it, perhaps, a sense of hope. *Is He taking me to my brother, finally?* I certainly hoped so.

We made it to the edge of the city, as far as where Dylan and Flannighans had become lost. Instead of following the narrow passage leading to Heaven's Warehouse, He turned in the other direction.

The trail made several detours thereafter. I had lost track of street names by then.

I had given Him a piece of me the night before. However, of all the names calling, I felt guilty the most for calling Him a terrorist. No wonder I felt so awkward around Him.

Today was my seventh day, and I still felt the burden of human DNA. I had no wings to fly with, no white robe with a golden belt. Well, I guessed, those things don't make one immortal after all. Last night had been an experience born out of anger and bitterness. Now I didn't know what to expect. Come to think of it, I don't have to worry much about wings, since neither Flannighans nor Dylan had any. This was a small consolation in itself, because if — of all beings and things created — Flannighans L. Molard in particular were to grow wings, I might as well say that something was wrong with them all.

The road eventually came to a fence. It felt old and looked odd in a way that evoked distant memories, perhaps even recent.

He lifted a small gate and motioned me to get in. I did, without paying attention. Then the gate closed after me. He looked at me with cold eyes and I suddenly realized I was inside the Gate of Exchange & Forgotten Hope.

I tried to flee back out, but my limbs became numb. My brain told me to speak, but my tongue refused words. My legs refused to walk. Everything in me became a burden — so heavy! I was hypnotized in my tracks. He looked at me as if from another world; from another dimension; from a different time — like a two-way mirror from a parallel world. I saw Him as so far away that I thought I could never reach Him, but then I knew He was right there on the other side of that window, or that mirror, or that see-through wall. My mouth opened wide as the blood drained from my face. And for the first time I felt the effect of loneliness, hopelessness, loss, fear and abandonment. He then entered the gate, took my right hand, gave me back control of my limbs, and we moved on.

Strangely enough, I saw no one languishing in pain. I just recognized the bizarre street names, and heard no musical madness. On the contrary, I heard the humming of a song called *Only You* that began with an uncountable number of voices, and I suspected Holy was behind it.

The humming was calm and strengthening. I'd never heard the song before, but the musical arrangement and the words were a feast for the soul. They spoke to the inward being, the exact words we long for, words that heal broken hearts and mend broken spirits. Holy sang her heart out in the early morning, my last morning, my last rising of the sun.

Who has brought you through the nights?
(choir) *Only you.*
Who has painted the midnight sky?
(choir) *Only you.*
Whose voice calmed the raging sea?
Planted the rocks upon the moon?
Whose bright star has found a way
For a deer to bear the pains?
(choir) *Only you. Only you.*
(choir) *Only you. Only you.*
Who has threaded you in the womb?
(choir) *Only you.*
Whose voice lifted up to the clouds?
(choir) *Only you.*
Whose law is written upon your heart?
Out of whose womb came joy?
Who brought forth the days of spring
Turned a barren land to your dwelling?
(choir) *Only you, only you.*
Only you, only you.

Holy called out the last word and shook every tree, every branch and every leaf until the forest itself gave in to a silent, swaying dance.

For forty-three years I had roamed the earth, I had never understood its mysteries, or felt the awe at its secrets. The sun

SEAT OF TRUTH

shone each day, sprang fruitful dwellings forth from barren land; the sea roared, stretched its might, but never beyond the shoreline. The universe, in my view, had been nothing but an abstract concept that could be discussed, reviewed, retouched, and redesigned. I saw the earth as a sessile painting, not as an instrument that, when played by its master, makes a beautiful dance. I was blessed with great health, was fortunate to have a roof over my head and clothes on my back, and I placed it all at the feet of my accomplishment, my talents, and my career. I failed to live a life He had well thought out and planned. But that song finally revealed to me why I dreamed the things I dreamed, how this marvelous design called Earth is a precious gift and an absolute proof of His artistic ability. And the words humbled me until I realized that I was indeed His creature, a speck of dust in the universe, the work of His hands, as Ms. Dylan had so beautifully put it.

The humming choir followed us into the murky woods. We passed several fields of wheat and tall green grass, rolling hills and ridges, and entered a forest dense with magnolias, walnuts, cedars of Lebanon and sequoias. We inched under beech trees like those of the Dark Hedges, trees I wasn't fond of. Rays of light I could almost touch pierced the branches. We pushed deeper into the woods until we stumbled upon a small arena that looked like a fighters' pit. Upon closer examination, it looked more like a slaughterhouse, hidden right in the middle of the forest and fenced with bamboo. It was an eerie environment. Although it looked familiar, I couldn't help but to wonder what this place was.

I looked around, half expecting to find Edmund lurking behind some trees, but I didn't see him.

We climbed the fence and landed inside. There was no gate.

148

Ezechias Domexa

In the middle of the ring a wooden cross, made of two beams lay on the ground. The wood appeared fresh cut, but there was no trace of wood shavings. There was also a small table near the fencing.

The Lord walked to the table and dropped the red duffel bag on it. Then he perched himself half on the table, with one leg upon it, and the other on the ground and crossed His arms. I gathered all this information from my peripheral vision.

Accounting is an exact science. My career had given me plenty of ways to acquire information that no other field dared explore. In a single glance I could gather an amount of Intel that would surprise must people. The Navy had taught me a great deal about espionage, too. So I used my skills.

We settled there in silence.

Then the Lord stood up and looked straight at me for the first time since the previous night. I knew His eyes were locked on me. As a human being I knew this much. I looked away, searching for something and nothing around the empty place. Finding everything and nothing.

Silence grew between us. Then He said, "Have I not been good to you, Mitch?" He waited for a reply. I kept my silence. "Was there anything you asked of me that I denied you?" I kept one arm by my side and crossed the other behind my back. My eyes darted around the ring, surveying, studying how well made the fence was, the perfect curvature of the bamboo, how there were almost no joints so that not even air could escape. I wondered who made it, what its purpose was, and how long it took to build. I counted the pieces that made up the ring: exactly seven hundred seventy-seven— a questionable and strange number. The fence wasn't quite a circle. It was arranged in a perfect heptagon — a seven-sided polygon — around seven pillars. *Even stranger.*

149

SEAT OF TRUTH

"You treated me last night as if you knew me," God said, "as if you knew the mysteries of things." He walked around the table now. "Was there even one day I was absent in your life?" He waited for an answer. "One minute?" A hint of sadness cracked His voice, and I felt the beginning of a breaking down in my spirit. "One second that I wasn't there, holding your hand or carrying you?" I remembered the pictures, all of them, in His bedroom. *Oh shit! He's right.*

My eyes grew heavier by the moment. I fought back the tears but lost. *Ungrateful.*

I dug my left toes into the soft soil and the smell of fresh blood rose from it. "Answer me!" He roared. It reminded me of His voice the night before. I fumbled backward and fell to the ground. Before I could regain self-control and stand, He was in my personal space. *How did He move so fast?* "Look me in the eye," He roared again, "and tell me!" I trembled like a leaf as I saw something in His eyes that I will forever fear.

He stormed back to the table and proceeded to open the bag.

He plunged His hand into the sack and drew out three flat-topped nails the size of kitchen knives and laid them on the table. *What is this?* I thought.

From the bag again, He pulled out a carpenter's hammer and laid it next to the nails. And finally, when He pulled out a whip with six thongs tipped with metal, I looked away.

"Don't you look away, son of Adam!" He thundered. I trembled at His calling me son of Adam. I managed to look the other way as water began to drip from my nose. "Here are your nails. Here is your hammer and your whip," He said. "Do what you do best: justice! For everything I did wrong to you, make it right." I remembered that Flannighans had said that humans come to judge Him. Whatever liquid I carried in my body instantly turned into stone.

150

He stepped forward, stood over the cross laid on the ground, opened His arms wide and closed His eyes as if invoking His own God. The large garment He donned dropped off mysteriously to reveal how His loins were girded in plain white cloth. He lowered himself onto the cross, crossed His ankles and spread His arms, and waited for me to crucify Him. Then I saw it.

I froze.

In a twinkling of an eye, as if someone had played some magic trick on my sight, I saw Jesus on the cross, not God. He was bound there with a brown leather belt so tight that escape was impossible. Adrenaline rushed through my veins. *Where is God?* I asked myself. Then I felt a hot breath behind my neck and swiftly turned. There He was, standing, staring at me. His expression void of compassion, or mercy, or grace; His eyes were red like coal fire, and in His hands he held the hammer and the nails.

I raced Him to Jesus on the cross, slid and shielded Jesus with my body. God came right up to me. I pushed Him violently. The nails and the hammer fell from His hands to the ground.

"Don't you touch Him! Don't you touch Him!" I yelled as I tried to unfasten the leather belt as fast as I could. But it wouldn't budge. It was too tight.

God came back in a fury and pushed me aside. He took one nail and grabbed for the hammer. I jumped onto His back and kicked His side. He fell sideways. He lost the nail again. "I will kill you!" I cried out. "I will kill you. I swear I'll kill you!" He jumped at my back, and drove me to the ground. I served Him an elbow to His rib. He jerked backward, but tackled me as I stood up. I fell down. His left fist connected to the side of my head. I felt the heat. He served me a powerful leg to the side. I blocked it, and pulled the leg up. He fell on His butt.

151

SEAT OF TRUTH

"Father?" Jesus said, almost pleading, as if already in pain. "I'll do it. I'll do it for Mitch."

I was broken.

God regained his balance. He came over and pushed me aside. I resisted, holding onto the leather belt.

"Then I will nail you with Him," He declared to me.

He fumbled and found the nail again, then grabbed the hammer in a hurry. He put one knee on my right hand and held it still. The other knee He put on my stomach, and held my left hand steady. I tried to kick, but I was under too much restraint. As I finally realized what was about to take place, I spoke in a much different tone, between gritted teeth, but calm, like a seasoned drug dealer or assassin: "I swear I will kill you. I swear on my mother's grave, I will hunt you down and kill you!" He used His knees to stop me from kicking Him. He held the nail to our hands, lifted the hammer high as could be and drove the nail into our flesh.

The hammer came down with such fury I almost didn't feel the moment the nail entered my palm. I screamed in excruciating pain, and so did Jesus. "Help! Help!" I yelled. "Flannighans! Please help!" — Maybe the people at the Gate of Exchange & Forgotten Hope could be useful for once. I jerked in pain. He grabbed another nail, still keeping His knees on us. He hit the hammer again and the nail entered our flesh, except this time I felt numb to the core.

Jesus withered in agony.

I continued to scream for help.

No help came.

I gave up.

"Please!" I whispered, begging Him to stop. "Please! I surrender," I pleaded. He proceeded with our feet. "You win. You win." I repeated.

152

"You! Men like you nailed my only Son on the cross." He searched for the last nail. "And you come all the way to my dwelling place to lecture me! I gave you everything I had. There's nothing left to give." He said it with so much rage and anger that I felt it in every breath He took, in every stare that seized me.

"What have I done?" I whispered. "What have I done again?"

When He had nailed our intertwined feet, my mind began to conjure a series of black and white images from my childhood to my last day on Earth seven days ago. It felt like a dream, but it wasn't — it was real.

My vision drifted on across the earth, now a post-apocalyptic world where everything was rubble and people — dead or alive — existed only inside giant, clear bubbles with their soul sealed inside with them, and they floated around the cities, all over the ocean. Inside each bubble I could see how the dead had lived their day-to-day lives and how the living still live theirs, like the library of heaven.

His thunderous voice had broken the sound barriers. His voice echoed into things and burst into every molecule, and now the universe looked like a chaotic cosmos, a dystopian world, a wasteland where everything is about to become extinct. Pieces of mountains suspended in mid-air, part of the sea rising like sheets of paper, and the roads, the cities, and the towns falling sideways. The laws of gravity and physics having no effect on anything, everything experienced weightlessness and stillness.

"Do you hear the calls and the cries of an insect in distress?" His voice rumbled. "I speak words your mouth can't even begin to form; language you can't even begin to comprehend. Declare your omniscience before me! Demonstrate to me the equation and the theory of life in just one symbol? Tell me how many breaths you took since you entered my Creation and how many times your mother thought of you? And show me the days that I

SEAT OF TRUTH

came to rescue you? Why don't you counter me about my science? Tell me where the sounds go? Let me hear the first words I spoke in all their fullness. Where do I store them?"

His deafening voice I heard everywhere, but could not look upon His face. He was everywhere and in everything that existed.

The earth turned upside down, sideways, inside out. All the laws of physics were broken, and surely it marked the beginning of all things, as if the earth was about to become void and soon darkness would hover over it.

Is this where it all started?

Is it how it all began? I wondered.

The towns looked ravaged by wars. Except it wasn't by war, but the breath of God, His thunderous voice. Half burned photographs partially hidden behind things; others were on the dusty floor, having separated from broken frames. Every memory, and story was still fresh around the fallen walls, around every dreams and joy this dystopian storm had stolen. Here, behold, the rags and ruins of what I used to call home — Earth.

Grey smoke covered the sky where mankind used to look for hope.

Hope.

What is hope?

The city resembled portraits, like the pages of a great American novel. They were sad and curious. The stories were parallel, yet they were one. They were childhood stories, filled with laughter and gaiety, filled with possibilities and mysteries, filled with hope and many things not yet known. Where was hope, the one thing by which mankind thrived in the midst of chaos, the one thing for which they lived, the thing that fueled them for the next sunrise and because of which no one wanted to die?

154

Hope.

Here I am, hovering over the cities.

There, on Okeechobee Boulevard, my Sunday school teacher, Mrs. Dorothy, floating in her own bubble. A simple peek inside let me see what had become of her. I had always known her hair was fake. I knew it was a wig, but no one believed me. *How about now, hey?*

Everyone had become so small and so old. They walked around in their bubbles like emptied shells, dragging their poor souls behind. Yet they looked happy.

Some souls had been so badly mistreated that they were discolored and full of holes, broken with unkept promises, emotional scars left by relatives, lovers, friends, and strangers. Their façades had finally peeled off and now they could be seen for who they really were in all their fantastically devilish daydreams.

Over there my old church assembly was singing, but only the few kids had hologram crowns. The rest were as phony as a phone booth. Hypocrites, unforgiving, avaricious, controlling freaks, selfish, lying, angry, full of resentment, and yet they were speaking in tongues, prophesying over each other — mankind's best method of manipulation: religion and speeches. Pity!

The world had become naked. Before it had been all façade —African wooden masks — people who think they can simply look at you and know your entire chromosomal structure. Mrs. Dorothy was one of them. She earned the award for Spiritual Police each year, as if walking around with a device, testing everyone's Holy Spirit level. *Ah!*

We knew so little about ourselves, let alone others.

There I was, floating in my own bubble. I could see my first day in kindergarten, all my college days. I wished I could go back and change some of them.

SEAT OF TRUTH

There was the lighthouse where Edmund, Flannighans, and I used to play hide and seek and skip rocks on the ocean.

How did everything and everyone declared dead still manage to breathe as if walking in a museum of the dead? This was the result of what had once been sacred turning into habit, everything habitual becoming popular, and everything popular becoming common until the origin of what was once truth became folk tales and ghost stories. This was the residue of cultural change.

Through all of it I still saw how connected their lives were, how their once-beloved world had become so insignificant. Everything had been decimated and dissipated with a simple touch, with a simple breath, cursed to turn into what it ever had been: dust.

Everything is dust, I now believed.

Everything is transient.

There are no more imprints. There is no more history.

Only memories.

The only things that moved were the brightly colored butterflies. In just one breathless moment they changed color each time their wings flapped, and they morphed into a different size and shape. I could see the last details of their molecules before they suddenly turned to powder. Dust.

Here came my son Matthew, running and playing soccer through the rubble by the main gate of the estate. Connie was inside with her guest observing him through the window.

My son, I thought. Will he grow to become someone like me — ungrateful, wicked, and dubious, a man of futile ambitions? Will he ever come of age to understand that mankind is like winter's wheat? Men rise and fall. Will he grow to accept that in spite of all his strength, all his power, all he can ever be is dust? And what will be left of us all is nothing but memory? Memories

156

are like caffeine; they keep us wide-awake. They keep our soul alive. They are strange, like surprises, and they're always near us. And soon we're faced with the ordeal that the passing time erases nothing.

Nothing.

And now all the fragile, broken fragments of the puzzle become whole. Like a sudden realization, it dawns on us like … Oh! It was that? It all made perfect sense now.

Memories.

The car crashed.

A bright Light overtook me in my black and white dream and brought me back to the fenced pit. I saw the hem of His robe trailed back into the woods. *He has left us here to die.*

And like that, He was gone. I died with Jesus on the cross.

CHAPTER TWENTY-TWO

Beauty of sight and sound

The episode ended almost like the first one. I woke up in His house again, this time on His couch. No one woke me this time. I awoke of my own accord. And it wasn't the kind of lazy awakening from tiredness, the yawning and stretching-forever kind. I bolted up like a rocket as if fleeing from a nightmare, inspected both sides of my hands, and made a quick assessment of the rest of my body. There was neither any trace of nail piercing in my palms, nor any broken ribs. I was whole — except I had experienced a felicitous attainment, a conscious awareness of perfect harmony with myself and with the cosmic.

What a comfort!

How mysterious! I thought.

At a single glance I could see how the flowers outside were fed. I could tell the number of nuclei in each branch, in each leaf, and in each grain of pollen. I could see how the nutrients flowed up and down and how they were distributed through branches, tree trunks and root systems.

How wonderful the wall of a single cell, its organelles! The chloroplast, which absorbs solar energy; the endoplasmic reticulum that facilitates the transportation of substances within cells, the ribosomes on the nucleus that produce proteins; how the cells produce fatty acids and store them as food in the form of lipid droplets. Everything is created with purpose and beauty. "On your seventh day you'll see Creation in all its splendor: the app, the bonding, the sensor, the physic, the distance, the motor, the colors etc." Ms. Dylan had said.

I saw the amazing feathers arrangement of a passing hummingbird: how the tertial features decrease air turbulence, the primary covert feathers allow air to glide over the wing; how the flight feathers provide propulsion; how the alula provides stability during flight and allows the hummingbird to hover and even fly backward. Everything is created with purpose and beauty.

What happened?

"There is something I wanted to tell you all." God's voice startled me as I was *oohing* and *aahing* at the mystery and beauty of Creation. He said it without a trace of hesitation. I looked around and saw a gathering in the family room. He was seated across from me, high on a recliner made of lambskin and bamboo. On my left were my parents, Mr. and Mrs. Gandalf P. Campbell; Flannighans and Atelia occupied the couches on my right; Jesus and Holy took two accent chairs that were next to Him. I was still avoiding her eyes. "Where's Dylan," God said, as if He had just remembered the little girl. "Dylan?" He called out in his baritone voice. I hoped He wouldn't tell her what I had said the night before about her.

"Coming, Grandpa!" she shouted from somewhere upstairs. She glided on the handrails, beamed with excitement as she ran into her Grandpa's arms and sat on his lap. "As you know," the

Lord continued, slowly rocking the recliner, "one day, all things shall be laid bare for all eyes to see," we all nodded in agreement, "even in the eyes of a seven-year-old girl." Dylan fidgeted and giggled while playing with her fingernails. "There should be no secrets between family, should there be?" He said to no one in particular, and everybody looked around searching for secrets. He leaned forward, straightened the child in front of Him, holding her a moment longer as if weighing His words, and said to her, "There's someone I'd like you to meet." He arched His thick eyebrows. "Ms. Dylan? I'd like you to meet your father, Mitch P. Campbell!" He then let go of the child, crossed His legs, and searched everyone's eyes for their responses.

What does He mean, "Ms. Dylan, I'd like you to meet your father, Mitch P. Campbell"? I don't understand.

The Lord now crossed his arms, as did Jesus, beaming smiles at each other and watching the whole family drama unfold in Heaven's family room. Holy rested her face on her right hand with a smile of pure joy and compassion, observing Dylan coyly.

Dylan let out a high-pitched shriek that sounded as if the kid had suddenly seen a ghost. She covered her mouth with both hands as she screamed her excitement and shock.

She looked at Grandpa in absolute disbelief as if to say, *You're kidding, right Grandpa?*

My heart dropped into my bowels. As everyone absorbed the shock, the silence grew longer and longer until I felt the throbbing of my heart again like foot soldiers in a battlefield. Dylan's gray eyes became wider and wider as giant bubbles of tears slowly filled them. But still there was that trace of joy her cute little round face always carried.

"Dad?" she whispered with a broken voice. I didn't answer. I couldn't. *My child? It's impossible!*

She attempted a step toward me, but her legs could no longer bear her, and she stopped.

I sank deeper and deeper into the couch as if a dream was carrying me away. The world was spinning like it had seven days earlier after the car crash. But this was the least of my worries, for there were many questions that needed answers.

Mrs. Campbell stared at me as if I had committed a crime punishable only by death, and death by any means. Her face was red with anger and contempt. She stood up, and my father held her hand in his. Everyone was waiting for an explanation.

I was still in the twilight of what He meant by the "meet your father" part. *I still don't understand ... Wait!*

The Lord spoke again. "He gave Simone Anderson two hundred dollars to get rid of her pregnancy when she told him her period was six days late." The episode was projected in front of everyone — a wild, passionate, erotic exchange with a beautiful ebony girl in a sorority bathroom during a party. *Oh!*

"Oh! Oh my God," I mumbled in deafened shock.

The girl with the hazel eyes had been on a spree that night just like everybody else. In the wee hours of the morning, she had emerged from nowhere with a pack of cold beer and limes. She gave me the last beer and I asked her to sit with me. As the hours wound down and the alcohol loosened my limbs, I now remembered, I found her beautiful and enjoyable. We smiled at each other, and from there it quickly escalated, but downhill.

Three weeks later we met again, coincidently, at a pharmacy. She told me her period was six days late. She then added that it might *just* be late, but she found it unusual and wanted to give me a heads-up. I gave her two hundred dollars and the name of pills I'd heard of. And that was that. I never saw her again. I thought I had buried the episode in the uppermost attic part of

SEAT OF TRUTH

my brain, but memories, however cold the original experience, always appeared colder down the road when they resurface.

"You conceived a child and murdered her in the womb?" Mrs. Campbell barked with rage and bitterness, ready to pounce at me. Gandalf held her still as if she were a bad dog on a leash.

Dylan took another tentative step, advancing toward me shyly, as if afraid I might hurt her, visibly shaking and choked with emotions. When she finally arrived next to me, she fidgeted and giggled a little, and more tears came to mix with her contagious smile.

I fell to my knees before her. I was mush inside.

She wrapped her little arms around my neck and slowly rested her head on my shoulder.

I was broken.

"Hi, Daddy?" she whispered. The girl was now sobbing on my shoulder and sniffling, struggling to regain control of her joy and composure.

Shame, or pride, or whatever you want to call it at this point, unlike what had been happening since my general admission to the Heavens, no longer held me back. I squeezed Dylan tight against my chest. Her hair smelled like fresh lotus oil and cinnamon sticks. And I knew at that moment that I could live my eternity, locked in her embrace.

I couldn't speak. How could I?

I was a coward.

When Mrs. Campbell came over to hug the child, I thought she was going to slap the back of my head. She held us together and said, "Grandma is here, baby! Grandma is here!"

Flannighans' expression I couldn't decipher. It was something between shock and a smile. The rest of the gathering came over into a group embrace filled with tears and joy and smiles and warmth.

162

After much wrangling with her emotions, Mrs. Gandalf took out a cake from a deep blue wooden liquor cabinet and placed it on a gate-leg table made of wood and something along the lines of granite.

The cake was decorated with petals and the words *Happy Birthday, Ms. Dylan* in heavenly calligraphy. Seven carefully designed candles, in seven colors, formed the number seven on top of the cake. Holy and Atelia were busy taking out bread and butter plates made of gold paper from a buffet next to the liquor cabinet for a symbolic birthday party.

Holy looked at her and winked. She and Dylan, I noticed, had matching rings on their wedding and index fingers.

When Dylan saw the cake, she was ecstatic. She gushed and ran to Jesus and buried her face around the hem of His denim shirt to hide her shyness and excitement.

Jesus took out a few dessert forks and ice cream spoons from the cabinet drawer with Dylan in tow and placed them on the wooden table next to everything else.

Flannighans wrestled out a bucket of ice cream from an ancient Frigidaire and began to add big scoops to each plate. Every plate, fork and spoon had the same inscription that was on the cake: *Happy Birthday, Ms. Dylan.*

Mrs. Campbell stood up and assumed control. She looked at Holy as if they had planned this. Then Holy started the intro of *Happy Birthday to You* on her magical cello. We joined in excitedly. By the time Holy finished the song, the candles had burned to their last flickers and began a firecracker display of unprecedented frenzy. The phrase, *Happy Birthday, Ms. Dylan,* was displayed all over the cake now in breathtaking changing colors, as we watched in awe.

After the fireworks, Mrs. Campbell cut nine pieces of cake that Atelia carefully placed on the plates.

SEAT OF TRUTH

Grandpa said Grace to Himself, and everyone grabbed a plate. Dylan, of course, couldn't have been happier. Everybody hugged her and kissed her Happy Birthday. She accepted it as if she had longed for this moment all her seven years of existence.

God finished his cake and ice cream before everybody else and abruptly stepped outside. I took the bait and followed Him. He stood by the main gate of His palace, where the two robust archangels acted as sentinels. He was contemplating Earth. He kept both hands crossed behind his back as if He was tired from the family drama. I walked over and stood by Him, just mere inches from the Omega. I assumed my position and began to think of convincing words to say. He spoke first: "You know, son," He began in a resounding voice, "a contrite heart and a broken spirit, We do not despise." Then He looked at me, and I immediately escaped His eyes.

"Thank you!" I said, staring down at my feet. "Thank you for your mercy and grace!"

We fell silent for a moment, looking at the giant globe that loomed before us.

"It is my understanding," He said, "that Ms. Dylan and you are quite fond of each other, are you not?" It was as if He was testing my sincerity. I took a moment to consider my answer.

"She's the fondest of all the dreams I have dreamed," I replied with a smile. I couldn't help but notice the beginning of a smirk on His upper lip, and He seemed very satisfied with my answer.

Silence. The globe was a blue hue — insignificant, unwanted.

"Are you ready to see your brother?" He asked distantly.

"Yes," I said with confidence, "I am."

PART II:
THE TRIAL

There are two days in a man's life:
today and *that* day. This is *that* day.

SECOND INTRODUCTION

Ahh! Entertained yet?

I hope you crave more, because that was just the icing on the cake.

You see, uh... these two fools, Mitch and Flannighans, escaped me only through a measly amount of luck, the kind of luck that defies all principles, especially spiritual ones. I had them almost at the tip of my tongue, could almost taste those vermin's little guts, as you discovered for yourself when the Cheater ... He ... um, snatched them from my teeth. And He claimed that I played with and preyed on innocence as if robbing them from me is not offending enough. They were the fruit of my labor, of working around the clock. I'd nursed them, pruned them, and reshaped them into bootleg copies of what they had been. They were mine.

Now, I know I made some rather unpleasant remarks in my earlier introduction. Some threats ... uh ... about when you find out who I really am, and so on and so forth — name calling, among other things. Look, I hope you don't take these things too seriously, because I am anything but frightening. Let's go back to our little adventure ... uh ... into the core of the predicament — the reason we are all here in the first place.

On another note, just so you know, after this we might not have another direct conversation. But I am so looking forward

SEAT OF TRUTH

to meeting with you in the same dire circumstances I am about to meet this fool, Edmund! However, you *will* see me parade in the courtroom pleading my cases.

For the rest of what is to follow I have taken the liberty of omitting a few details irrelevant to the situation at hand by simply leaping to the essential parts so we can make the best use of our time. Because, believe it or not, I don't have much time left.

Here is a brief outline of what's coming, although chronologically misleading and confused — again, my memory is as cloudy as the peak of Mount Everest — but you'll get an idea.

What you're about to see is a movie.

A feature-length movie filled with drama, spies, corruption, lies, betrayal, ecstasy, secrets, destruction and death.

It features:

A forgotten maid who can't stand the sight of me, and the feeling is mutual.

A beautiful marriage.

A law student.

Good old college days.

An unfortunate blessing (humans call it "good luck")

A law firm's dissolution.

People who are in the wrong place at the wrong time.

The other side of the world.

The residual of greed.

Oh, uh … the death of a bad man … I think? Anyway, I can't recall all the details, okay? But somehow somebody gets hurt, *badly*.

Eventually, an insight into how I play my game with humans.

Then will come the closing arguments, and I will walk out of here with great fanfare and a soul.

Here again, I entrust you into the capable hands of Mitch, with whom, I'm sure, by now you're head-over-heels in love, aren't you? Every human loves a great story with a great leading character. He will introduce to you a few characters of his own acquaintance. And from time to time, as you now recognize my voice, you will know when I speak. Every human does. However quirky or smart they might sound, they all know my voice.

At this point I can only hope that this document will be kept secret, out of reach of human hands. That would be too much of a scandal for my business, and potentially ruin my few remaining days. Mitch, the monkeys are all yours.

CHAPTER TWENTY-THREE

Beyond and above the unimaginable

One of the features I found pretty cool in the Heavens — and you will too — was the means of transportation. Traveling in heaven could be really fun. I could fly at any imaginable speed and pass through anything without a special suit or armor like the superheroes back on Earth hid behind. The joy of immortality excited me and nearly turned me into a reckless citizen of the Heaven.

During the previous seven days, since my general admission, the Square had been a rendezvous point — a hangout. Now when I abruptly landed in the Square after testing my flying abilities, I stood slack-jawed. The Square had been transformed into a stunning architecture of divine creativity. The Courthouse had taken over the entire Square. It was a massive open-air structure mimicking a Roman amphitheater where gladiators entertained spectators.

The main entrance boasted seven staggering columns that resembled bands of light made of diamond and turquoise dust. The second, fourth and sixth pillars sat on heptagonal bases

170

made of opal, amethyst, and sapphire, and on top of them three flags of charge had been erected. The rest of the columns sat on heptagonal and hexagonal bases. All seven columns were filleted and fluted and adorned with an assortment of gemstones.

The three flags of charge carried three different emblems: the first one, a white lion on a green background; the second, a yellow eagle on a red background; and the third, a blue *fleur-de-lis* on a white background. Formulas were written on the columns along the curves, and mystical symbols and shapes, barely visible, covered them as well.

Despite the colossal exterior of Heaven's Courthouse, stepping inside it was even more astonishing. My eyes climbed the sprouting arcades twisted into mesh, their arcs joining high above to form a hovering vault where a pure light ascended to illuminate every joint. The tiers of seating had a dormant glow when I stared long enough. Each seat had a name, and I found mine in the seventh row, near the entrance.

My father sat in the first row, calm and composed as if he knew something the rest of us didn't.

My mother sat alone, the sole juror on the jury bench below God's Throne — the Mercy Seat — and behind it Planet Earth loomed so close one could almost touch it and count the grains of sand from any country.

The central stage where gladiators would have normally faced off in battle formed a perfect semi-circle with an empty chair set in the middle. *This,* I said to myself, *is the Seat of Truth that sucks human depravity out of their filthy gutters and exposes every lie, every secret, every vile thought, and all the stains on the very fabric of their souls that have been masked throughout their lives.*

The Seat of Truth was made of dark grey oak, without much aesthetics. It had been used since the beginning of time, and people from every walk of life had sat on it — generals and

171

SEAT OF TRUTH

civilians, doctors and movers, executives and farmers, pastors and servants, truck drivers and politicians, presidents and clerks, judges and lawyers, chefs and actors, royals and commoners, musicians and garbage collectors, electricians and architects, photographers and carpenters, kings and beggars, roofers and conglomerate executives. All had graced it.

So it was aged.

It had no armrest for comfort. After all, this wasn't the place and time for such indulgence. There was also no leather belt to fasten subjects here against their will. After a lifetime of playing the game and haggling with the world for pleasure, it was time to testify, time to answer for one's life.

The spectators waited. They watched like hawks the mysterious chair supremely placed in the ring, waiting to tell them another story.

The ground in the ring was a flaky substance. It wasn't black, red or grey. It was simply dust from which we had all come.

People chatted here and there, mostly in whispers.

After a few moments, a formidable presence swept onto the scenes, sending a shock wave through the audience. He was dressed in a hot red and black priestly robe that reminded me of the creepy inscription at the Gate of Exchange & Forgotten Hope. His features were hidden under a hood. He carried a long scepter that exuded mystery and ancient knowledge.

He stopped in the center near the chair and planted his scepter in the ground.

"I'm Counselor Tshembow. The regal prince of Earth, son of the morning star." The crowd booed him. "I'm here to claim what is rightfully mine."

God came out of nowhere, took his time to walk the few flights of stairs, both hands behind His back, and joined Counselor Tshembow at the Stone of Creation. He wore a

Ezechias Domexa

lavender shirt with His slogan *"I am God alone; beside me there's no other Savior"* and the back — you already know what it said— *"… and I'm not showing off,"* as if He knew everyone thought He was. He wore the same khaki pants I had seen Him in seven days before. *Can He at least change His pants, for His own sake?* I wondered.

The two camped on each side of the empty chair facing the audience.

Everyone fell silent.

"As the court knows," Tshembow began in a British accent, "I am in all truthfulness, in the business of souls as well — and ladies and gentlemen, it is a thriving business. I am here to collect the soul of young Edmund P. Campbell."

The crowd roared their disapproval: "Not in here. Not in here. Not in here."

"If Edmund's Counselor agrees to simply hand over this worthless soul, I will leave at once so that the things not yet revealed to many might remain so." God kept His hands behind His back and listened attentively, nodding to Tshembow from time to time. "If on the contrary, Your Honor," Tshembow turned to God as if giving a warning, "the Counselor wishes for trial — which in my wisdom I'd advise against — I will call to bring forth the Book of Remembrance where all is written."

"Counselor Tshembow," God spoke in His deepest voice "you are very familiar with the procedures of the court and our agreements regarding souls, are you not?"

"Yes, I am so, Your Honor."

"Then you should know that by no means can I deliver a soul without proper audience, shouldn't you?"

"Your Honor, given the evidence at hand, it is a hearing of no consequence—"

173

SEAT OF TRUTH

"Do you know unto whom all hearts are open and from whom no secrets are hidden, Counselor Tshembow?" God snapped.

"I certainly know the boundaries of my knowledge in soul matters —"

"Then you would equally know Counselor, that a proper exchange demands an audience, wouldn't you."

Tshembow looked nervous. "Trial it is, then, Your Honor?"

"I'm afraid so, Counselor."

"It is settled then." Counselor Tshembow said with much attitude, and a few mumbled words. Then God left as He had come — quietly.

They had spoken as if they were legal colleagues when it came to human souls and lives. What was it about the relationship between them that could not be broken? And what agreements, I wondered, could they possibly have about human souls to mandate such mutual loyalty and respect?

"Demons?" Counselor Tshembow called out. "Bring this fool's sheets of transgression and iniquity," he raised his hand in the general direction of the audience, "that they may know and see with their own eyes. Then, perhaps they will better understand."

A herd of other creepy individuals entered the arena. Some were limping, others had crooked bodies and weird shapes, but the audience feared them not. On the contrary, *they* were the ones trembling. Each carried a placard of one of the seven deadly sins as if they were street protesters. "This boy once dared calling me funny," Counselor said, now in a Scottish accent, "in one of his miserable prayer quests, his weekly yadda yadda." He paused and rifled through a load of folders as if looking for something important. "If I could, at that instant have snatched the very living breath out of his disgusting little guts, I

174

would have made my point." By now seven little demons stood in single file, each holding high its placard: Pride, Greed, Lust, Envy, Gluttony, Wrath, Sloth.

After much shuffling, the court was ready and settled. The bailiff entered.

CHAPTER TWENTY-FOUR

Land of the truth and nothing but the truth.
The things we believed when we were children.

A tall, robust Archangel came from behind the Throne. In his right hand he carried a green and purple staff that radiated the same elements I had noticed on my body after the car crash. Swiftly he extended the staff over the whispering audience and a hush fell over them.

A line of musicians appeared out of nowhere and surrounded the entire Courthouse.

The Archangel raised the staff. As he slowly brought it down, a familiar song began to take shape: *Amazing Grace*. And let's just say ... the musicians killed it.

Flannighans showed up at the end of the rendition just in time to tell me that this was Heaven's national anthem. "Why is *Amazing Grace* the anthem, not *Rugged Cross* or *Power in the Blood?*" I asked him.

"*Amazing Grace* is the only hymn that expresses salvation as a whole in just a few short sentences," he said, crossing his bony legs, "for grace is the very core of salvation. In other words,

176

grace gave way to the cross, not the other way around — make sense?" He looked at me for confirmation, mimicking my daughter, Dylan.

After the rendition the Archangel spoke as if announcing a boxing match: "All bow!" On those words everyone dropped to their knees and prostrated flat on the floor. "The Courthouse of Heaven is … in session," he said. "God Almighty; Alpha and Omega; the Lord of Hosts; God, the Creator; the Beginning and the End; the First and the Last; the One who is, who was, and is to come is … presiding!" All in Heaven shouted with joy and excitement. The Seraphim and the Archangels flapped their wings causing thunder and quakes that shook every corner.

Then a total silence reigned.

Although prostrated on the spectacular floor, I tilted my head from side to side searching to see if God, might this time, arrive in all His Glory and Might, with an army of fearless angels in a majestic entrance. Maybe on a cloud of high wind, or beneath lightning bolts with mighty beasts we know nothing about.

Drumroll, please!

Oh boy! I was so disappointed.

Amid all the excitement, He showed up in the same shirt except, this time, not the khakis pants, but cotton sweatpants – one leg rolled to below the knee, and tennis shoes — surprisingly, Nike.

No army.

No horses pulling Him in a chariot of fire.

No fanfare.

He came alone.

"You may be seated!" the Archangel ordered the audience after the Lord had lowered Himself onto the Mercy Seat. His mood I could barely decipher.

You've got to be kidding, I thought. *The Lord is wearing Nike?*

177

SEAT OF TRUTH

"Today," the Archangel announced, "we're going to see how young Edmund P. Campbell lived his life back on Earth. Mrs. Gandalf P. Campbell, his mother, sole juror, must find a place for him among us, in the stars, or at the Gate of Exchange & Forgotten Hope, according to the Book of Instruction Before Leaving Earth. May justice be rendered at last!" The Archangel bowed and disappeared behind the scenes.

In terms of trial procedures, the differences were few. In an earthly courtroom the bailiff said, "All rise!" instead of "All bow!" Earthly judges wore long black robes and their hearts were filled with prejudice. They were not interested in moral values, or justice. Earth's courtrooms were filled with trained witnesses, a bunch of crooked minds seeking favors from high school pals for a piece of the pie, willing to sell out any soul. But God, although dressed in a simple shirt, wasn't bluffing, for He put His Word above His name.

He did have a gavel, and the Big Old-Fashioned Book in which all articles are written was wide open before Him. This was not the constitution of a mundane government institution peddled in the streets while the essence of law was ignored, and money and favors took priority. No, it was nothing like that. This was where the statement "the truth and nothing but the truth" was really sincere and truthful.

Please do understand that this was no ordinary time for tricks and gimmicks. That kind of trial has no strategy.

Now, because you are accustomed to *trial by fire, mistrial, re-trial,* and all such wonderful little words and phrases the system itself has blessed us with, I feel compelled to lay forth a few rules for your own amusement and understanding about trials in the Heavens.

Rule #1: The case is never dismissed in Heaven, because everyone shall one day give a full account of his life.

178

Rule #2: You can't plead insanity, because everyone is fit for trial in Heaven. The guilty or the sinner must die, or otherwise there must be a substitute. He took it all upon Himself so we might be sane according to the Old-Fashioned Book.

Rule #3: All evidence is admissible, regardless of the means of obtaining it, for all things shall be laid bare for all eyes to see. No more secrets. Enough!

Rule #4: You can't make a deal. There is no dealing. Unless you repent, you will likewise perish.

Rule #5: There are no annulment or gray area or technicality because Grandpa said, "Therefore, I put before you life and death: choose life so that you might live."

Rule #6: There are no appeals or purgatory. For it is appointed unto man to die only once. After death, comes the judgment.

Rule #7: All kids get a free pass, for the kingdom of Heaven belongs to such as these. In fact, Tshembow never bothers to come claiming babies' souls for they have a heart like Jesus.

The rules are simple and self-explanatory. They are Heaven's Miranda rights in the *trials of Life and Death*.

Now all deeds and procedures were done, all *i*'s dotted and *t*'s crossed. The court was finally ready and settled. They brought him out.

He came out in a cage covered with yellow fabric, hovering above the chair.

After maneuvers were done, the Archangel stretched his scepter and slowly the yellow cover dissolved and the contents beamed up gradually, like in some sort of Star Trek current. There, on the Seat of Truth, in the middle of the court, was Edmund P. Campbell. And the audience gushed and exploded in applause.

CHAPTER TWENTY-FIVE

Nothing lasts forever, except the Word

Nothing was missing as far as I could see. He had all his body parts. He had not undergone any transformation of any kind. He was in fact Edmund P. Campbell as men knew him back on earth.

Yet, a streak of nearly imperceptible change did show due to the last washing he had been given at the funeral home. He had remarkable freshness and had been given a handsome haircut before being installed in his expensive imported casket, the best the funeral director could come up with.

I remembered the ordeals the funeral director and his staff had gone through. Under Mrs. Campbell's burdensome concerns, everyone at the funeral home had grown nervous. Any move, however small, had to be made delicately.

One of the embalmers had accidentally twisted one of the dead man's fingers, forcing it to fit properly into a white glove. It had nearly cost the poor man his job. Mrs. Campbell had screamed in excruciating pain as if the guy had just hurt Edmund.

Ezechias Domexa

The dead man's measurements had been sent via email and fax to a top Italian fashion house so they can ship in the latest suit in their newest collection. A pair of $2,000 shoes just days from hitting the runway found themselves on a dead man's feet.

After many hurdles and headaches for the funeral home staff, Edmund was finally ready for the funeral service at Emmanuel Baptist Church. Properly packaged, handsomely laid down in his impressive costume. It was a handsome, charismatic Edmund P. Campbell send-off — very inspiring.

But this person I was looking at was not the man my mother and I had buried just a few months before. It was a completely different person in every possible, imaginable way.

He came with nothing: no fancy shoes, no top-of-the-line casket, no expensive suit, and no jewelry — in fact, no mundane glamor at all. Oh vanity! What a waste! If only man knew!

He had lost all manner of his earthly dignity. He came in his natural outfit: naked.

His head held straight; he saw everyone he had known during his glory days.

The look on her face was completely unrecognizable: the hurt, the pain, the suffering were so vivid that every shred of joy in her seemed to have been depleted. But I felt a connection between the two of them that God alone could comprehend. She neither spoke, nor swallowed, nor even blinked.

A soft, rhythmic drumming began in the silence. It sounded far-off. Soon a bass note hummed along with it, and a grinding voice I thought was Peter Gabriel began to sing a lyric that spoke the story of many.

Am I All Alone?
I was born in the night of a full moon
In a fields of dreams, and joy and laugher

181

SEAT OF TRUTH

Among giant men, with smiles of hope,
With love and games and dance and songs
  One winter day I settled down as expected of
    all man
Later in that same year my twin boys were born.
Never knew the price from whom all blessings flow
For the vile that stains and dwells in me has
    grown so strong
Oh! What have I done wrong?
Am I all alone? Am I all alone?
Where are the friends I walked with all these long
    years?
Where is my father? Has anyone seen my mother?
What about my brother? Have you seen my wife?
Oh! Am I all alone? Am I all alone?
What have I done wrong?
A wife and two newborns, a job and a mortgage
Little time left to question my own existence
As the years went by, old age crawled in slowly
Feeling the sadness and weakening in all my bones
I questioned my provenance, got answers here and
    there
But the vile that stains and dwells in me has
    grown for so long
And of course in the end I thought I would have
    more time
Oh! What have I done wrong?
Am I all alone? Am I all alone?

The music faded away as it had begun, slowly. I never learned who had sung that song. In fact, no one in the Heavens knows. It is believed to be the story of mankind, according to Flannighans. As only him could say something like that.

182

With all the strength she could possibly muster, my mother whispered the only word and the only name she could: "Edmund?" in a desperate tone, out of rage, out of hope. She visibly fought the urge to withhold her emotion as tears streamed down her cheeks. Edmund seemed to attempt to return the love, only to bow down in shame. The tears in his eyes proved his regret about the course of life he had chosen to pursue with the few short years God had granted him. He looked at everyone, and once again confessed that he had had choices about his destiny. And today, he stood alone before the Throne of the Mighty God of the universe with his choices about to be unveiled and judged. He had never known that a day like this would come.

Who would have thought the life of a man so full of energy and will, a man who had planned for the next fifty years or so, would come to an abrupt end in the prime of his life? But time has its own agenda and it moves faster than most of us think. He never knew that the moment he opened his eyes he began to die, as someone once said.

After many unspoken words and a flood of heart-wrenching emotions, the trial was finally ready to begin.

CHAPTER TWENTY-SIX

The million-dollar question

In a slow, sweet, and authoritative voice the Great Judge spoke.

"As you all know, sadly, as often as can be, Counselor Tshembow and his team come here to collect souls. Souls that are so precious to me; souls that cost me everything; souls that can't be bought, but by the blood of my beloved Son Jesus."

Tshembow and his team fell to their knees at the mention of the name of Jesus. "But because of my justice, my infinite and absolute nature to be truthful and just, I find myself obliged to invite them to bring forth their accusations before the court in the trial of my own children. So today he comes to collect the soul of one of them. May justice be rendered at last!" The crowd cheered.

"What are your accusations against my son, Counselor Tshembow?" God asked bluntly.

"Oh, uh! Your Honor," Tshembow said in his British accent, "Edmund knew full well that the penalty for sin is death — eternal death, as you guys call it up here. He died in

complacency, without the Son. So I am here to collect his soul."
The crowd roared in disbelief. "Yes, he did die without the Son,"
Tshembow confirmed as he turned to face the audience.

"Do you have proof for your accusations, Counselor
Tshembow?" God asked with a piercing glare.

"Yes, I do. Your Honor." He produced a list of
transgressions in a folder: the seven deadly sins. God studied
them and handed them back.

"How does the defendant plead?" God asked, now looking at
Edmund for an answer.

The crowd chanted: "*Not guilty! Not guilty! Not guilty!*"

"Order! Order! Order in my court!" God said. The crowd fell
silent.

Edmund kept his head down.

Everyone was waiting.

"Not guilty, Father," a sweet voice echoed from far off. And
there, at the back of the court, between two large pillars, stood
Jesus. He was dressed in a large purple priest's robe crossed over
with a golden sash and belts. He walked slowly and looked
ravishingly handsome. Behind Him trailed a white veil that filled
the entrance. Tshembow cast a sudden look in the general
direction where the voice had come from. His eyes opened wide
in shock and surprise. With much uncertainty, he whispered
Jesus? as he again fell to his knees. The crowd went wild with
excitement. The Alpha and The Omega looked at Jesus from the
far end of the hall and smiled with an expression of complete
satisfaction, as if to say, *that's my boy!*

Jesus walked up the aisle confidently and came face to face
with Counselor Tshembow in the center. Edmund and everyone
else seemed to breathe a sigh of hope.

An angel came and removed the trailing robe, and Jesus was
left in a cream and purple ephod.

185

SEAT OF TRUTH

"Let it begin!" Tshembow shouted in a high-pitched voice. And his team cheered him on. A little.

It was a face-off, with one Counselor on the right of the chair, the other on the left.

Tensions were high.

Expectations were uncertain.

Everything was about to be revealed.

God opened His mouth, and a voice I had yet to experience shouted as if thunder had reverberated throughout the Heavens. The voice echoed and resonated; it drilled into every part of us. It came as if with every single letter pronounced. "Edmund P. Campbell, what have you done on earth with your forty-two years, six months, two weeks, five days, seventeen hours, twenty-three minutes, and thirty-six seconds?"

A jolt hit Edmund hard at the mere stating of his full name. I'm sure you've been called out by your full name, including your middle name, especially when caught doing something bad? *Oh boy!* I thought.

Eternity stiffened. Everything froze, and every eye was on Edmund.

What a moment!

In his other life, he was used to asking the questions. He had been the one calling the shots.

The first time I saw him in action, he was beyond impressive. Some public relations firm had sued the family business for millions over contractual terms of engagement. This, of course, attracted the attention of the press and everyone with a basic certificate in anything legal or paralegal. After three weeks of wrangling with the system, invoking all manner of laws, it was enough. The court was filled with reporters, colleagues, judges, and everyone with an interest in law. Edmund gave lethal blow after blow to his opponent and paraded his extensive knowledge.

186

He paused from time to time, walked around in his expensive suit as if he owned the justice system. He called on article after article, witness after witness, case after case, strutting in the courtroom proud as a peacock, and showing off his academic prowess in legal matters. He stood before the jury of twelve men and women and charmed them with witty remarks and clever exposition, as was his expertise. He brought them to their knees in the end. The verdict was an obvious one.

After a thriving few years he was featured in the glossy cover of a law review magazine as the new face of the Melon, Bulk and Ellis firm. Donned in a dark grey suit, crisp baby-blue t-shirt, Windsor knot-tied cravat and in bold title, The Future Face of Melon, Bulk and Ellis Law Firm.

Who truly knows the future?

Now Edmund P. Campbell, JD and a strategist, could not plea-bargain. How surprising life can be! He couldn't plead *Not Guilty by Reason of Insanity*. Could this really be happening? It is really abhorrent how one minute you can be making plans and the next you're no more. How sad and strange! Life is indeed a lonely, winding road.

He could call on no trained witnesses, or doctors with degrees in psychology who would play the game with words that none could find in the dictionary, just to confuse the jury, to cover the lies. Those days were over.

Edmund knew without knowing how he knew that there was no space to play in these procedures. He also knew that this time, he could no longer afford the tenderness and the presumption of innocence his peers would have granted him for his reputation. No more favor.

No psychiatric evaluation was needed: everyone was, and will be perfectly fit to stand trial in the Heavens someday. It's a one-time appointment before the Mercy Seat, and that's it. No

SEAT OF TRUTH

leather briefcases filled with documents, no fancy suits to impress people, no jury in seclusion, no one is angry — it is where all appearances are banished forever.

Edmund seemed to ponder at how he used to call the shots, how he used to pose in the courtrooms as if he owned eternity. Except this time he wasn't the one running the show. He was on the hot seat, the Seat of Truth.

He opened up the gate of his extraordinary memory and began to empty the contents of a human soul that was once a mighty fortress of secrets. The best you'll ever be in the end, and the most you'll ever be left with, are memories. For the time that passed erases nothing, no matter how long that time is.

Edmund seized the moment to collect himself, as if he had come from afar with all the details possible about his own life, to tell a sad tale of nearly forty plus years of foolishness and a vagabond life.

Please take a seat. Let's see how it all plays out, shall we?

CHAPTER TWENTY-SEVEN

Birth of a Legend.
Every birth is registered in the Heavens: year, season,
month, week, day, hour, minute, and second.
A small party and an unwelcome guest.

On November 19th of 1973, a clear Monday morning, at exactly 10:34:27, Heaven and Earth registered the birth of Edmund P. Campbell, weighing five pounds and seven ounces, in a West Palm Beach Medical Center. It was a boy.

Autumn was already halfway through. With temperatures in the 70s throughout south Florida, the sun began to warm the empty blue sky. It was a beautiful day.

Edmund measured twenty-two inches long. Born naturally blonde. He appeared hairless to the naked eye his mother pointed out, but he was full of hair.

With bright eyes, a narrow nose and cute little ears, he was an almost ridiculous replica of his father. He was forever tagged with two nearly invisible scars — if one might call them that — one hidden right under his little left butt cheek, and a small purple dot on his left groin.

189

SEAT OF TRUTH

He carried another scar on his left cheek too, that seemed to grow each time he smiled.

His fragile little body carried 60 ounces of purified liquid water and a rather small supply of unsullied blood, precisely 6 ounces, running up and down between his little heart and the rest of his little body at high speed. All had been neatly fashioned in the matrix of the womb of his mother, Mrs. Gandalf P. Campbell.

He had no earrings, no piercings, no tattoos, no shoes, and no clothes. He came naked.

His little fingers moved frantically, as if already trying to claim stuff. He was praising the name of the Lord because the Old Fashion Book said: "Out of the mouth of babes and nursing infants, He ordained praises." But who can understand worship in waving hands, constant crying, and whining?

He was born into a wealthy family, to Mr. and Mrs. Gandalf P. Campbell, well known and respected in the West Palm Beach community. They named him Edmund P. Campbell. He joined his brother, three years older, Mitch P. Campbell.

The delivery room was almost full. Besides the family, those present included a woman named Atelia, the boys' nanny. Three doctors and four nurses were also visibly present. There was, however, someone else that no one could see — someone who was not invited, someone who wasn't welcome, yet he was present: Tshembow was there.

Tshembow was there as much as everyone else was there.

He had come to ensure the damnation of the boy, to sow the seed of lust and pride. Then he'd sit on his ass and watch the boy grow in the fullness of life with which comes death.

He was there because the child was conceived of sin. Yet he was sinless.

190

He touched him, yet could not harm him. He held him, yet could not take him. He wanted him badly, yet could not have him. Not yet.

Not now.

He envied him.

He had as much interest in the boy's safety as everyone else, for his gain lay ahead. So he'd lie down for the child where the boy might have hurt himself. He wished not to kill him — not now, at least, for his soul would be forfeited. He was to babysit, play, protect, and smile. The boy smiled plenty too. He knew not the consequences of the fruit of knowledge and death. For him Tshembow was funny. How innocent! But Tshembow hated that word. He hated the boy's wiggling little feet; he hated his constant smile. But he admired his weekly growth, for with the spread of life comes the responsibility of choice. He looked at him and licked his drooling mouth. He patted his boney skeleton head; he scratched his ass; he wiggled like a dog playing with his own tail; he roared around him like a lion, lurking in the shadows, waiting. He knew the law because he had been there when it all began.

The child opened his beautiful grey eyes and met for the first time the woman who gave him life and smiled at her. He stared at her for a long moment and moved his eyes across the room setting them on his older brother Mitch. He wiggled his little feet and smiled even broader. His brother smiled back while holding his little fingers.

The baby turned and set his gaze on his father and recognized him immediately.

He switched his eyes from one doctor to the next until he reached Atelia. He blinked at her and smiled and then closed his eyes for the longest sleep in his babyhood. And just like that, the race for his soul had begun.

CHAPTER TWENTY-EIGHT

Some very important people-
A maid with no last name
Edmund's childhood stories
A small family gathering
Starring Atelia and the Campbells.

I thought the people we met throughout our lifetime were random, total strangers we weren't necessarily meant to have any relationship with. How many falsehoods could anyone hold?

In our lifetime, explained my daughter Ms. Dylan, we meet many people from all races and all walks of life. That's because they have a purpose in our life. It is a mutual responsibility. Some people come into our life to cause drama, some to ask us questions, some to love us, others to hate us and steal from us; another bunch to backstab us, to borrow and never pay us back, to put us down, and to tell on us; others to manipulate and control us; some to support us, help us, stand with us then leave without explanation. Some to break our heart, humiliate us, cause us unbearable pain; some to betray our trust, abuse our good basic nature; others to help us and feed us; a few to pray with us.

Some of these people come into our lives to stay for a while, and others stay longer than a while. I later learned that there are also those we meet only once in our lifetime and never see them again. It wowed me to discover there were people created just to smile at us in a very specific place — at the bus stop, at the train station, at the ticket counter, in the workplace, at the library, in high school, at the bank, at the barbershop — and it might happen only once. And just like that, they've served their purpose in our life, and they're gone. And likewise, just a few will stay until the end.

Ms. Dylan had told us that life is like a movie, except everybody is the main character in his or her own story — the others are extras. She also told us that those stories have no title. When I asked her why, she said all the stories are really part of the big story, which is called *The Story of Us All, the Story of Mankind*. Because they're all connected to Oneness.

I smiled.

Let me tell you the story of someone in whose tale I played a small role — more than an extra, I would say.

Let's just say that I was very close to the main characters. See for yourself.

Introducing Atelia: The Maid of Honor

You have already met her. But let me show you how our lives were purposefully brought together.

Atelia's coming into our lives was no accident, but a carefully engineered plan. Now I know. It all makes sense.

SEAT OF TRUTH

She wasn't married and had no kids, no relatives whatsoever. In fact, no one really knew her last name. Atelia's life is one of the saddest, funniest, and yet most captivating tales, and you wouldn't want to miss it. However one might look at it, it had purpose beyond ordinary sight.

Not that she couldn't afford a man, as she always put it — she just could not stand the idea of marrying someone or being owned by a simple man. The prospect of spending that much time with a total stranger wasn't appealing to her, she explained.

She left West Palm Beach for the second time for an arranged marriage that didn't happen. Three days after she left our house she came back with all her luggage, never unpacked. She protested mightily that she couldn't stand so many rules: being behind somebody twenty-four hours a day, seven days a week, for the rest of your life — and emphasized on the numbers too.

Every man has an incurable and intolerable defect, one that certainly can't be fixed.

The second arranged marriage — one she considered to be an unforgivable insult — also caused a four-year break with her best friend Daniela who had arranged the affair.

It was something to listen to, when Atelia is telling us tales of men and women and their outrageous adventures in love, loss, pain, and redemption. Every story ended happily ever after. She loved happy ending stories.

Some nights, during our nightly storytelling she claimed that she was from the western part of Puerto Rico. Another night she'd come from somewhere in the Caribbean, born to a wealthy family, and her parents had divorced but sent her to live with her grandmother in West Palm Beach.

One particular night I picked up my geography book that had a large map of the world and the flags of all the countries. I asked her if she could show us where she'd come from. She

194

looked at the map, puzzled, and pulled it closer. "If you were from Puerto Rico...," I said, pointing on the map to the location of Puerto Rico and the corresponding flag. But Atelia's finger wandered into western Brazil and she said, "I think ... I come from there."

"Impossible! That's Brazil," I said.

"No, no! Not from there," she replied quickly in disgust, as if Brazil were diseased. Then she returned to the map and made her way to Europe. When her finger stopped near the Arabian Sea, near Russia, and seemed to be certain this time, my dad said, "Enough geography for one night."

She was between six to seven years old when she came to live with my grandparents, she said. In fact, she later recounted that she was used as currency to pay back a loan to Gandalf's father. While bargaining on the phone, the debtor looked at her as she — coincidentally — was passing by and suddenly found the solution for his debt crisis. "Oh! I ... I have an idea," he said, gazing at her longingly.

"What is it?" Gandalf's father shot back.

"I found something."

"You found *what?*" he barked.

"A little girl."

"A little girl? Where did you find her?"

"Look, let's not get hung up about all that. I know you need someone to play with your kids and do basic cleaning." And just like that, the debtor drove her over to a warehouse and settled his delinquent account.

Atelia had no recollection of birthplace or her birthday. "Anyway, that's not important," she always answered. Some nights when stories were told around the table, she claimed to be my great-grandfather's distant cousin. In other episodes she remembered full well her mother's name: Sephora. She said

195

Sephora was a guitarist and that she still remembered songs that her mother had sung to her in her crib.

She delivered her stories with grace and a sense of privilege and never said anything impudent. Her eyes, although filled with hurt and pain, were warm with secrets, and above all, hope.

Generally speaking, neighbors agreed and disagreed with many of those accounts. Some, for instance — the Hamiltons — believed they had seen her among other kids who came with their parents from a non-denominational Baptist church in Jacksonville Florida, on a mission in West Palm Beach. The parents probably forgot her. The neighbors thought someone would notice and would later come back for her, but no one did. However, other families — the Crawfords and the Moets, for instance — insisted that they had seen her long before the mission even came to the county. They said her mother was indeed a blind guitarist, who took off with a bass player to Nashville Tennessee, in search for fame and left the child with someone who later died of a bizarre combination of maladies. The Eisenbergs however, had a totally different theory. They swore on anything holy that the mother was indeed blind but not a guitarist — a pianist instead — who married a far away soldier of some rank, traveled abroad, and left the child with the missionaries.

If, in fact, Atelia found difficulty in tracing her true origin and parenthood, she found her calling in matters of the kitchen and in raising two boys. Entrusted with two young boys, Mitch and Edmund, over time she mastered the arts of nutrition, and wowed private and elite society with her culinary prowess — and that, the neighbors would testify to. Predestined to instill a sense of love in the lives of a loving family, to teach two boys how to love, how to pray, how to share and read, she was the carrier of something greater than could be perceived by the naked eye, and she accomplished perfectly what she was created for, hence the mutual hatred between her and Tshembow.

CHAPTER TWENTY-NINE

Some law practitioners
How to practice law on earth
The beginning of the fall
Why does Death always tackle
humans from behind?

After four years as an undergrad in Florida, followed by three rigorous years in a respectable law school in New York, Edmund P. Campbell strolled down the streets of Manhattan with a big smile. He had just received news that he had nailed the bar exam. He could not help but celebrate.

Today he could plan his future.

He had been offered a great position at a prestigious law firm that he truly admired and where he was articling, despite his parents' lamenting plea that he come home to practice law in the family business. He would deal with the family later. Now he wanted to savor the moment alone. He wanted to take the opportunity to thank himself with a pat on the back: the sleepless nights, the fatigue, the research papers, and the long hours of internship in the attic vaults of mega firms. He needed a break. He needed a drink.

He entered a well-known steakhouse in Upper Manhattan and ordered a full meal. As he sipped red wine quietly in a corner booth, he grinned at his future. More so he was smiling at what he had found four months earlier, something he had shared with no soul. But did he know that anything that is not shared becomes a secret, and that secrets are burdens, and that burdens are the very weight that bring us all down? He smiled at all the possibilities — the glory and the recognition. He seemed to think that he had found the Holy Grail.

More wine followed. *How often did you find the Holy Grail?* He asked himself time after time.

Four months ago, he had driven to a Salvation Army store on the outskirts of Toms River, New Jersey, to buy a defunct computer on which to save a few things he deemed necessary. Upon his arrival the store was closed, but he found two Mexicans, hard at work, unloading a truck of used electronics goods. "Hey guys, you think I can buy a used computer from you?"

"No hard drive, fifty bucks," the thin one said as he negligently grabbed a computer box and handed it to Edmund. He paid the money and disappeared.

As soon as he got home he inspected his bargain to see if the Mexicans had looted him of fifty bucks, only to notice that there was a hard drive present.

He quickly hooked the computer to a waiting monitor and switched it on. After passing a series of Windows protocols and antivirus screens, the computer screen flickered, and opened up with all the icons, bypassing all password parameters.

He looked at the screen, puzzled. He clicked on one icon and began to read, and then closed it. He clicked on another icon,

SEAT OF TRUTH

read it, and closed it. He couldn't believe what he was staring at. He bolted upright, locked the door, closed the curtains on his tiny windows, and started shaking.

For four straight months he read the trail of emails, documents, depositions, banking statements, tax filings, contact names, contracts, propositions, evaluations, offers, real estate transactions, government relations, offshore account details, land ownership statements, and every juicy and scandalous detail of a firm he had, during his law school years, thought was a fairy tale.

He lost half his weight in the wee hours of the night printing, copying, organizing, classifying, and categorizing box upon box of printouts in chronological order.

His roommate had long since declared that law was not for him and had moved out of the tiny two-bedroom apartment, although they had agreed and sworn — on paper — not to break the lease. Lodging was hard to come by, especially in New York, and the price tag that came with it was too often exorbitant.

Edmund used all of his savings to buy a fancy copy machine. He hauled it into the now-available tiny bedroom. He planned to call his folks for backup, particularly his brother, if it came to that.

He gave up all social activities at the firm and with former classmates, and he stopped taking phone calls from the Korean girl he had met on his orientation day at Mellon, Bulk and Ellis — Seo-Yun something. They had been touching each other in the parking lot since day one until they became dizzy and turned pink. Since then she had talked nonstop about getting married and starting her own family. During one of their episodes of frolicking, she asked him if and when he wanted to get married, and he couldn't remember if he — as he was ripping off her clothes — had said yes or no or maybe, or if in fact he had made

200

any promises. He waved at her from a safe distance and hurried into a closing elevator. He was too busy.

Was it luck or faith that brought him these documents? He again asked himself. But the answers to that question and to so many more proved elusive.

He had bought extra locks for his apartment door and for the tiny windows. He learned from the Internet how to install an alarm and monitor it from a distance. He became more suspicious in the streets than he had ever been. He looked over his shoulder unnecessarily, glanced in his right and left mirror anxiously, as if he were being followed.

At first he was skeptical about the authenticity and potential of the documents. But the more he dwelled into the murky world of the business dealings of the law firm of Alt and The Rosenbergs, the more he was convinced that the horrible stories of law breaking at the firm were indeed very much true.

No stories could ever come close to describing the Alt and The Rosenbergs myth, usually known simply as Alt & The Rosens. The firm was a one-stop boutique for anyone who could afford prime fees for government relations (foreign and local), land ownership and acquisition, offshore accounts, tax manipulation, big-shot lobbyists, and anything dirty that was not advertised on the menu.

After Edmund had organized everything — case studies, files, faxes, judgments, corporate dossiers, and depositions — he pondered his next move. *Who should I tell?* That question alone was nearly novel-length because it raised even more questions — actually the real ones, like, where did you find them? How did you get them? No one would ever believe him.

Or should he go to Alt & The Rosens and tell them what he'd found?

He played it out in his head. It didn't sound pretty convincing. "Hi, Mr. Rosenberg, my name is Edmund P. Campbell. I work for Mellon, Bulk and Ellis. Last week I found your hard drive in a junk truck, and it's full of corruption-related documents that the Feds are looking for, but I wanted to give it to you."

No.

Not a chance.

They would just shoot him on the spot.

Despite his struggle, deep down in his heart, he knew what he wanted to do.

****

He retrieved the offer letter he had received earlier from Mellon, Bulk and Ellis and considered his next move.

He mulled over the idea for two weeks, playing out different scenarios in his head, how to approach them with what he now knew. The good thing though, was that Mellon, Bulk and Ellis had offered him an associate position. There was no way he would want to risk this wonderful offer and the law firm's reputation, especially that of the great man whom he considered his mentor.

One early morning during his internship he had stumbled upon Alex Mellon Jr. in the elevator struggling with a few boxes. He quickly offered his assistance and helped the great man all the way to his vast corner suite on the top floor of the fifty-seven-story building that housed the fourth largest law firm in New York.

A cute secretary quickly brought fresh bagels and orange juice. As they ate, they talked nonstop about nothing but law — after all, that's what had brought them together.

Alex Mellon Jr. and a few founding partners of the firm had been smiling secretly at Edmund's skills since his first week.

They admired his ambition, his ideas and approaches. They had closely studied his research and agreed that his recommendations were beyond impressive. But Alex had never met him in person until that morning.

Edmund had dazzled him with his legal prowess and how he fancied himself and dreamed to even best him someday. That morning a mutual friendship was born. It was an immediate and genuine bond forged around the judiciary system.

It was the great man, Alex Mellon Jr., who took Edmund to his first court trial. He gave him his first case. And boy! Edmund had been born for this.

Edmund had never met the six founding members of the firm personally. During his first week of orientation at Mellon, Bulk and Ellis, he sat in the middle of nearly three hundred prospects. He had only seen profiles of the founders from the lectern as they took turns replaying old battles from their lengthy careers. Oh, how they loved to talk while half of the interns were asleep!

Edmund replayed the scenes over and over again and went for it.

"Let me see if I get this straight." Alex Mellon Jr. sat upright in his fine leather chair. "You want me to convene the partners for an emergency meeting without me knowing why. Am I correct?" the great man said sternly after Edmund had made his pitch.

"Yes, you're correct."

"I'm afraid that's not possible!" Alex said.

"Everything is possible, with a little push." Edmund was matter-of-fact with his mentor.

Alex laughed at what he was hearing, more so at what he was thinking: *Either this boy had found the Holy Grail of all legal matters or he's full of shit.*

SEAT OF TRUTH

"Your father once said, 'the biggest battles in the courtroom are won by gut feelings, not by what you can find in books.'" Edmund knew if there was someone who could bring the old folks together, it was Alex Mellon Jr. The partners respected and trusted him. He was a baby boomer and had a sense of discipline that they cherished. In a way, he had not only kept the old wolves' truce — their work ethic and their vision for the firm — but over time he had inserted his own modern twist, making the firm a fusion of the aged and youth. "We don't have much time sir, do we?" Edmund added and left his superior's office knowing full well he had him.

Alex Mellon Jr. remained in his chair staring at the sun rising in the distance. The boy had specifically asked that only the *founding* partners be at the meeting, not those who had made partner over the years, he thought. He had been in court a few times now with Edmund. The boy had proven time after time that his skills as a defense strategist were unmatched, and most partners knew that.

He reckoned that it wouldn't be an easy task to convince some of the old men that a twenty-something recent law graduate, lucky enough to have been offered a job was asking for a private meeting. *Is he asking for a raise already?* His refusal to disclose the reasons for the meeting was mysterious and strange, oddly uncomfortable but curious.

Alex Mellon Jr. was not a founding partner, but he was the son of Alex Mellon Sr. — the link between the founding partners and the currently active firm. He pulled some strings and succeeded at bringing the men together at one of their Hamptons vacation homes for the secret meeting.

CHAPTER THIRTY

Everything that is sparkled isn't gold.
— Law firm dismemberment
The beginning of the fall.

The meeting took place on a late September evening after the men had eaten enough roast lamb, and had drunk enough vintage wine. They made a few pleasantries about politics, the economy and the stock market. The waitress came to refill their coffee cups and retreated into the kitchen. Mellon Jr. stood up and cleared his throat. Every eye now focused on him. He smiled shyly.

He was a man of few words.

"I took a big chance in trusting someone I had the pleasure to work a few cases with and to bring you here not even knowing why. You have taught me" — he turned to his father, who sat next to him holding a cane — "that sometimes it's a gut feeling that wins us the biggest battles, not our savvy in matters of the law. Tonight, I have taken that advice, hoping there's something in what Edmund Campbell has to say. Edmund?" He turned to him, but the look in his eyes said, *It had better be good, or I swear* ... "I present to you the founding partners of Mellon, Bulk & Ellis. Please state your business."

"Thank you sir," Edmund said as he leapt to his feet, pulling his chair aside to make some room for himself. "I'm honored to have finally met the legends that brought this great firm to be what it is today. I've read your bios, how you've built your way to greatness — you're nothing short of inspiration. Although

205

I've yet to officially accept the firm's offer of one hundred fifty thousand a year as an associate, I consider myself family already." He noticed some faint fake smiles among them. Then he went straight for it. "Your first court date with Alt & the Rosens regarding the Wyndell Group is two months from today." Every jaw at the table dropped, every body shifted left and right in shock, as the men searched for answers as to why he had raised this. Edmund let it sink in. It did.

"How did you know about this?" one of the more elderly men barked, standing weakly, leaning for support on his chair.

"It's best that you don't know, Mr. Bulk. I'm here to tell you we can win the whole thing without ever going to court. But Project Fox has to be done *my* way." Bulk looked at him as if he might just kick him in the groin.

Project Fox, as the case was now referred to, was almost a myth in the firm for many years, and for good reason. No one really knew what it was about, who was involved, or if it was even real. In fact, it was so secretive that the files were kept on a different server, one that only the founding partners and some chosen senior partners were allowed to access, and occasionally a few lucky executive assistants.

After Edmund admitted how much he knew about the case, he explained — with legal implications and security cautions — that the founding partners' being left in the dark about his knowledge would be better for all. "Believe me," he said, "it's best that none of you know what I know and how. Simply let me lead the defense strategy team. Let me call the shots behind the scene."

Ellis let out a loud laugh as if he had just heard the best joke ever. But the laugh was really showing how impressed he was with this twenty-something lawyer who seemed far ahead of his time and career. If what he said was true — and all of it was — Alt & the Rosens was going to be history.

"What about *your* safety?" Mellon asked him, showing a little compassion, a little caring.

"It's the law, gentlemen. May the best firm win," Edmund said smugly, and they all laughed.

A few tales about Edmund had found their way into the founding partners' Hamptons vacation homes before this. The six founding partners had never expressed much enthusiasm to meet him personally, however they had unanimously selected him as the best future lawyer for their firm and had agreed to offer him a higher salary as an associate than his peers. They had gone through all the interns and selected the few lucky ones who had proven their worth. Edmund P. Campbell had gone beyond. He was ambitious, smart and intelligent. He was ruthless.

But little did Edmund know that some eighteen years later, those documents would be the last nail in his coffin and the moment he decided to use them, his destiny was forever altered.

***

Two months after that evening meeting, Edmund P. Campbell led his Mellon, Bulk and Ellis team to worldwide victory. Under his brilliant strategies he crippled the massive firm of Alt & the Rosens into financial ruin and shame. By midafternoon that last day, the twenty-four-year-old recent law grad's name was spreading like wildfire and sending shockwaves through the world of law pundits. Before sunset there were talks of major law firms circling around like vultures to yank the boy out of sight. He was one of the many products that law schools around the country were putting out onto the streets as if they were coming from an assembly line, to defend the law, to bring justice, to bring balance to the system, and to serve.

SEAT OF TRUTH

Edmund was so unique in his skills as a defense lawyer that professors, partners, associates and judges agreed among themselves and feared as well, that such talent would ruin many lives.

Mellon, Bulk and Ellis officially added one more weapon to their defense arsenal.

The firm offered him all the top perks: private planes, private dinners, private this, private that. They bounced him through rich and glamorous circles where he could contemplate the glitz and glamor of his bright future. At the time young Edmund felt he could go on like this forever.

For the welcome ceremony they flew him to Barbados for a long-weekend retreat, where the firm's partners lived in lavish style, in over-the-top multi-million-dollar beach condos with young gals as complementary gifts to do with as they pleased, and no one really cared. Edmund was the new kid on the block. He alone could send big guys running and hiding into the safety of bankruptcy and plea-bargaining. In the grip of plain selfishness and belligerence, he let himself get caught up in the sad reality of a sophisticated society driven by success and greed and attention seekers. He thought he had wings that could take him to the moon.

Back home in Florida, however, it was a different story. In spite of all his success, accomplishments and money, his thriving career wasn't well perceived by his parents. There were murmurs and groans and expressions of concern. There were always questions, until he returned home some years later. For the love of his father, Gandalf P. Campbell, and to fulfill his dying wish, Edmund left Manhattan and came to Florida to establish his own strategic consulting firm.

CHAPTER THIRTY-ONE

How long to plot a revenge?
The residual of resentment and greed
The things that keep us wide awake
— Live each day as if it is your last.

The law firm of Alt & The Rosens had remained closed for the majority of the past fifteen years ever since a twenty-something law grad laid bare their secrets and sent them into hiding in shame and public disgrace. Except for the caretaker who came once a month to make sure the lawn stayed somewhat short, apart from that, the place seemed abandoned and haunted. The Feds had used it for their lengthy investigation after the raid, then had turned it over to an international corporation that negligently passed it down to a secret real estate firm attached to none other than Alt, the oldest of the Rosenberg brothers and the leading man behind the firm's success.

The senior partners scattered across the country, licking their wounds in solitary retirement, lost in twilight horizon about what had really happened. How had their lies been exposed? The law

SEAT OF TRUTH

firm, once a powerhouse, had faded faster than smoke into the clouds.

If truth be told, there wasn't much to mourn about, really. Because sadly, Alt and The Rosens law firm was where embezzlers learned how to trick the system; where thieves came to hide their stolen goods; where liars mastered their craft. In other words, Alt & the Rosens was a crooks' college.

They had created mayhem in several different markets, and then waited to reap the benefits. Although law enforcement had questioned the coincidences and their apparent good luck, the firm had always remained innocent in the eyes of the system, never having been proven guilty.

Their wildly successful tactics were later revealed in the manipulation of stock markets, in staging major construction accidents, in causing fires, in contaminating pharmaceutical products, and in twisting arms and legs among other things.

Stories about Alt & the Rosens were no secret. Anyone with a basic certificate in anything legal heard them — every vile joke, bit of fast cash, and bridge burner. That was how professors woke up sleeping students: with a potent dose of legal fairy tales about Alt & the Rosens.

The young partners and associates however, rebuilt their careers. One can always start over, and that's a good thing.

Alt & the Rosens, brothers and criminals, founding partners were in their late sixties now. After the fall their appetite for late-night bedroom games had rapidly declined. Their only interests now were golf and fishing on good days, which seldom came. Grudges and the thought of revenge consumed much of their quiet lives and they lived with an eternal howling anger that they weren't able to move past, so they grew twice older than the average citizen of their age.

They had fought mightily in high courts, but document after document was produced. The epic fall of Alt & the Rosens became inevitable — the end of nearly one billion dollars in assets, half a billion a year in revenue, and offices spanning thirteen countries and four continents.

The law firm of Alt & The Rosens was known for its aggressiveness and coercion of clients into spending fortunes for all sorts of services. Although numerous complaints were filed against the firm, no government could prove anything. So it had thrived. But this time, at the height of the fall, multiple branches of law enforcement had raided their headquarters in Manhattan and other offices worldwide, and prison became a sanctuary for most partners.

The Rosenbergs had vigorously maintained their innocence. They had worked hard on the phone, pulled strings, drawn on resources, and called in favors owed by politicians, senators, friends and governors to avoid prison time. In the end, all assets were seized and sold at public auction. With what little was left, their wives walked away.

Fortunately for the men, the judicial system slapped their wrists with a measly five years in prison each, five years of house arrest, and ten years of probation, and the state bars revoked their licenses to practice law.

Alt, the eldest of the brothers had lost his penthouse in New York and his second home in DC. Federal thugs had hauled away the private plane and the yacht the partners shared. Alt retreated to an old barn in the Midwest where he milked cows, rode horses and cursed his ex-wives and everyone else in the world.

The business of law practice is fragile in its very nature. Friendship and loyalty are hard to maintain. The other law firms laughed their butts off and celebrated with expensive

SEAT OF TRUTH

Champagne and caviar the fall of the mighty Alt & The Rosens. "Hypocrites!" Alt Rosenberg declared as he turned off the TV and flung the remote control somewhere behind the couch.

Over the years Alt Rosenberg had managed to begin a casual, but equally pricey relationship with a former partner at Mellon, Bulk and Ellis. Slowly but surely new pieces of information began to fit the puzzle. What he had learned so far proved very useful and unsettling. None of the partners at Mellon, Bulk and Ellis were aware of documents, the acquaintance explained. They were simply to take direction from the defense strategist, the new kid. Names were not revealed until later.

Alt Rosenberg had always maintained that someone must have gotten their hands on their servers, or worse, the firm was sold out. But who would do that? Or someone must have been watching.

At their most recent yearly get-together, Alt had gone to a locked cabinet, retrieved a heavy folder, and dropped it in front of his brothers, Sheridan and Brad Rosenberg. The two looked at it as if it were contraband. Alt undertook the difficult task of telling them what had really happened and who had destroyed their lives and bourgeoning careers. After he had explained in crisp detail, going from document to document, and video to video, both his brothers were stunned. And then he showed them a trap he'd devised for payback. The three brothers shared a smile.

***

The setup had taken some years to prepare, he told his brothers. Ten years, nine months, three weeks, and four days, to be exact. The traitor, as Alt referred to Edmund, was to meet a man by the name of Wong Dan Lee in China — supposedly an insider in a medical supplier and manufacturing conglomerate, Manu-Med

212

Corporation. This informant had privileged and classified information that Edmund's firm could use for leverage. Manu-Med Corporation was looking for a strategic consulting firm for their new venture in the south Florida market. They were looking for someone who knew the system well. The informant had proven extremely resourceful with inside information, and was extensively conversant concerning the business of Manu-Med Corporation.

Edmund took the bait.

CHAPTER THIRTY-TWO

Who needs a license to kill?
Who wants to die young raise your hand?
The uncertainty of the system and the cunning of man
The fall of a hero.

The two-level airplane landed at exactly 10:00 a.m. local time outside Hong Kong International Airport where a line of cabs waited. Edmund stepped out of the entrance and a black limousine pulled right in front of him. The driver quickly identified himself, and with no hesitation Edmund accepted his invitation and took a seat in the idling vehicle. Then they took off.

The Mandarin Oriental Hong Kong hotel was the top portion of a majestic structure boasting an incomparable view of Victoria Harbor surrounded by gleaming skyscrapers. Edmund sat in the high hotel suite stuffing cash into a brown manila envelope admiring the view of the island below. This was just a tip for the informant, who had offered all the inside info about the family that owned the medical supplier and their business model.

At the first sign of the afternoon rush hour, Edmund left the hotel and headed in the general direction of downtown. He ventured deeper into the abyss of the main marketplace and exited into a street known as The Mask. Everyone entering it had to wear a mask. He grabbed a mask from a kiosk, dropped some change for it, and lost himself in the world of fakers, or so he thought. But someone was watching, videotaping him all along.

He found his informant and exchanged his brown manila envelope for a thick folder without speaking a word. He made some quick detours and unnecessary stops, as if he knew someone was following him before entering his hotel lobby.

With this exchange, Edmund unknowingly infiltrated a small and equally dangerous underground gang that sold deadly poisons in the black market — poisons that had been used in various crimes throughout Asia. This new trend had left Asian governments speechless and facing a rapidly increasing crime rate. For the tons of money that had poured into forensics labs and technology, taxpayers had not seen much of a result.

For four days Edmund did nothing but read the documents, page by page, accessing the free Wi-Fi to supplement his research on the Zhao Ho Kun family. He clicked and studied the pictures of the man he would soon meet, or so he thought. He read extensively about the man's love for nature, about his devotion to his family and his employees. Then he read about his wife, Wu Li Chun, an outspoken woman, a devoted mother, and a fierce advocate of fair wages. She had been featured in several high-profile Hong Kong and Chinese fashion magazines, but was known as a down-to-earth philanthropist and a generous contributor in charitable circles. Then he read about the only son, Zhao Jia Cheng, a big fan of Western culture and sport. In fact, as a Miami Heat fan, he usually attended NBA playoff

SEAT OF TRUTH

games. According to the informant, he was also down-to-earth, harmless and friendly.

He read about the family as if he was about to interview for a mission on Mars. He now knew about the warehouse hidden in a forest — not even the government knew about that.

He studied their business ventures in Asia, Europe, and North America with great interest. Manu-Med Corporation, according to *Forbes* magazine, was the largest medical manufacturer and supplier in the world and the twelfth richest company, with fiscal revenue near two hundred billion dollars. The management team had done a marvelous job of diversifying their portfolio with business ventures in various fields, making them a worldwide go-to for medical supplies.

On Edmund's fourth day, as he was clicking and reading frantically, he heard a soft knock on the door and suddenly remembered he had ordered food and a ride to the airport. The maid entered with a tray of dim sum and kindly notified him that his ride would be ready whenever he was. He thanked her, tipped her, and headed for the shower.

***

Nearly one hour later a commotion took place in the hotel lobby, but almost no one knew about it.

When a high-profile person has died suddenly — especially if death raises doubt — and in the case of a prominent CEO such as the head of an international company, containment is a must, to maintain what is known as "shareholders' interests," in financial jargon. You wouldn't want anything less than that. Usually the family offers a simple statement about some vague ailment, a minor flux, which causes no panic whatsoever, while they put things in order behind the scenes. And later, the Board

216

would ensure a transfer of leadership for the shareholders' peace of mind. Then all hell can break loose.

The ambulance staff entered the hotel as Edmund exited the elevator. Outside, he noticed two ambulances and two fire trucks idling. He entered the waiting limousine and left Hong Kong for good, never suspecting that the man he was to meet on his next trip in the near future had just been murdered two floors above him. And that *he* was framed as the killer.

CHAPTER THIRTY-THREE

— The hunt for a killer
How far are you willing to go?

Although attempts on the life of Zhao Ho Kun were nearly impossible, there were people who would secretly cheer if he was dead.

The plot to kill the CEO was conceived at the heart of a new building under construction in downtown Hong Kong: the Mandarin Oriental Hotel.

There was a constant rat race in the hotel industry between Asian elites. Every month some new guy would claim the hottest, biggest, tallest hotel, making competition tiresome for serious developers. The Zhao family wanted to make a point. To attract international big spenders, the Zhao Group — a subdivision of Manu-Med Corporation — began the construction of a new hotel, and Zhao himself gushed that he would spend two weeks vacation each year in his new fortress. The Mandarin Oriental Hotel would be designed to the top magazines' tastes, with state-of-the-art features and presidential security for the super-rich according to preliminary reports by

Forbes magazine. Back when Alt & The Rosens law firm was at their prime, Alt Rosenberg had negotiated the contract for the company that ran the network cable for the building's infrastructure. So he infiltrated his men to plant and plan future chaos and mayhem that would later bring fortune to their firm. Thus, Alt & The Rosens had had their seed in the Presidential Suite for years. Two floors below, they had established a fiber-optic connection that supplied video and audio feeds from a series of concealed pickups in lighting fixtures, mattress, power outlets, frames, door knobs, cabinet tops, and so on. The most dangerous piece of equipment lay dormant in the shower pipes where a micro tube containing cyanide was hooked up to a needle ready to launch at the remote touch of a button.

Alt had made arrangements to reserve the suite two floors below the Presidential Suite in Edmund's honor.

***

The family's head of security was a man named Liu Han. He was a man of few words. He watched over the Zhao family as he did over his own. When it came to the safety of the Zhao family, nothing and no one could stand in his way even if it meant losing his life. He shared little with his subjects.

Liu also monitored the family assets and business locations around the world from an old warehouse where four dozen workers reported to him. With the family-owned global GPS satellite system Liu could detect every happening down to when Ms. Wu left her bedroom to go to the restroom.

Now his entire staff worked around the clock where Mr. Zhao had been killed. The hotel manager had willingly provided videotapes and the guest list for the last four weeks. Every face was scanned through a government database, and background checks on every single one of them were ordered.

SEAT OF TRUTH

An emergency family meeting was called at a quiet estate on the Chinese mainland where the family had resided for decades. At the gate, four heavily armed men bowed before Liu. He wasted no time proceeded to the front door, and was ushered inside.

He entered a large conference room containing half of China's antiquities and then another one that led to an exquisite yard not far from a majestic waterfall that delivered a breathtaking view. There, in the middle of a garden, the family sat around a small table with three chairs. Liu grunted something under his breath, bowed politely before his hosts, and quickly took his seat.

The meeting was quiet.

A basket of fresh fruit had been placed in the center of the table. Jia Cheng, the only son, protector of the family fortune, picked out a peach and calmly began to peel it. The newly widowed Ms. Wu was staring off at the view, seemingly unaware of anyone else's existence, sipping the last drops of tea from a tiny cup as if it had been magically refilled.

"Who did this?" Jia Cheng asked, with no emotion whatsoever. The head of security had kept his head down since his humble salutation knew the question was addressed to him. He raised his head and looked back where he had come from as if the answer was waiting out front.

"We don't know for sure," he said, "but the Ting and Cho families are suspected — they've caused trouble at times." He turned to look at Jia Cheng. "We have people in place, and we're expecting answers soon." His demeanor was not so certain.

"Can we think of anyone else?" Wu Li Chun questioned, wrapped in a long, silky patterned robe that looked like a nightgown. Once again with the same lack of confidence, Liu cast a distant glance over the landscape as if it might tell him

220

where to look for the killer. After a second of thought, knowing that he could not keep Ms. Wu waiting for long, he said, "We do not want to guess, but —"

"Neither do we," she broke in calmly. On that last note the head of security rose from his seat and exited the way he came. He knew exactly how to proceed.

CHAPTER THIRTY-FOUR

—What's the price for one soul?
—Who can escape the power of the grave?

Alt Rosenberg scheduled the phone call for 8:00 p.m. Beijing time, exactly six days after the death of Mr. Zhao. There was no way the call could be traced. After all, it was being made from a long forgotten warehouse in Singapore that housed a host of hardware with relay capabilities.

He spoke calmly and with confidence. He had asked to be put on speakerphone so everyone could hear him: he wasn't in the mood to repeat himself.

His intimate knowledge about the murderer proved genuine. His demand was for one hundred million dollars in exchange for all the details. The Calm-Spoken man ordered that their futile efforts at monitoring a few innocent rivals be abandoned. He explained that the head of security had set up major surveillance solely based on rumor and that the killer would never be found.

After twenty uninterrupted minutes of crucial information about the family and its business practices, the son buckled. He agreed to pay under the terms and conditions offered.

The instructions they had received from the Calm-Spoken man were accurate. They had found the equipment and chemicals, and they had found the connections between the lower floor and the Presidential Suite. They reviewed the video of the man clicking on his computer keyboard at the exact time Mr. Zhao was showering. A team of highly skilled software and hardware engineers had reconstructed how the connections were established, how to access them, and how they operated. The last piece of evidence was found in the back seat of a chauffeured limousine: a remote control device.

They had conducted tests in sophisticated laboratories and concluded that a dose of cyanide from the showerhead had indeed killed Mr. Zhao Ho Kun, which the toxicology report confirmed. It was a major break.

Jia Cheng sat on his balcony gazing at the waterfall in the pale moonlight. He was deep in contemplation. He allowed himself a moment of quiet time to breathe alone. The Calm-Spoken man had promised to call back with the last details. So they were waiting. It wasn't long before Liu knocked on his door.

One week later the last phone call came from the informant. The Calm-Spoken man gave the latest details about payment arrangements, for the other half of the funds, this time into a Swiss numbered account. Within days the money had been received and then vanished without a trace, as had the first installment.

All documents were sealed inside the same manila envelope Edmund had given to the supposed informant: a copy of his passport, his fingerprints, a copy of his driver's license, his boarding pass, and his last known address in the US were mailed to the Zhao family. As soon as the package was received, the head of security called a closed-door meeting.

SEAT OF TRUTH

They examined every item through microscopes for days. They wanted to make sure that this was indeed the man they were looking for. And they called on the best man for that job: Danny Lee.

Jia Cheng opened a side door and stepped into an impressive library with Liu and Danny following close behind. He selected a book, and suddenly gears and pulleys began to rumble somewhere inside. The bookshelf gave way to another room. They found Ms. Wu inside waiting.

Without speaking she handed to her son a small red box. He took it from her. And with the same care she had given it to him, he turned to face his head of security and Danny. He looked at Danny with cold, lifeless eyes and said, "Kill him."

Danny took the red box and turned around quickly as if he were already late for the killing.

Within hours, travel arrangements were in place and the final countdown of Edmund's life began.

CHAPTER THIRTY-FIVE

The countdown of a soul.
Each soul has a countdown,
And the clock begins at birth:
Tick tock, tick tock, tick tock

Danny claimed his window seat in the Jumbo Jet at Beijing Capital International Airport and began meditating, counting the beads in the wooden necklace he wore. He closed his eyes and took a mental inventory of his career as an assassin. Fourteen hours later the airliner landed at Dallas International Airport. He entered Customs.

"Next person in line!" a tired lady in bifocals called out. Danny came forward. "Welcome to the United States of America!" whispered the lady as she accepted the tourist's passport for inspection. She pulled herself away from the document to create enough space so her reading lenses could pick up the information. "How long are you planning on staying in the United States, Mr. Danny Lee?" *Or Mr. Assassin,* she should have asked.

"Three weeks."

SEAT OF TRUTH

"What is the nature of your business in the US, and where are you traveling?" Her eyes were locked on her monitor as if reading from a script.

"Pleasure," Danny said, with confidence. "In Miami Beach." She raised her head and looked at him, as if doubting his pleasure capabilities.

"Do you have any meat, carry any weapons, live creatures, or dangerous substances in your suitcase?" Now she was staring back at the monitor.

"No. Just my medicine." What Danny really meant was, *Yes, there's poison in my necklace beads, because I am going to Florida to kill the man who killed my beloved boss.*

"What kind of medicine?" She waited for answer.

"Heart medicine."

"Do you have your prescription?"

"Yes, I do."

"Can I see it?" A prescription was obviously not a problem for the Zhao family to have obtained. They would trade the Great Wall of China itself to revenge the death of Mr. Zhao if it came to that.

"I've had the same problem for many years," the woman said. "God knows what you're going through, my dear. I've tried every doctor in America — can't find a good one these days."

Danny showed absolutely no sympathy or compassion for her. He bowed respectfully, grabbed his passport politely, picked up the suitcase containing his heart medicine, and an arsenal of poisons and walked away avoiding more advanced medical questions about heart problems.

226

CHAPTER THIRTY-SIX

A discovery at dawn
—The city that smells death
— Story of a murderer

He found him at dawn the following day. He found him exiting from a high-end clothing store in downtown West Palm Beach. Danny watched him from a safe distance as he entered a black convertible Porsche. He followed him and took down his license plate number before Edmund could disappear at the next intersection.

Two hours later, Danny was enjoying Edmund's workout routine. Though *kung fu* would have definitely been more enjoyable, nonetheless, sprinting and the life on the beach sustained him for now.

For three weeks Danny followed Edmund everywhere he went, snapping pictures of him.

Danny sat in the southwest corner of a popular outdoor bar sipping iced tea like many tourists. He easily blended into the diverse culture of this part of the South with the flock of Asians looking for a tan. He had just finished a late lunch, and now it

SEAT OF TRUTH

was siesta time. He was admiring his subject jogging back and forth rather than the inviting beachfront.

At this time of the year the streets of West Palm Beach blossomed with tourists: pedestrians, bikers, skateboarders and lovers roaming the lively city.

It was early April.

The afternoon displayed once more the beauty of the South. Out in the streets you could tell it was the spring season: light fabrics, clingy tank tops, belly buttons barely covered and no one caring.

A windless, empty blue sky stretched beyond the beach.

The shouting from the bar and the kitchen, the constant yelling, the clanging of plates and utensils and beer bottles, and the loud conversations made a perfect atmosphere to monitor Edmund's workout routine: two traffic lights southbound and three northbound for a total of one mile. Danny had mapped it.

The energetic runner would do that distance four weekdays, from 6:00 to 7:30 in the evening.

He ran four miles a day.

He watched how Edmund's chest rose and fell, all because of one simple mechanism: breath. Although the details were a mystery to him, he knew that it was breathing that caused that motion — and time allowed it, too. "Keep breathing! You're about to run out of this precious commodity," he said to himself.

"Time kills everything," he heard someone say nearby.

So do I, he wanted to reply. He smiled instead. *How many human beings can truly say that?* He thought.

He looked at how Edmund's firm legs moved on the hot pavement with stealth, rhythm, torque; how the soles of his shoes stamped the ground with discipline and will.

He watched the limbs that would soon be lifeless. He admired how his chiseled body held itself harmoniously, how the eyes guided it, the hands balanced it, and the legs carried it forward. This whole structure would soon collapse and be called defunct, a corpse, remains, a thing, and Danny chuckled at the fragility and uncertainty of life. He imagined how a simple breath of life would soon flee the body at the sound of a well-crafted, poisoned bullet. Abandoned to rot at the mercy of nature. He chuckled again in the late afternoon. No one saw him smile.

For the past few weeks he had dreamed of taking Edmund somewhere, preferably to an abandoned warehouse, one of many the Zhao family owned, to question him until he confessed. *Orders are orders — I must comply,* he reminded himself. *What if I drugged him, or something?* He thought again. *No! Kill him!* Said Jia Cheng's calm voice in his head.

He had sent an encrypted email to China two days ago containing photos of his target for confirmation. Within minutes Edmund's pictures had been downloaded and closely examined by a support team of assassin in a secluded place half a world away. The team huddled shoulder-to-shoulder, facing two large monitors, eager to see the face of the man who had killed their boss.

The young technicians mounted a few tools together, joined by wires and other necessities and quickly converted a conference room into a sophisticated high-tech station. They began switching on equipment and waited until all protocols were approved, ready, and in place.

Jia Cheng entered the room and the chatter stopped altogether.

A young female technician took the only seat. She struck a few keys, and two large projector screens side by side flickered to life. Screen number one displayed a perfect passport photo of

SEAT OF TRUTH

Edmund P. Campbell with all his personal details. Screen number two displayed the newly received pictures for comparison — a young and handsome Edmund in an expensive blazer and black jeans, about to enter his sport car.

The technician struck another key and Edmund's face filled half of screen one.

The young woman tech-savvy hit a few more keys that put a beard on Edmund's face. What a transformation! And then, at the touch of another key, the beard was gone. What followed was a rapid parade of different shots of Edmund with large reading glasses, with sunglasses, and without.

This is Edmund bald ... and Edmund not bald. He slowly grew a long mane like a rock star, and then short hair followed. One click changed his nose and another carefully put it back. The last picture half-filled screen two. "One thing remains the same." It was the voice of the head of security. "The eyes. It always comes down to the eyes and their shape. They never change. Please remember that people."

The technician selected the option *Compare Images,* and the software began counting percentage ratios for facial recognition against screen.

The room became colder. Everyone sat silently, waiting. They had labored day and night for over six weeks.

All eyes locked on the screens as they prayed, or invoked something, anything that could put an end to this madness. Who could blame them for wanting to go home to their families, to the normalcy of life?

The screen reached 70 percent, 80 percent, 90 percent. Then it reached 100 percent and stopped. And the word *Match* in neon green flashed on both screens. The entire room let out a breath. There were hugs, high fives, and embraces.

230

The passport photo and that of Edmund in jeans in a blazer getting into his car were a perfect match. They had found their killer. What a relief.

The head of security cleared the room. He turned and looked at the last man remaining and said, "Sir, it's your call now." So casual is the assassin's dialect.

Jia Cheng stepped forward, leaned over the young female technician. He clicked on Reply, and typed a single sentence: *Have a nice flight.* And just like that, young Edmund, unknown to himself, or to the world around him, had only fourteen hours left to live.

Justice was about to be served.

The system is working. There's no doubt we have our guy.

How foolish is man's wisdom?

Danny's disposable pay-as-you-go phone buzzed. He looked at it and read the four-word message from another continent. He snapped out of his kidnapping daydream, went straight to his hotel room, and spent the night working on the deadliest poisonous bullet he had ever conceived in his extensive assassin career.

The bullet was handmade, coated with a liquid extract from a rare scrub tree found in the mountains of east China that Danny had mastered and turned into a deadly chemical compound. It reversed cell function without damaging the tissue or skin, especially when combined with a violet-colored layer of cyanide. No doctor would be able to determine for certain the true cause of death because there would be no sign.

To perfect the bullet, Danny heated it with ultraviolet rays, which would camouflage the poison should any test be performed on it.

The sound of the weapon firing the bullet would trigger the adrenaline of the victim, accelerating the heartbeat and allowing

SEAT OF TRUTH

the chemical to work wonders in a very short period of time. As long as the bullet touched the skin, five miserable minutes would be the life expectancy.

***

Just hours later, in broad daylight, as Edmund was having tea with his mother, a weapon designed to make a very loud noise was fired in a public place. The bullet brushed him just above his shirt collar, by the neck, and before paramedics could arrive, he was gone. Just like that, one bullet brought to an end the last chapter of his life.

CHAPTER THIRTY-SEVEN

The Womb
An intimate moment
The last dance

Six days after the loss of his only brother, at 6:30 p.m. sharp, Mitch P. Campbell pulled slowly into the parking lot of Solomon & Sons Funeral Home and Cremation Center. There were a few cars already in the lot.

A valet approached the sedan with a solemn face and opened the door. Mrs. Campbell exited the car slowly. Mitch walked by her side up the few stairs, almost as if they were walking down the aisle. A young funeral assistant welcomed them into a lavish waiting room where friends and family were sitting in silence.

They exchanged hugs and kisses. Some with a few words of encouragement, others with tears or a pat on the shoulder, and the rest with simple nods that conveyed nothing short of pain and loss and sadness and heartbreak.

Mrs. Campbell spoke about Edmund as if he were sleeping next door.

SEAT OF TRUTH

After small talks and enough condolences from everyone, the assistant funeral director came out and whispered to her that they were ready.

Mitch stood first and offered his strong arm to his mother. She was a rather large-framed woman. Today she needed all the support to stand up. All maneuvers had to be made with absolute delicateness. After all, she had just lost the man — the boy she had thought would be one of her pallbearers, the one she thought would make her final arrangements. So she was fragile.

It is expected, in all known cultures that a child must bury his parents, not the other way around. Mrs. Campbell hated the world and all therein. She hated people for who they were; all seemed destined to oblivion. *The world has no sympathy, no compassion,* she said to herself. Who could step into her shoes and pretend to really know, feel, and understand? And where is God when it hurts like this? Where is the Rock? Where is the Fortress? How could she pray with such a knot in her throat? Someone had yanked her heart out of her ribcage; and now she felt as if she were falling into a bottomless pit with no one to catch her.

She thanked her friends and family and then excused herself.

She followed the young assistant through an open door. They passed a space where an assortment of coffins were showcased and entered a private sitting area. On the left of the plaster wall, more exotic coffins were advertised. On her right, a floor-to-ceiling glass panels had a door in the middle that read *Preparatory Room One* where unspeakable tasks would soon take place, or already had.

The funeral director was waiting with his staff. His head was bowed. So were those of his assistants.

234

In this business, it is an absolute must that we convey respect and dignity for the dead at all times the funeral director had explained to the young apprentices earlier. We must keep solemn composure even if it meant faking it. He went on to educate his prospects — all Solomons — the proper etiquette of internments and dealing with the dead and gave them a short history of how Solomon & Sons Funeral Home and Cremation Center came to be.

It was a well-crafted atmosphere in which to handle the dead.

Solomon & Sons Funeral Home and Cremation Center had been sending people back to wherever they came from for three generations now. They offered world-class funeral services that many saw as corporate feasts.

They had received the body, or remains, or corpse — whatever you want to call it — from the county mortuary after legal procedures had been completed. Now their duty was to prepare it to the utmost excellence and present it to the loved ones undisturbed.

The funeral director greeted Mrs. Campbell with a fake look of sadness that could easily have passed for madness but she didn't notice. How could she?

They had a quick and quiet exchange, after which he unlocked the door of Preparatory Room One.

Generally speaking, funeral directors do not let families into their preparation areas, however Mrs. Gandalf Campbell had made a phone call and special favors were granted.

She pushed the door open. The light came on, and the inside became as clear as daylight.

She entered the room alone and shut the door behind her. And there, in the empty room, young Edmund lay on his back on a single white marble slab. How strange, surprising and unbelievable was that? She had had tea with him not long ago. It seemed like yesterday, and although he was gone, she still refused to believe it.

The smell of death and pain and loss stung the air. *Great Is Thy Faithfulness*, played in the background.

Is this my son? She thought.

She stared at the boy for a full minute and painfully smiled. Then she kissed him. Again she kissed him, this time on his left cheek. He was cold. *How come my son is so cold?* She said to no one.

She walked slowly around the table as if time and space no longer mattered. She looked at what was left of him and couldn't decide whether it was love, destiny, or maybe death, or a combination of the three that robbed her of joy.

She was now singing along to the tune.

The words cut through her like a butcher's knife through butter. They fell from the ceiling speakers onto the floor, crashing into pieces like sharp fragments of a broken bottle. The despair cut through her because there was no power in them, no magic, in spite of the lyrics' lucid truth.

The words had no effect.

In her heart they meant nothing.

Her soul spoke, fully awake, but yet it lingered between dream and reality, between despair and anger. She wished young Edmund had been Lazarus, who was fortunate enough to have the Savior Himself shed tears at the sight of his tomb and call him forth from the grave.

Confusion, anger, bitterness, and hatred clogged her windpipe. Her heart spoke again. She searched and reassessed her heart for the things it whispered to her seemed outrageously disappointing and unfair. "Yes, unfair," she managed to mumble.

Is it fair to rob a mother of her joy? The heart said to her.

Have you not pledged allegiance and faithfulness to Him no matter what? She fought back.

236

Now where is the source of your joy? Her heart countered.

Have you not said yes to His way, yes to His will? She questioned her heart.

What about your loss, your pains — did you count them? The heart said to her.

She was tempted to count the wounds, the time spent in supplications and prayers, the penances, the pilgrimages in the name of love. She reproached her heart and accused it of treason, but somewhere in the bowel of her soul, she knew the worthiness of her words. Then she wept.

She wept upon realizing that the life of her precious son had ended and now she was looking not at the charismatic lawyer she had raised, her well-versed son, but at his cold corpse.

His remains.

A thing.

A young man, who had gone to a prestigious law school, belonged to private clubs and dated the elite, was now a corpse.

She kissed his cheek, but held him in her gaze. She looked at her charismatic lawyer son, the man who had stood at the head of the family's legal business team and who she had seen in the courts exuding all manner of law to keep the business growing. She looked at him, and the echo of him leaving her for college struck a chord. She had never wanted him to go. Although Gandalf had tried to wow her with the prestige of the university — as if that was supposed to console her — she had never wanted him to grow up in the first place. The influence of society had filled her with dread. She was always afraid of losing him.

A woman's second child is believed to be the one most expected, the one best prepared for. Edmund was that child, a joyful child, and the one who gave her the most kisses, the most hugs, and who confided in her the most. In his mother's opinion the world was too cruel for such a young and fragile soul.

She touched his chin and kissed his forehead.

She ran a hand through his short, healthy locks and spoke for the first time. She spoke as if the dead could hear her. But could this man, the one stretched out on that cold marble hear her, really?

"You're not dead, baby. You're not dead. I know that." Nearby water dripped from a faucet. She took a small towel and dampened it. "I know you don't like cold water. I know, baby. I know that." She washed his face with the towel cautiously, as if she might break him, or wake him up.

The tune had changed to *Hallelujah! Lord Have Mercy*. She attempted to sing along, but the words came out of her mouth like venom, like poison. If anything the song was upsetting. She experienced a deafening weightlessness as if her existence was no longer terrestrial. She felt dull and void of sense and value.

She dabbed the face of her son as she continued to sing despite her pain.

As she worked her way down, she noticed the small scar by his left buttock and remembered the Monday of November 19, 1973. She seized the moment to revisit the momentous Sunday afternoon, forty-plus years ago when her father had arranged her marriage.

238

CHAPTER THIRTY-EIGHT

The past
—If only we can turn back time.

If it had been up to her, she would have spent her life in the safety of celibacy, like Atelia, away from matters of the heart and motherly love. She would even welcome the life of a nun, especially because of what had had happened two weeks earlier, on that Sunday afternoon.

***

Two weeks before she was engaged to Gandalf P. Campbell, she had accepted a date for an afternoon promenade along the shorelines of West Palm Beach with a prospect.

In the late 1960s, West Palm Beach was in a burgeoning economic renaissance with a rapid growth of goods coming in. Many new and prospective businessmen sought family status to establish esteem. So she had agreed to go on a date.

They had been walking for an hour, chatting about life, business, and music, but mostly about family. The man had told her how he had been seeking her affection and that he was ready and willing to ask her to marry him. She hadn't had the time to properly ponder and digest the sudden request — on a first date — when their stroll along the shore reached a difficult passage, almost a dead end. The man, of course, wanted to continue to take advantage of the afternoon. However, in order to move forward it was necessary to cautiously walk around the edge of some sharp rocks.

The man made the small mistake of attempting to hold her hand to aid her to walk safely across the stones. She bolted sideways and stared at him with defiance and resolve, then leapt into the nearby sugarcane field and took off. The man chased after her thinking and hoping that it was a joke. It wasn't until his running abilities proved insufficient that he realized he must have done something terribly wrong. At that moment he swore to show her that he truly loved her.

Mrs. Gandalf P. Campbell's story
A beautiful wedding

Two weeks after that episode — I remember it full well, it was June 1968, an ordinary afternoon — my father summoned me under the coconut tree that served the family as a living room on any warm day. He ordered me to sit down, and he told me that he needed to talk to me about life.

He cleared his throat and began to inform me that he had found me a husband — a good man — with whom I could start my own family and start making babies as soon as humanly possible.

He told me nothing about this husband, except to ask me to prepare a good meal because the man's family, himself included, was coming the next Sunday to meet mine, and if possible, to select a wedding date.

240

Like any hopeful young woman in the market for a future husband at the time, I wasn't excited about the news of a man being chosen for me without my input, especially after the episode I had had with my date on the shoreline two weeks earlier. Nevertheless, I did as told under the circumstances and prepared a good meal.

My father had done his own evaluation of me the night before and concluded that the product was ready to go. "At seventeen years old," he declared to my mother, "Marie Grace knows basic kitchen matters, basic cleanliness, basic knitting. She's more than ready."

"Why are you in such a rush to get rid of her? Can't she finish school, at least?"

"Mary Grace knows basic reading and basic arithmetic; that's enough knowledge for a woman's brain."

With a hefty dose of oil — which my mother considered a major investment — she massaged my head as if it were not part of my body. She brushed my hair until my scalp turned pink. I put on my best dress and floundered into a pair of tight-fitting high heels that belonged to my mother, took a good look at myself in the broken mirror, and wondered for the first time: *Is this real? Is marriage the only honor my family craves? Who is this man, anyway?*

To top off the package, using an ancient brush, my mother dusted a last layer of white powder on my neck and ears and ordered me to go sit down under the palm trees and watched the oncoming traffic.

My father had already taken his position under the trees. His reading glasses fell to the tip of his nose as he pretended to read a newspaper. Not long after, two cars entered our small farm. The occupants waited a few seconds to let the dust settle. Doors

241

SEAT OF TRUTH

began to open, guests started to come out, and suddenly my heart stopped beating.

I didn't look at him. I refused to. He didn't look at me either.

On my mother's advice I had taken the charge to serve the guests, walk around the table to refill either glasses of water or wine before I sat down. She had said this was how to win a man's heart, which I didn't want to. As I was serving, I stole the occasional glance from behind him — a quick stare at the back of his head to see what a husband-to-be looked like.

Of all the men God created on earth, of all the places on the planet my dad could go looking if he had to be so crazy as to hook me up with a man, of all the men in all the towns in the state of Florida, and of all the states in the country, of all the men in the Caribbean Islands, even from the reserves, he brought me Gandalf.

Dinner was served and compliments were made. I was praised for my cooking abilities, service and kindness. I know I wasn't the best version of a human being at the time. But I figured it was an evaluation, or plain flattery, because the virtue of kindness I didn't have at the time.

I never spoke to him that day.

The parents spoke and made their deal as if I were a bargain from the flea market. On the spot they decided on my wedding date.

"Gandalf, are you able to provide for this young woman and the children you will have with her?" His father said loud enough.

Children? With whom? I wanted to ask, but I let it pass.

"Yes." He replied. He was ready and willing, and immediately began an inventory of his assets.

* * *

242

Now, forty-six years later, she wished it were all a joke, or a bad dream. This pain would have been unknown to her. This night would have been avoided.

She wept again.

The clock on the wall struck the half-hour. It was 8:30.

She had thirty more minutes with her son. But for her, the time to abandon her son to the worms, to the starving insects and the heat of the South had not yet come. She was not prepared to release him into the realm of the dead.

The funeral home director had come into the room and removed a small box from a secure vault, held it as if it contained live creatures that might escape at any moment, and presented it to her. "This belongs to you until tomorrow. It is a pin for the coffin," he said. She looked at the director and said thank you.

**

Precisely fourteen hours later, a black hearse delivered Edmund's remains to the front door of Emmanuel Baptist Church of Sinai, with traffic having been stopped at every intersection along the way. Pallbearers carried him to the altar as family and friends watched with red eyes and quiet sniffles.

On a clear Saturday morning, Edmund P. Campbell was mourned at a lavish funeral service, laid in a $20,000.00 Promethean polished gold casket with his name spelled out on the red velvet.

His favorite color was on full display inside the church. Light yellow roses lined both sides of the aisle, up to the altar where three large pictures of the late lawyer had been placed under the funeral director's guidance.

Emmanuel Baptist Church was congested. Dignitaries and state officials, youth groups, and charities had secured good

SEAT OF TRUTH

seats. "Today," Pastor Brian Watson began, "we are celebrating the passing of a great man, a humble man, a personal friend, Edmund P. Campbell." The mourners applauded in a standing ovation.

What a freak show!

The preacher smiled as if he knew the mysteries of life and death. "We know that he's smiling on us from Heaven." *Who knows these things?*

The church choir, the elderly choir, and even the youth choir performed.

A team of twelve talented Boy Scouts rumored to have been sponsored by the late down-to-earth philanthropist performed a sketch that depicted the circumstances in which they had met the harmless man.

Representatives from charities and little children's sport leagues expressed their grief and testified that Edmund's good deeds had not been found lacking.

There were many eulogies; he was a great man and a great friend. He was a warm and generous person. He was a good Christian, an angel. The compliments were overwhelming. And the funeral was both entertaining and touching.

After they had worshipped the dead body long enough, they took him to a nearby cemetery where a prominent space reserved for the rich waited to receive his remains. They lowered the casket onto the ropes, pushed a button, and the expensive casket descended into the bowels of the earth, into the pits of darkness, alone.

And just like that, young Edmund was no more.

244

CHAPTER THIRTY-NINE

The heart of man
How much we truly
Know about each other?

Heaven's Courthouse and its citizens were amused and in shock as they watched in silence and disbelief. Every last detail of Edmund's life was put on full public display for all eyes to see and all ears to hear. Edmund, without choice, watched it all unfold until the last moment of his passing.

CHAPTER FOURTY

The Art of Dying
Who knows exactly how to die?
The Stone of Creation

Tshembow rose from the Counselors' bench and slowly walked into the center of the courtroom. Edmund had his head down, looking at the dust, staring at what he had become. From dust to dust, ashes to ashes.

"Who among you would dare to argue that how to die isn't something mankind can learn?" Tshembow yelled at the astonished audience. "Let him bring forth his feeble arguments and counter me. Dying, of course, is a virtue that mankind *must* learn. If abilities and skills can be refined and developed, we can conclude that death has its own learning curve also.

"We've already collectively agreed that the sum of all lives is conditioned to accomplish something. How can death be different, huh? Mankind writes all kinds of songs, poems, novels, and dissertations" — he fell into a French accent — "about the life they witness for just a little under a century, but did so little about death, their last resting place. The universe and everything therein was designed with purpose. Whether it be scientific, spiritual, or mathematical. It is not the product of cosmic coincidence as I led the scholars, the scientists, and billions of others to believe.

"Because of attachment to things of this life, mankind negates all reality that threatens to rob him of everything he holds most dear. He ignores the ringing bells of death, thus most people die in fear and wish they had more time. They tremble upon seeing death because they have no knowledge of it.

"A bit of warning is always a good thing. Something like 'Ready, set, go!' can go a long way. In death, however, things are a bit different." He raised his voice this time, in his British accent again. "There is no warning. Death either tackles you from behind — mostly when you're certain you're not being watched — or it hits you in the face from looking behind. You see, either way, it's always a surprise. Thus one must prepare for it. Ladies and gentlemen, the dead are not dying — the living are."

Edmund felt a rising dread grip his body as he attempted to keep his head straight, but he couldn't. He wondered how he had been so much of a fool for lack of wisdom and knowledge.

"Death is nothing but another state of being," Counselor Tshembow continued, "be it good or bad. As in the case of Edmund, there is often no harmony between the spiritual and the material. Edmund left the world in a state of fright, regret, and burden. It happened so fast that he didn't have time to properly arrange his affairs, to right his wrongs, and to diligently ponder what might await him in the next life. The accused is therefore guilty as charged. I must collect his soul at once, at the Gate of Exchange & Forgotten Hope." Tshembow turned, then raced to the Counselors' bench as the inside of his priestly robe flashed fiery red velvet.

SEAT OF TRUTH

Jesus had sat with his legs crossed the whole time. He was now staring at Edmund, blinking from time to time, as if weighing how best to defend him. The last note of a song called *Ocean* lingered in the background. Everyone was expectant — not of a miracle, though. Not this time. The time for miracles was long past. It was now time for reaping.

Jesus stood up and started talking as if He was going to free the prisoner. But instead He walked closer to the edge of the circle, which was called, according to Flannighans, the Stone of Creation.

"Do you remember Calvary Counselor Tshembow?" Jesus said.

"Oh no! Not again," Tshembow said, throwing his hands in the air. The crowd laughed out loud. "I don't want to talk about it." He searched God's face for approval. God smiled dimly.

"That's where it all began, Counselor Tshembow, wasn't it," Jesus said.

"Well, if we must go back, let's go way back to the beginning of all beginnings," an angry Tshembow yelled, quickly rising to his feet. "When earth was — was void of light and — and ... our Father had the crazy idea to make them in OUR IMAGE — OUR RESEMBLANCE. I have objected to this ... this experiment. You — you were young, Counselor. I was at the left hand of Your Father, Our Father, remember? This experiment has gone terribly wrong...this...disease has spread, and now no one, not even the creators, I mean *us,* can contain it."

"Counselor Tshembow, I have a simple question," God said, arching his thick eyebrows. "Why are you ranting?" He added calmly, "Your visits are numbered here, Counselor."

"Thank you for the reminder, Your Honor," Tshembow said.

"Answer the question!" God ordered.

"What does Calvary have to do with this?"

248

"It has everything to do with this trial," Jesus said, pacing slowly, waiting for Counselor Tshembow to answer.

"My patience is wearing thin, Counselor Tshembow." God said, glaring at him.

"Yes, I remember," Tshembow mumbled.

"LOUDER!" God shouted at him.

"Yes, yes, I remember. I was there."

God rolled his eyes as if to say, what am I to do with this guy?

"Of all your accusations," Jesus continued, "which one did you find me guilty of?"

"We've been through this many times, Great Counselor."

"Did I not bear your lies?"

"I told some lies —"

"All of it," Jesus cut in. Now He faced the audience. "You have seen and witnessed how Counselor Tshembow manipulated Alt Rosenberg and the others; how he filled them with rage until greed and revenge consumed them. You have seen how far Tshembow pushed them and maneuvered them with his lies in order to harvest Edmund's precious soul. This will not stand before the Court!"

"This one," Tshembow quickly stood up, his face contained, and pointed at Edmund, "is a proud sinner. He belongs to me."

Jesus had been standing near Mrs. Campbell with his right hand resting on her left shoulder. He raised his chin as if searching for someone in the audience, and then He spoke.

"Every deviant and perverted mind you take hold of, every hypocrite who still calls upon My Name for favor, every atheist you turn away from Me, every murderer who takes life without mercy, every vile mind you condemn with guilt, every blind person who fumbles through the streets, every liar and thief who thrives among my nations, every rapist who preys on the weak

SEAT OF TRUTH

— my blood has paid for them all. How dare you?" He pointed at Tshembow, who stood on the other side of the Seat of Truth. "I carried the sins of all, did I not? Answer me before the Great Court!" The crowd roared their support.

"Everybody calm down. Calm down," Tshembow said, looking around with his hands spread wide, trying to appease the wild crowd. "Sons, daughters of Zion, hear me out. Edmund has nothing in common with any of you here." He paused for effect. "You have heard from his own account that he has chosen the wrong path, *my* path. And he knew full well that the price for my followers is death, eternal death — the Lamb said that Himself. The defendant slept around, he hated, he robbed; he was prideful and selfishly ambitious. For all I know, he broke every single one of the Ten Commandments."

Jesus quickly stood and defended His client. "Your Honor, Counselor Tshembow is right. The accuser is a fornicator, a hater, a covetous man, a liar, and a hypocrite, among many things. But can the Counselor explain which of these transgressions were excluded from my forgiveness?"

"Ah! The Blood of the Lamb, the Well of Emmanuel," said Tshembow with sarcasm. "Yes, Counselor, you bore the sin of all, for which you acquired your only Name, the Name by which every tongue shall confess, every knee shall bow, including my own. But they are fools and fools and fools that fall in love with the very things that destroy their soul. Does it not clearly state somewhere in the Book of Instruction Before Leaving Earth that they should present themselves BLAMELESS? SPOTLESS? Not partake in the unfruitful deeds of DARKNESS? UH? It is written: Let all bitterness and wrath and anger and clamor and slander," Tshembow raised his voice, then paused again for effect, "be put away from among you, and so

250

Ezechias Domexa

on and so forth. And after all of that, you still call him…son?"
He laughed at his own idea.

The song *Before the Throne of God Above* had just begun, but the
introduction was much longer than Selah had originally sung it.
Jesus stood lazily, both hands behind His back, and walked
toward a floor-to-ceiling window that overlooked the
breathtaking view of a brook, which threaded among tall trees
through a lush valley. Then, with His back to the audience, He
spoke.

"From the Garden of Gethsemane to the High Priest's home,
from the house of Pontius Pilate to Herod's Palace, and up to
the hills of Calvary, I still remember the fresh scent of My blood
in the sand of eternity, Counselor. It penetrated the soil so deep
that it gave life to everything that was dead and straightened out
every crooked thing. My Father, Our Father, was by my side, and
hosts of the heavenly army were waiting. I bore the sins of all."
He spoke distantly now.

"With all due respect, Young Counselor," Tshembow replied,
"You did carry the sins of all. I have no objection. And yes, for
the thousandth upon thousandth upon thousandth time, it was
my plan to nail you on the cross. I admire your courage. If it had
been up to me, the world would still be in need of a Savior
because I wouldn't do it.

"Edmund scorned the law of Your Father, Our Father, and
the trace of it remained in his memory before the son of Adam.
For the book of the law has not been found on his lips. He
rejected knowledge, so knowledge must reject him today because
he died from his own proclivities."

This last statement hit Edmund like a rock. It pierced him like
an arrow. There was a long silence as the audience awaited Jesus'
response, but He leaned closer to the windows, staring at
something below.

251

SEAT OF TRUTH

The music died down. Tshembow walked to the floor-to-ceiling windows to see what Jesus was staring at. It was a woman, a beautiful woman. They both admired her, as she stood staring back up at them. The musicians stopped altogether as if they knew the moment was coming.

She wore a long, light pink and yellow dress with short sleeves. A red sweater rested around her shoulders with the sleeves loosely hanging around her neck as if she was slightly cold. She tucked a wisp of hair behind her ears.

"Who's this woman, Flannighans?" I whispered, leaning closer to him.

"His mother, Mary."

She looked up for a good while and smiled. Her soft grey eyes were full of pleasure and promise and love. Then she continued her solitary promenade.

"Your mother looks lovely, Counselor," Tshembow eagerly offered.

"Thank you, Counselor Tshembow," Jesus said without looking at him.

The long silence was interrupted by yet another revelation from Counselor Tshembow, as if this piece of new information was his best tactic to win the trial. He turned directly to God and said:

"Your Honor, I'd like to remind the audience and especially the jury that the defendant slept with his brother's wife on countless occasions and with her he produced an offspring named Matt—"

"How dare you!" Mrs. Campbell growled, bolting straight like a rocket, ready to escape the jury bench and pounce at Tshembow. God shook His head at Tshembow as if to say, what a jerk you are for bringing this up. But He kept his manner calm.

252

The revelation came to me as yet another blow. *How could this be? When and where? No! No! No! No!*

"Sorry, Mitch, you never had a son. Matthew is your nephew," Tshembow said, looking in my direction and watching me turn purple.

If such a revelation had come to light in an earthly courtroom, God helps us all! World War III would be unavoidable. We'd have been called to the judge's chamber, and the nasty exchanges would have been unstoppable in a court of law. All manner of litigation and lawsuits, threats and swearing, even fighting — all would have been options.

"Tell me this isn't the truth, baby! Please tell me!" Mrs. Campbell pleaded with broken voice as she buckled under her own weight and collapsed on the floor.

As the audience watched like they had never seen a woman collapse before, another woman stepped down into the court and came to her aid.

It was Mary.

She undid the red sweater from around her shoulders as she walked toward Mrs. Gandalf Campbell's jury bench. She took her by the elbow and slowly raised her up onto wobbly legs. Mrs. Campbell grabbed hold of the bar for extra support. The all-too-shocked audience felt the love. Mary straightened my mother on her trembling legs, wrapped the sweater around her waist, and tied the sleeves in a knot. Mrs. Gandalf Campbell's body responded, quickly straightening, as her strength was restored. They exchanged a few words, holding each other's shoulders as only two women could. *Teamwork.*

God looked aside and scratched His neck as if a giant mosquito had bit Him.

Mary then walked directly and purposely into the Stone of Creation. She kissed her Son on the forehead, then Edmund.

SEAT OF TRUTH

Then she stared for a moment at Tshembow and his acolytes. And it was only at that instant that I realized it was a good thing concealed pistols were banned in the Heavens, for from the look on Mary's face, she would simply shoot them all in the head and get it over with. What mother wouldn't?

Tshembow looked at me and saw the flare of anger as the blood drained from my face.

"Oh, you're surprised? So was I," he mused and laughed at the audience.

I searched my brother's demeanor for answers, but he kept his head down, still staring at the dust beneath him. He seemed to be pondering what this all meant. The ghost of his former self had long gone. His shadow had been replaced by his true identity, his worst enemy – himself.

No more performance.

"Your mockery," Jesus said to Tshembow, "I bore it all. You have preyed upon his innocence and kept him from the truth. Edmund owes you no blood," He added as He turned around and sat back down.

"Is that what this is all about?" Tshembow said. "Keeping him away from the truth? I never wanted to keep the sordid creatures away from what they considered truth, but from the path to Oneness," he boasted. "All I did was place a tiny, little, mini seed of self-righteousness – the only state mankind strives to maintain. At this stage, all I do is sit and enjoy the inevitable collapse, as is the end of everything that is built upon me.

"The effect of unraveling a soul is something I find quite amusing. From the early Stone Age to this very last hour as we speak, I've remanufactured great minds and artists to lay out the new definition of things. And slowly, a deluded view on spiritual matters would override their universal faculties.

254

"Man began to seek and perceive things with excessive fondness, and this produced an excellent opportunity to derail more souls than I had ever hoped for.

"This trend has been made possible by the spread of collective teaching in social media. I'm able to play on human nerves with simple words like *loan, credit rating, delinquent* and *collection, mortgages, marriage,* and by midday a man could easily miss seeing a traffic light. This produces the dangerous habit of worrying, which the Old Man eternally forbade.

"Such crafty work, too, begins as early as in the nursery as you have just witnessed. Hence, the new meanings of words — worldly definitions — become the very DNA with which it appears they have been created.

"For instance, major print and social media identify a spiritual family based on financial success: the house, the title, and the occasional business travel have become the symbols for spiritual progress. Unsuspected debilitating affliction of the mind leads them to believe that by the mere works of attending church and performing well, they can be one of the lucky few who, miraculously attain everlasting joy.

"Let them believe that only what is desirable in their own eyes is pretty, even in the precious sight of little babies! Thus I am reproducing a new breed of human being with no sense of truth, no sense of self, no memories of history, but instead, with false hope based solely on their own clairvoyant minds. They don't understand that the mechanics and mysteries of life found only in the practice of good virtue and in yielding, and even in the depth of chaos — pain and loss — lies also a well of peace and joy. It suffices that they turn to Him." Tshembow pointed at Jesus, then he continued his narrative.

"Let them be moody, unpredictable, and devious above all! Do not let them suspect that they were born to help, not to destroy; to support, not to criticize; to love, not to judge; to unite, not to divide; to share, not to be selfish; to accept, not to be prejudiced. With such a mindset their breed will become less and less interested in learning, thinking, seeking, but a generation of self-entitled perverts. Of course, I didn't have a say in their making, but I will redesign them into a replica void of all faculties.

"Mankind does not find meaning in living, so I keep them running around all the time looking for something that resembles it. When they find out the next big thing is equally empty, I provide them with self-help books: *Find Your Inner Self, Discover the New You, Harvest the Energy Within You, Create the Perfect Life You Deserve, The Five Steps for Prosperity,* and so on. Over time, because of the depth of their compulsiveness, even in the face of evidence, blindness will still prevail.

"Consider the last century of schooling of the mind. It produced the rational tendency to feel good and dream big that easily generated the illusion of belonging. These are the very individuals who become subtle victims of psychological distempers.

"I will lure them into thinking they can fix that broken system: that they can end famine, war, poverty, illiteracy, diseases, racism. That way they will never come to the real knowledge of the word peace, which is simply the presence of God — not the absence of war and bad news. Be that as it may, there will always be bad news and war and everything else. With a little distraction they will forget their basic fundamental instinct and confuse the meaning of joy, which isn't having plenty, but is a knowing and a longing for home. These are the gems of the heart they must miss at once.

"You know, I enjoyed going to those little ... those little sessions." Tshembow now spoke with sarcasm. "You know, those little sessions where they swap little stories, little tales of *yeadi yeada* to subtly flaunt their accomplishments: the flourishing career, the house, the bank accounts, the beautiful spouse, and the oh-so-well-raised kids who seem to be doing so well academically. They call them...uh — oh! *Blessings.* You know, during those...emotional moments, those moments of tears and weeping, even sobbing among those brave enough. Some call it, I believe, enlightenment? Prosperity therefore has become the hallmark of spiritual progress. However, underneath that comportment – that false humility – lays the dangerous seed of some misplaced and misguided sense of self-righteousness. I know that scent, walking with that ideal public persona, but it's all under *my* control, however humble or spiritual they sound.

"John Newton's *Amazing Grace* cost me dearly. Although he brought a great many worthless souls into my kingdom, thanks to his early delightful foolishness.

As you can see, for every great mind you created, I produced my own bootleg. For every God-given virtue you imbued them with, I added a little...a little sparkle, a little...a little color, if you will. You gave the world David, I came up with Goliath and Nebuchadnezzar; you created Pascal, I came up with Nero and Vlad the Impaler. You brought forth the apostle Paul; I countered with Joseph Stalin and Ivan the Terrible. You called upon Elijah, the great prophet; I brought in King Herod and Vladimir Lenin. You gave the world Billy Graham; I came up with Adolf Hitler and Francois Duvalier. You raised Lazarus from the dead; I brought back Freddy Krueger and Jeepers Creepers. And the race can go on and on."

Edmund was bewildered. He sat in eerie silence, astonished at how he had been so much of a fool as Counselor Tshembow spelled out his true identity — how he had cast his spell over fancy works of art, hidden treasures, history, museums, philanthropy, architecture and an inexhaustible madness for carnal pleasure.

"His longing for glory and self-righteousness," Tshembow said, gesturing at Edmund, "if memory serves well — and I'm sure it does — doesn't fall far from the tree. Made to Your likeness, Our likeness, I told you so … for he craves the same thing we both do: glory." To which God frowned and temporarily looked aside.

"For his years of vulgarity and frivolities," Tshembow continued, "mankind's *mea culpa* for euphonious words and futile projects is alarming at best."

Edmund looked as if he wanted to vomit. He felt like regurgitating every bad thought he had ever had, every bad word he ever uttered. He ached to empty his soul of every vice, but then again, they were now part of him. He couldn't escape his own shadow now, could he? He felt for a second that he had been cheated, but he knew full well he had not been, he had had choices.

"Perhaps," Tshembow said, "had I had the idea first, or had I had some input into their design, I would have given them more legs to wander about like zombies, more hands to take things away and to fight with and murder each other, and of course a bigger head to store worthless ideas and nonsense. Because man's sustenance depends on things beyond himself, he craves only public recognition.

"Supernatural life is imbued into the heart of each man so that he may achieve greatness. In the composition of his atoms, in the structure of his soul and spirit and body and mind, within the boundaries of his own making lies all he ever needed. Because anything that is not within his reach, might as well be within his will if he choses to.

Ezechias Domexa

For the Great Book of Life says, 'Ask, and it shall be given unto you; seek, and you shall find; knock, and it shall be opened unto you.' Then he would be wiser, more beautiful, smarter, and more humble than he is, or can ever hope to be. For your Word says, 'They shall be like Him.'" He pointed at Jesus.

"For amusement," Counselor Tshembow said with a laugh, as if he too, could not believe what he was about to say, "I have sometimes opened up a discussion among the great minds, between the past and the future — what they called an 'interesting debate,' forget the present. That single idea, spread into a consuming flame, harvested me more souls and lives and minds and hearts and homes and sons and daughters and nieces and nephews and uncles and aunties and daddies and mommies and doctors and lawyers and nurses and teachers and musicians and singers and carpenters and electricians and chefs and actors and kings and princes and queens and students and artists and many more than I care to name.

"All I did was give a mere suggestion, and there would be another enthusiast who would extend it, perfect it, elaborate on it, and in the same episode confuse more souls than necessary. Eventually their ideas spread abroad and across. Over time they took other forms and meanings in each culture and movement. When the so-called great minds mingle together — UN, UNESCO, EU, AF, WHO, AU, NATO, the religious leaders, men and women of state, lawmakers, queens, senators, governors, princes, students, judges, kings, scientists, taxy drivers, engineers, philosophers, mechanics — the result is a beautiful, ugly, confusing, skull crackling mess of fancy ideology based on no spiritual value, but self-righteousness.

"You give the world peace; I add alcohol and drugs. You shower them with grace; I teach them to boast. You give them mercy; I blend in a little noise. You fortify them by faith; I

259

SEAT OF TRUTH

whisper to them doubt and fear. You promise them daily bread; I worry them with a future they may not see. You give them love; I invent religions. For all I know, in all the ages, man's longing for trivial ambitions has never changed. They are *les amis de la confusion*. Hauled and mauled into the density of history, between truth and illusion, mankind has done most of my work. A primal species, still living in his prehistoric incubator, that is what mankind still is, after more than two thousand years.

"All great men rise and fall. But history teaches these baboons nothing for the next generation falls into the same cadence. So I will not go down alone — not while there is still time. Not while there are still new ideas, new roles, new technologies, new governments, new career opportunities, not while there is still history to be made. I will walk over the cold corpses of these men and women who were once brave and mighty, beautiful and handsome, powerful and accomplished. Upon their decaying bodies I will retrieve their one true worth: their souls. For mankind has leapt into falling in love with what I hold most dear. I simply respond in kind, Counselor," Tshembow said with confidence as he walked over to the window.

With his hands crossed behind his back, he examined the earth as if it were diseased. From the floor to ceiling windows he observed how flocks of humans wandered about their daily lives.

"Look at them running, hurting each other, gyrating between legalism and lawlessness and thriving in façade and moral decay and arrogance," he said. "Look at them rushing into new things, new deadlines, new realities, new compromises — restless, defenseless, purposeless, vague, oblivious and sadly unaware that they're already living on borrowed time. Will they ever get it, I wonder? Your darlings..." He looked over at Grandpa. The

260

Lord frowned and turned to cast a thoughtful gaze at Adam, as if to say, 'it's all on you, son. It's all because of you.'

Tshembow now turned to the audience, as would a professor to his students. "I will teach them how to play on each other's nerves with mocking smirks and patronizing compliments while the mind whispers vile things. They must evaluate each other quantitatively — for the purpose of business and gathering together— but subjectively in spiritual aspects and other matter. Thus, their compassion will extend solely to their immediate entourage. They will do for one what they would not for others. Such deeds will produce the fruit of passion, which causes blindness, considering that blindness is the product of fanaticism. And the main residue of fanaticism is seeing things the way one would like them to be, not the way they are in reality. Furthermore, they will see others as *different, but the same* not as *the same, but different*. There is a major difference between these two constructions. The first part of the construction, repeated in the wrong country, can easily ignite World War III. Or is it World War IV? I have lost count. The latter part — as innocent and truthful as it is — can still stir an intellectual debate that will invoke old wounds of color and race, and ethnicity and religion, and postal code, and continent until they are practically at each other's throats.

"Let them not be fond of the present, but run around like mad chickens and waste the precious commodity of time. It is also paramount that they never suspect that today's love is the same as yesterdays, and the same as it will be tomorrow. Encourage them to believe that tomorrow's love is going to be better, so they can neglect and procrastinate the present. Let them come in with their sour faces as if they knew better."

Tshembow strode to the center. The assembly watched him closely as he continued to tout his achievements. "I encourage them to fist fight each other for hope — a better tomorrow — in a world still torn apart by conflicts and suffering. Compassion will become a thing of the past once they think they can make a difference in their own strength. Now because they have no anchor, disappointment will follow and consume them." Tshembow said with a tight-lipped smile. "This will only shift them a world away from the path to Oneness and into the cosseted royal life they daydream. That will allow me to hurt them with impunity because they lose inhibitions and the ability to answer correspondently.

"The world is so full of noise. It is easy to get them distracted in life and lose sense of purpose. It will seem harder and harder for them to focus on what is really important. They can't help it. Pride. Health, family, bills, little puppies, little kitties, Chihuahuas, society, and neighbors will drown them into the fabric of time to make them forget about the things that matter the most. Even though those things are right in front of them.

"I will turn every culture, every mind, every home, every heart, every city, every country into a maze of distraction. I will steal their beloved sleep with the excessive demand of societies and technologies. And for lack of sleep and proper rest, they will become restless each morning, which will cause them to gain weight, or lose weight, or stay in between, but dissatisfied regardless.

"I will teach them to toy with the innocent idea that love changes according to circumstance and under the weight of time, like they do. That way '*I Am the same yesterday, today, and forever*' will eventually sound more like a long-ago saying from the land of forgetfulness. The more they think of the past — failure, regrets, opportunities, mistakes — the less Love seems a reality. And the more they worry about the future, their home, employment, school loan, marriage, babies, 401k, vacations,

262

family competitions and birthday cakes, the less likely Love is possible. That creates doubt and self-condemnation, which are the very things the Old Man sternly discourages.

"Let them believe that a piece is missing in the equation of Love, and that social media has nearly figured it out for them." Tshembow stopped to catch his breath. Then he resumed speaking calmly as though what he had been talking about was not really important, but only the following: "Knowing full well they must all answer to the call of death as they once did to life, this is what this trial is all about. To the victor the crowns, not to a vessel of dishonor." He walked back from the window and took a seat next to Jesus on the Counselors' bench.

CHAPTER FOURTY-ONE

The Call For Closing Arguments
Who can convince a jury of right and wrong?
What's a good or a bad verdict?
Drumroll, please!

Jesus' Closing Argument

After he spilled his guts about how he ruled the world, Tshembow relaxed on the bench and crossed his legs. The musicians began a solemn rendition of *There Is a Fountain Filled with Blood*. The piece sounded just as Selah sang it.

Jesus stood up with a handful of dust He had been gathering. He looked left and right and slowly released it into the air. It slowly fell, spreading on the ground. He spoke in a raised voice: "Dust to dust. I know what it is to be man, for I was once flesh." He turned around sharply. "I have been tempted too, many a time. I have experienced fatigue, weariness, pain, anger and hunger. And from the Stone of Creation I have felt every emotion known to man.

"I have watched over Edmund from the very day I opened his eyes, until the last time Tshembow closed them with his

264

vicious lies. I've carried him, holding his hand, pushing him more than he can remember. I snatched him from treacherous tricks and accusations." He turned to face Tshembow. "You have pushed him over the edge too often and he has lost his way too many times, but he has redeemed himself. I saw him fight battles in his quiet and desperate moments and I have responded by strengthening and fortifying him. Who can dare to understand how much I love Edmund? I know how many time he thought of his mother; I know how many thread of hair he has; I know how many words he spoke since his existence, only I know where and how I stored them. I therefore demand that the verdict be against the seven deadly sins," Jesus finished, and swiftly found the bench.

Tshembow's Closing Argument

"Well, he will be found guilty of every one of them," Tshembow blurted as he rose from the bench, waving both hands in the air.

He scanned the audience for a moment. "Ladies and gentlemen," he began. "The evidences are undeniable, aren't they?" he asked but no one answered. "In the case of Edmund P. Campbell, you have seen it and heard it from his own lips — not from the lips of Moses sitting over there." He pointed at Moses, who was nodding while playing with his long white beard. "Not from the lips of Abraham." Abraham nodded, and then rested his face back on his left hand. "And certainly not from Adam, the Fallen Man." Everyone turned to look at Adam, who quickly buried his face in his hands. "But from his own lips.

"Bound by the futility of his mind, following the deceitful lust of his eyes, his vessel was not ready to receive the plenitude of Your grace, Your Honor. Having not been redeemed from his empty shell, his heart was but a thriving cold field, void of Light. The Burden Bearer's gift of life had not been redeemed in the proper salvation scale." He paused for effect. "Young Edmund

SEAT OF TRUTH

lived his life not according to the Book of Instruction Before Leaving Earth, but according to his own ambitions. The Word says, 'Everyone shall one day give a full account of his life.'

"Human beings know full well that they must all answer to the call of death as they once did to life. Hence my defense rests: not on my own lies" — he raised a finger — "but on the fruit of his lips; the contents of his memory, as memory is all that will be left of all man." Tshembow had concluded and walked lamely back to the Counselors' bench. He gained some small applause from his acolytes, as his closing argument seemed to seal Edmund's fate for a trip to the Gate of Exchange & Forgotten Hope.

CHAPTER FOURTY-TWO

Grandpa's Verdict
— Guilty but not condemned

God cleared his throat and surveyed the audience expectantly. He considered Edmund for a good minute, appearing undecided, and then the crowd. There was faint chatter, as if they were guessing at what He might decide, but still they were attentive. He looked in front of Him as if reading from some ancient tablets the proper procedures and formalities. Then He spoke.

"I will render the verdict on the seven deadly sins in the case of Edmund P. Campbell, and Mrs. Gandalf P. Campbell will determine the final verdict and his fate." The crowd went wild with applause.

All eyes were on the altar.

"For accusation number one: 'Does the Courthouse of Heaven find by a preponderance of evidence that the defendant is guilty of the sin of Pride?'" The Lord scanned the audience,

SEAT OF TRUTH

who had stopped breathing. After a pause that lasted no more than a few seconds, the Lord said: "The verdict is: Not Guilty."

"Not guilty, Your Honor?" Counselor Tshembow shouted, springing to his feet. God cast him a glare and Tshembow quickly found the bench again. The crowd chanted: "Not guilty. Not guilty. Not guilty." Jesus smiled at them.

"For accusation number two," said God, "'Does the Courthouse of Heaven find by a preponderance of evidence that the defendant is guilty of the sin of Lust?' — The verdict is: Not Guilty."

"What?" Tshembow shouted again, standing up. This time Grandpa didn't pay attention to him, but a subtle smirk formed around his jaw, as if to say, Wait for the bomb. Again the crowd celebrated with the slogan, "Not guilty. Not guilty. Not guilty." Tshembow's legal team, obviously confused, searched for answers between them.

"For accusation number three — 'Does the Courthouse of Heaven find by a preponderance of evidence that the defendant is guilty of the sin of Greed?' — The verdict is: Not Guilty.'"

"Oh, come on! Your Honor?" Tshembow put his hands on top of his head.

"For every accusation brought before My Throne of Grace," the Lord concluded as He closed the Book, "the defendant is found not guilty because all sins are covered under the blood of the Lamb."

"Are you kidding me?" Tshembow yelled. God smiled with the audience.

On God's last words Edmund gained some composure, and looked around the court for the first time as if to say, *Is it true? Am I to be freed?* He searched left and right like a curious child searching for answers.

268

Ezechias Domexa

"However …" God added, and Edmund was jolted back into reality. "Although these counts are now decided, the jury must also know the state of the soul at time of death. I will give full permission to access the thoughts of the defendant to properly render the final verdict. May the Counselors and the jury approach my Throne." All three of them, Jesus, Tshembow, and Mrs. Gandalf P. Campbell hurried before the Throne.

The Great Judge extended His hands over them. They closed their eyes and plunged into a deep dream. It went on for a good twenty seconds, then they woke up and quickly found their respective seats. Tshembow smiled satisfactorily, while Jesus showed no emotion.

***

Mrs. Campbell went back to the jury bench, sat down to process the new information she had just received.

She looked at Edmund in a way only a mother could.

The womb.

Their eyes locked in an invisible link, like a network of love only they had access to. Everyone felt it. It seemed as if the umbilical cord that once joined them had grown stronger and stronger with each passing moment and slowly transformed into a solid rope that seemingly became an unbreakable cable. She wanted to touch him, hug him and kiss him all over. She wished he had never come of age or maturity. She had always wanted to have him for herself — forever.

After a moment of deliberation, the Great Judge cleared His throat. "May the jury rise!" the Lord ordered. Mrs. Campbell stood, her eyes resigned. "Has the jury reached the final verdict?"

"Yes, Your Honor. I have."

"What is your verdict?"

269

CHAPTER FOURTY-THREE

A mother's verdict
Who has the courage?

Mrs. Gandalf Campbell turned slowly and faced the Almighty. The red sweater that had been wrapped around her waist over her light pink robe seemed to give her some strength. *Tis So Sweet To Trust In Jesus* began to play softly in the background and it reached a part of me I didn't know existed.

"Lord, my dearest King, my Redeemer and Savior," Mrs. Campbell began with trembling voice. "On account of my son, I have seen with my own eyes and heard with my own ears what mankind, all mankind is capable of. I have loved my son from the moment you opened his eyes until his last dying breath in my arms." God nodded understandingly. Her voice grew heavier now. "I have watched him grow, day and night. It is a mother's greatest joy to see her child walk, talk, laugh, and play." Now her words became broken. "As a small child...I remember him singing...for you...in the children's choir...the youth choir. He sang for you when he was sick and sad.

"My fondest memory of these days is of a particular night he knelt down before his bed and sang songs and asked you for toys and games and candy. You must remember that night. He was two years old." The Lord nodded with a hint of sadness and remembrance. She braced herself, holding onto the bar in the jury box for support, as if she might go into shock at any moment.

She paused and sniffed.

"I watched my son that night ... until I caught a fragment of ... of who you truly are. Love. And in your name, I loved him. I've loved him with every fiber, every ounce, every drop, every second, every molecule that you have created me with. And you know that." She reached down for the sweater and tied it tighter. "But ... my good King? Of all the good virtues you imbued him with — like devotion to his family, kindness to others, patience, and his dedication to good cause, is there one good thing left ... for which you might spare him ... for a mother, for me? I know no other help." She waited for a reply, her eyes ravaged by tears. The crowd gave her a standing ovation. She scrutinized the audience and gained some strength from the applause. She turned to God again, this time as if her strength doubled. "I too have sinned, Your Honor."

"Mrs. Campbell, be careful with your next line of inquiry — I must warn you!" God said sharply.

"I have done unspeakable things before your sight too, Great King."

"Tread carefully, Mrs. Campbell!" God leaned forward on His Throne.

"I have killed the very man whom I swore to love until death do us part, and have kept it a secret —"

SEAT OF TRUTH

"Mrs. Campbell, this is completely irrelevant to the matter at hand!" God barked at her, now on his feet. The audience roared in surprise.

Mom? You killed Dad?

"The court must know Your Honor, how wretched I too am, shouldn't they? You said all things shall be laid bare for all eyes to see and all ears to hear, didn't you, Great King?" she challenged. She descended from the jury bench and walked into the Stone of Creation. She paced now with confidence, hands behind her back, before plunging into the next part of her narration.

The next song broke the long silence. It was *Now You Are Free*, but the heavenly version.

"You lost us once," Mrs. Campbell said, "in the Garden of Eden, on account of one fallen man. He touched what was forbidden, and all mankind suffered death. The result of death is decay that inevitably produced a genetic chaos in all living things and beings. I know now why you sealed off the Garden of Eden: to save Adam and Eve from eating the Tree of Life. They would be eternally cursed and the Great Exchange for the Cup of Redemption would not have taken place. You'd rather die than leave us in the dark. This is the evidence of the love you have for us." She turned to the audience, who were on their feet applauding. She waited for the cheers to die down. "This is truly a demonstration of love for your son, Edmund P. Campbell." The audience nodded, and now she found more strength in her voice. She looked at God again, with resolve, then added: "There's nothing you created in me that allows me to let go of my child, however wicked he may be. And therefore, because of my right to the Tree of Life, my Crown of Incorruptibility" — she raised her right fist and the crowd cheered — "I am giving up my place to my son that he may live among the Stars. I will

272

go with Counselor Tshembow to the Gate of Exchange & Forgotten Hope in exchange."

"It is forbidden!" God barked. "You have no right to change the rules and the theories of life."

"You've changed them often, for me, haven't you?"

"You're out of your jurisdiction, Mrs. Gandalf P. Campbell." His features turned to stone.

"I'll take them both," Tshembow blurted.

A sudden debate erupted in Heaven among the inhabitants. The Courthouse was in chaos. Everyone was talking.

"Can she really take his place?" one voice questioned.

"She's incorruptible," another said. "She should be able to."

"There cannot be two Saviors — the Old-Fashioned Book forbids it," one was heard saying.

"Yes, but what about her right to the Tree of Life?" another questioned. The discussion rose into a heated debate, and everyone was practically shouting.

"Order! Order! Order in My Court!" the Great Judge yelled, smashing His gavel on the bench. The court became silent again.

"There cannot be another Savior!" the Lord called out.

"I can do as I please with my right to the Tree of Life," Mrs. Campbell countered.

"It is not feasible," God roared.

"What has become of my right to the Tree of Life, Your Honor?" she questioned Him seriously.

"Mrs. Campbell, the Stone of Creation and the rules over souls were written before you ever were. The principles that govern life rested upon your shoulders when you agreed to deliver a final sentence so that your word would not come back void. So I'm waiting for your sentence."

Mrs. Campbell had moved back toward the jury box. She walked slowly now into the Circle of Justice, the Stone of

273

SEAT OF TRUTH

Creation. She kissed Jesus and said, "Thank you!" She unfastened the red sweater from around her waist and restored Edmund's dignity by girding his loins. Smiling, she kissed him on both his cheeks and said; "Now you are free. You are free, my son." Then she surrendered her wrists to Tshembow, as would a criminal to a court martial. She turned to God and said: "This is my final verdict."

"It is not acceptable! Not in my court," the Lord cried out. But the crowd cheered in joy for the mother.

I surveyed the wild audience from top to bottom, and then my eyes met Edmund's for the first time. We stared at each other for a good ten seconds as only two loving brothers could, as if we were exchanging secrets without speaking. He tipped his head ceremoniously as if to say thank you. I winked at him and he smiled broadly.

As for Mrs. Gandalf P. Campbell, she had done the unexpected. I didn't see that coming. And boy, my mother knew how to put on a performance! God looked at me as if to say, 'are you part of this little family montage, boy?' But before I could make full contact with His fiery eyes, I walked out of the Court with my hands tucked in my coat pockets.

274

CHAPTER FOURTY-FOUR

The Tree of Life
I wonder who is next

One can never really experience the beauty of sound and music until entering the Heavens. When I stepped out of the Court, a breeze began to blow, and a single soft drum rhythm broke out. Then a cello joined in, carrying just two notes longer and longer. A husky voice began to sing; at first I thought it was Peter Gabriel. When the second voice entered the rendition, I looked left and right for Donnie McClurkin. Instead I found Dylan waiting on a bench.

The music started to drill its way into our skin, tissues and bones and into our very beings. Dylan filled us two cones with rainbow ice cream from a jar nearby. We took our first bites and smiled at each other and held hands walking away. As we turned left onto King Joshua Road, we heard the loudest applause in all the Heavens. I wondered how they'd worked things out.

"Court is adjourned!" I heard the Archangel declare. "Next case!" he called out.

It could be you.

SEAT OF TRUTH

Forever is too long to gamble with life. The thing is, you just don't know how close you are to the front of the line.

Are you ready to meet the Maker?

AUTHOR'S NOTE

All characters in this novel are purely fictional. Any similarity to a real person is coincidental. To begin with, there is no street in Asia that is called the Mask. And definitely nothing described in this book about the Heavens is real, but I wouldn't mind if there were ice cream there. Anyway, who knows?
The streets, however beautiful or pretty they sound, are just the product of the author's imagination.

The city of West Palm Beach is real, as far as I know. None of the organizations, churches, the law school in Manhattan New York, the chemical company in Asia, corporations, hotels, magazines, associations and charities are real. A few names of streets in Florida might, or might not be real. I just don't know which ones.

Writing and publishing a book is not so solitary as one might think. It takes a whole lot of friends, helpers, editors and marketing folks to bring it to fruition.

Thanks to my legion of beta readers for their invaluable feedback and insight. Too many to name here; I might get myself in trouble.

I'm very fortunate that the whole team working together in various stages on my debut takes such a proprietary and committed role to produce the book.

Thanks to my editors: Stephanie Fish, Joe Milligan, Daina Doucet for making the reading smoother and the writing shinier. My gratitude to the book production company, the Book Makers, for such a great, finished product. Thank you, Tracy.

Special thanks to the book cover artist and production: Felix Hernandez from Dreamphography. You guys rock.

Abdias Laguerre, thank you for the Book Trailer and production. Your vision is beautiful.

And special thanks to my beautiful photographer, Jennifer Wood, your shots work wonders.

Many thanks to friends and family and colleagues for cheering me on and always asking me when the book is coming out. Your words of encouragement moved me beyond the imaginable.

Heartfelt thanks to my kindergarten teacher, Ms. Emma, who taught me how to read and write. Thank you for holding my hand to draw my first *i*. It was so difficult, but you made it seem so easy. I still remember my first *i*. It took the entire length of the page. LOL! Thank you!

My ARC team: Karen Warankie, Natalya Bogatchenko, Patrycja Kubica, Anne, Midrady Althouriste, Dail Domexa, Joyce Meghan, Lucy Njoki Wambui and Jennifer Dickson. Thank you guys for your valuable input.

Special thanks to my worship team at NHC for their continuous prayers, and to my little besties at Kidsville for the thousands kisses and hugs.

To my spiritual leaders: Bishop Brian Warren, pastor Ellen McFarlane, pastor Derrick Coke, pastor Clifford Ivory, pastor Demola Orekoya, pastor Sharon Osborne and pastor Edner Petit-Frere, thank you so much for your teaching and prayers.

And finally to my parents: Rev: Henry C. Domexa, Lujanita Milien. My uncles: Wisly, Maxo, Celuinor, Jean. My aunties:

Celitane, Violette, Adou. Little brother: Milbentz, Twonsend. Little sisters: Marie-Ludia, Hendy, Lunie. And the nieces and nephews and cousins I can't name.

From fans to friends and family, I could not have written this book without your unconditional love and support.

From my heart to yours,

Happy Reading

Ezechias Domexa

QUESTIONS FOR DISCUSSION

1. The story is told from the point of view of multiple characters. What was it like experiencing the mind of Tshembow? Does his sense of humour surprise you?

2. Throughout the novel you understand the different perspectives of righteousness from Grandpa, Mitch, Flannighans, and Tshembow. Debate Holy Spirit's perspective on righteousness, does She have one?

3. Which character do you most identify with in the novel, and why?

4. French culture is often referred to in nuanced ways throughout the book. Care to take a guess as to why?

5. Why did it feel as if the Holy Spirit was uncomfortably close to Mitch at times? Why do you think Mitch struggled with the presence of Holy Spirit?

6. In the book, the dynamic between God and Dylan is much closer and more playful, whereas Mitch's relational dynamic with God is very tense. Also note that Mitch is a highly judgmental

character. In what ways do we project how we think God should be?

7. Describe ways in which Mitch identifies with an orphan spirit throughout his life. How does this affect the moral compass in his spiritual walk?

8. Abortion is cast as a redemptive act on behalf of the aborted child in the novel. If Dylan's destiny after being aborted was not mentioned, what do you think her fate would be after death? Do you think all unborn children are forgotten even if they are mere cells being formed? Is there an afterlife for zygotes?

9. Flannighans' character is portrayed as gay and drug addicted. Do you think the LGBTQ community can enter the Heavens?

10. Compare the thief on the cross mentioned in the Bible to the character of Flannighans. How did their story, up until the very last moments of death, parallel? How were they different?

11. The Baobab tree is compared to being like a human. What does this snippet reveal about the nature of the human heart?

12. Notice the mutual respect between Grandpa and Tshembow. On what principle order is this exchange sustained?

13. If you could collect your dreams from the warehouse of heaven today, which ones, past or present, would they be?

14. *"Immortality is a gift to all man. But eternal life is a choice. In the end we're all going somewhere."* Where do you wish to spend your immortality?

15. Dylan surprises readers with her extreme wisdom. However, her illiteracy is emphasized as a major quality lack. How does her gift contradict the prerequisites for acquiring such knowledge here on earth?

16. Why do *you* think Edmund's final fate isn't fully disclosed? What is your conclusion?

17. Discuss how Tshembow uses his wisdom to rule the world? What are some of his tricks and tactics to distract Christians? What are some of his platforms? Explain!

18. Forgiveness, betrayal, resentment, redemption, family secrets, happen to be recurring themes throughout the novel. Discuss how the Gandalf family related to them and to yours?

19. How big of a role does Atelia play in the life of Mitch and Edmund? Does Atelia fit a broader definition of the word 'motherhood'? What is our responsibility in the life of someone else's child? A stranger's?

20. The Gate of Exchange & Forgotten Hope bore the inscription *Abandon all hope, you who enter here*. What is your sense of this place? Discuss and reflect on the words: abandon, hope, gate of exchange and forgotten.

21. How is femininity used as a tool of healing and comfort in the novel? Consider Mrs. Gandalf, Connie, Holy Spirit, Atelia and Dylan.

22. What's your story? Are you ready to meet your Maker?

CPSIA information can be obtained
at www.ICGtesting.com
Printed in the USA
LVHW110136190422
716593LV00018B/607/J